Alice-Miranda and the Christmas Mystery

Books by Jacqueline Harvey

Alice-Miranda series
Alice-Miranda at School
Alice-Miranda on Holiday
Alice-Miranda Takes the Lead
Alice-Miranda at Sea
Alice-Miranda in New York
Alice-Miranda Shows the Way
Alice-Miranda in Paris
Alice-Miranda Shines Bright
Alice-Miranda in Japan
Alice-Miranda at Camp
Alice-Miranda at the Palace
Alice-Miranda in the Alps
Alice-Miranda to the Rescue
Alice-Miranda in China
Alice-Miranda Holds the Key
Alice-Miranda in Hollywood
Alice-Miranda in Scotland
Alice-Miranda Keeps the Beat
Alice-Miranda in the Outback
Alice-Miranda in Egypt

Kensy and Max series

Clementine Rose series

Willa and Woof series

That Cat

Alice-Miranda and the Christmas Mystery

Jacqueline Harvey

PUFFIN BOOKS

PUFFIN BOOKS

UK | USA | Canada | Ireland | Australia
India | New Zealand | South Africa | China

Puffin Books is part of the Penguin Random House group of companies whose addresses can be found at global.penguinrandomhouse.com

First published by Puffin Books in 2023

Copyright © Jacqueline Harvey 2023

The moral right of the author has been asserted.

All rights reserved. No part of this publication may be reproduced, published, performed in public or communicated to the public in any form or by any means without prior written permission from Penguin Random House Australia Pty Ltd or its authorised licensees.

Illustrations by J. Yi © Penguin Random House Australia Pty Ltd
Cover design by Louise Davis © Penguin Random House Australia Pty Ltd
Typeset in 13/18 pt Adobe Garamond Pro by Midland Typesetters, Australia

Printed and bound in Australia by Griffin Press, an accredited
ISO AS/NZS 14001 Environmental Management Systems printer

 A catalogue record for this book is available from the National Library of Australia

ISBN 978 1 76104 894 4

penguin.com.au

We at Penguin Random House Australia acknowledge that Aboriginal and Torres Strait Islander peoples are the Traditional Custodians and the first storytellers of the lands on which we live and work. We honour Aboriginal and Torres Strait Islander peoples' continuous connection to Country, waters, skies and communities. We celebrate Aboriginal and Torres Strait Islander stories, traditions and living cultures; and we pay our respects to Elders past and present.

*For Ian, with whom I have celebrated many memorable Christmases,
and for Sandy, who would have loved this story.*

Prologue

Delia Wickham picked up the box containing the only things her sister had left in the world – a framed photograph of a smiling young girl, her wedding and engagement rings, a patchwork quilt that had been sewn by their grandmother (Delia had one almost the same), a pile of magazines, some bric-a-brac and a china teapot of indeterminate origin. Most of the woman's wardrobe had been donated long ago. Delia would drop off what was left at the charity shop on her way home, along with some of the other things she didn't want to keep.

'Thank you, Louisa,' Delia said to the woman sitting behind the reception desk at the nursing home. Her only sibling, Maggie Phillips, had died there the previous week.

'It's no problem at all. I'm sorry for your loss, Miss Wickham,' Louisa said. She gave a tight smile. 'But at least Maggie's not suffering anymore.'

Delia knew that was true. After a massive stroke had rendered her sister in need of twenty-four-hour care, the doctors had predicted Maggie wouldn't live long. But, stubborn as always, she'd gone on to prove everyone wrong. Delia couldn't quite comprehend that it had been almost fifteen years.

'Have you been able to find her daughter?' Louisa asked, nodding at the photograph sitting atop the box.

Delia shook her head. 'Unfortunately, no.'

'Sad, isn't it – the way families can drift apart,' the woman said. 'Maggie's lucky she had you. We've got residents who haven't had a visitor in all the time they've been here.'

Delia felt a twinge of guilt that her own visitations had been few and far between. It's not that she hadn't wanted to come – it was just difficult with her job. She'd worked for Elliot Turner since she was a young woman – initially as his personal assistant but then, after a time, she took over the complete running of his household. She'd never married or had children of her own but neither of those things had been on her wish list. Her days were happy and fulfilling – though she always regretted never getting to know her niece, Aster.

It wasn't what anyone expected. Years ago, Maggie and her husband Stuart had lived only a few miles from Delia. He was a doctor at the local hospital; she was a young woman revelling in new motherhood.

When tragedy struck, it changed everything. Maggie's husband Stuart was killed in a car accident when Aster was only a few months old. Days after the funeral, Maggie packed up the house, took her baby and moved to the other end of the country. Delia tried to maintain contact, but her sister cut her off. She really didn't know why – but at the time she'd put it down to grief. Over the years she'd tried to find her, but Maggie had moved house and the pair completely lost touch.

Delia would never have known her sister was so gravely ill if it wasn't for the police who somehow managed to track her down. When she made the long journey to Maggie's home to see what she could find out, the next-door neighbour was shocked to learn that Delia was indeed alive and well. Maggie had told her that her entire family was dead – apart from her daughter. The neighbour also said that Maggie's niece, Aster, had taken up with a young fellow her mother considered completely unsuitable – and then the pair of them disappeared. Apparently, Maggie reported her missing, but it was only months later that she had the stroke.

From what Delia learned, it seemed that mother and daughter clashed constantly. Maggie treated the girl like a possession and hence she had run away.

While Delia had done her best to find Aster since then, it had been without success. She'd even hired a private detective who concluded that the girl had most likely left the country years ago.

Delia vowed to her dead sister that she'd redouble her efforts. After all, Aster was the only family she had left.

Chapter 1

Alice-Miranda set the last candelabra down at the end of the long table. 'I love Christmas, don't you, Millie?'

Her best friend looked over from the fireplace where she'd finished hanging a row of white stockings from the mantel.

'You know what they say, *it's the most wonderful time of the year*,' Millie sang – a broad grin on her freckled face.

The pair were putting the finishing touches

to the dining room decorations, having earlier been helped by a veritable army of girls and staff. Most had now headed back to the boarding houses to pack, given it was the last night before the Christmas holidays. It seemed strange to be leaving school on a Wednesday morning, but that's how the term calendar had fallen.

In the centre of the vast room, the school gardener, Charlie Weatherly, stood atop a giant ladder pinning the last of the fairy lights to the ceiling. 'Can someone flick that switch for me?'

Millie scurried over to the panel.

Instantly, the twinkling lights transformed the space into a festive wonderland. Later, when the candles were lit, it would be even more gorgeous.

'Wow!' the girls gasped.

Charlie leaned back to survey his handiwork and agreed that it was very pretty, indeed.

'Hello?' a tiny girl with cascading blonde curls called as she swung open the door. Britt Fox, who everyone considered Alice-Miranda's Nordic twin, was on exchange for the term – although she'd recently confided in Alice-Miranda that she was hoping to extend her time or, even better, change schools permanently. Britt had said that while she loved her friends back home in Oslo and missed her parents terribly, there was something about Winchesterfield-Downsfordvale Academy for Proper Young Ladies that had her heart from the very first day. It was quite likely to do with the students, who she adored, but it wasn't only that. The classes were always interesting and she'd never felt more challenged when it came to her studies. Alice-Miranda could only agree with her.

'I thought I'd come back and see if you needed any more help, but this looks amazing!' Britt exclaimed, unwinding the scarf from around her neck and removing her woollen gloves.

'Do you think it's enough?' Alice-Miranda asked.

'Enough?' the girl echoed. 'This is better than the windows at Steen and Strom – that's my favourite department store at home. It's incredible.'

Decorated in a silver and white theme with touches of azure blue, the hall looked like something from a magazine, with giant wreaths on the walls, stockings over the fireplace, candelabras on the tables, a huge Christmas tree covered in silver baubles in the corner and fairy lights strung across the ceiling. In only a few hours, gifts would be piled high beneath the tree, purchased with money raised by the girls at a cake stall and mufti day. There had been a committee in charge of liaising with several local charities to find out what was needed most. The podium where the teachers' head table usually sat had been transformed into a makeshift stage with a curtain. The staff would be seated with the students for dinner this evening.

Tonight was the annual school Christmas feast for the girls, staff and a few specially invited guests. It was to be followed by a talent show, which had drawn fierce auditions over the past few weekends. Caprice had already told everyone she was the star, of course, given her singing prowess, but apparently there were some other impressive acts too. Miss Reedy and Miss Wall had overseen the tryouts and had asked the girls not to share anything about their performances so that everyone would get a surprise. Tomorrow the students would leave for the holidays – although this year Alice-Miranda was hosting a group of her closest friends at Highton Hall for an early Christmas celebration before they all went their separate ways.

'Where did you get everything?' Britt asked.

'Mummy sent it from Highton's. The stores change the theme for Christmas every year and that means most of whatever was used the time before is donated after the season to various hospitals or charities, but this was left over. I told Mrs Parker that she can have it all for the village for next Christmas. She was very grateful,' Alice-Miranda explained.

'No, she wasn't,' Millie rebutted. 'Myrtle said it was a pity Winchesterfield had to have the Highton's hand-me-downs and she could only take it all if the school could find somewhere to keep it. Apparently, she doesn't have any space at home and the village hall is overflowing – which I know it's not because I was there a few weeks ago helping put things out for the trivia night. That didn't sound very grateful to me.'

Britt giggled. 'Mrs Parker certainly says whatever is on her mind.'

Charlie Weatherly clucked his tongue. 'Yes, that woman has a gift.'

'The gift of natural rudeness,' Millie said, to great guffaws of laughter from the man.

Alice-Miranda looked at the three of them. 'You know she means well.'

'Yes, most of the time I'd agree with you, Alice-Miranda,' Charlie said.

'I wouldn't,' Millie replied.

'You wouldn't what, Millicent?' Myrtle Parker said loudly. Millie shrunk behind Britt, hoping that the woman hadn't just heard their earlier conversation. It didn't pay to cross her – Myrtle had a memory like an elephant.

Alice-Miranda came to Millie's rescue. 'Oh, hello Mrs Parker, how are you this afternoon? Do you know if Mrs Derby is coming this evening?'

Myrtle pursed her lips and pulled her shoulders back while adjusting the string of pearls around her neck. This afternoon she was wearing a beige skirt and a matching cardigan with pearl buttons – very demure considering she often preferred bold floral prints that looked as if she'd repurposed some curtains.

'Last I heard, the baby hasn't been well so I'm not sure. Honestly, I'd be staying home if I could in this ghastly weather,' Myrtle replied. 'She'd be mad to bring the little mite out.'

Louella Derby, Winchesterfield-Downsfordvale's beloved school secretary, had not long ago had her first baby – a boy she and her husband, who was the local constable, had named Daniel. Surprisingly, Myrtle Parker had taken over Mrs Derby's role prior to the woman's maternity leave (as Mrs Derby had been terribly unwell during her pregnancy). To the amazement of the children and staff, the Headmistress, Miss Grimm, had kept Mrs Parker on once the baby was born and despite some early hiccups, it seemed the two women had come to a workable arrangement. Things had improved dramatically once Mrs Parker stopped impersonating a guard dog, keeping everyone out of the office – and to be fair, she had helped Alice-Miranda and her peers solve a mystery while they were on their recent Queen's Colours expedition in Egypt.

'Is Mr Parker coming?' Alice-Miranda asked.

Myrtle rolled her eyes. 'He said he wouldn't miss your performance for anything.'

The girl grinned. Reg Parker was one of her favourite people in the world, and even more so since he'd started teaching her the drums a while back. It wasn't something his wife approved of, but the man was in his element. He now had a small group of students and his own pocket money – most of which he spent buying delicious treats for his charges or vinyl records to add to his extensive collection.

'Anyway, you lot had better get back to the boarding house and change for dinner,' Mrs Parker instructed. 'And make sure that you take some umbrellas with you. The weather is bad and only getting worse.'

On the other side of the dining room wall, a huge crash followed by a loud yelp caused everyone to jump. Fortunately, Charlie was already down the ladder or he may well have fallen off.

'Good heavens!' Myrtle gasped. 'What on earth was that?'

'It sounded like Mrs Smith,' Alice-Miranda said, running towards the double doors that led through the servery to the kitchen beyond.

Seconds later, the girl arrived to find the school cook, Doreen Smith, standing over an empty roasting pan, the contents of which was now spread across the flagstone floor.

'Oh, for goodness sake.' The woman mopped her brow with a handkerchief.

'Mrs Smith, are you all right?' Alice-Miranda asked, rushing to her side. Millie, Britt, Charlie and Myrtle were gathered behind her.

'Yes, dear. I'm sorry to have startled you all. I lost my grip. I suppose that will teach me for not waiting for help these days – these pans are so heavy. Mrs Jennings was just collecting Miss Grimm's afternoon tea tray and I've sent Ginny to the greenhouse to find some rosemary for the lamb,' she said. 'I fear I'm getting too old for all this.'

Alice-Miranda and Millie had already found some tongs and were picking up the pieces of turkey from the floor. Britt grabbed a cloth from the sink and was wiping up splatters of grease.

Doreen Smith sighed. 'At least Fudge is in for a treat.' The school's caramel-coloured cavoodle was always far more enthusiastic about human food than his own.

'Will there still be enough for tonight?' Alice-Miranda asked. She could see other cuts sizzling away in the cooker as well as two large legs of glazed ham sitting on the bench.

'I think we'll be fine,' Mrs Smith replied. 'As long as no one's too hungry.'

Myrtle Parker wrinkled her lip. 'Well, you'd better hope there's enough, Doreen, because I've just come from the supermarket in Downsfordvale and the shelves at Kennington's were practically empty – particularly of anything related to the festive season.' She turned to Alice-Miranda. 'You'd think your father would be used to the Christmas rush by now.'

Millie frowned. 'You do realise, Mrs Parker, that Hugh is the CEO. He doesn't actually do the ordering.'

Myrtle's lip twitched again. 'Of course, I do. But Kennington's have a problem – mark my words. At least this time they're not poisoning people. Though it sounds like your father could do well hiring more reliable staff who check on things properly.'

'Like you, Mrs Parker,' Millie said, biting her lip.

'Yes, exactly,' the woman replied.

Alice-Miranda shuddered at the memory. The food poisoning scandal had been a ghastly time made worse by the fact that it was one of Kennington's own scientists who was responsible. Fortunately, no one died. The child was keenly aware, though, that it didn't take much to ruin reputations.

When her parents, Cecelia Highton-Smith and Hugh Kennington-Jones, had married, their wedding had been reported as the most magnificent retail merger the world had ever seen. Given her mother was one of the descendants of the Highton's department store empire and her father was heir to the Kennington's grocery chain, the couple certainly had shopkeeping in their blood. Over the years, Alice-Miranda had seen her parents go through several difficult times and the girl knew that any sort of scandal could have a terrible impact on Kennington's and Highton's and the thousands of employees relying on them for their livelihoods – not to mention the shoppers who trusted their brands.

Millie looked at Alice-Miranda and rolled her eyes.

But Alice-Miranda was worried. Kennington's should be bursting at the seams with stock right before Christmas. Something wasn't right, that's for sure. She'd call her parents later and see what the problem was.

Chapter 2

Dolly Oliver glanced up at the television screen in the corner of the vast kitchen at Highton Hall. A recent addition to the room, she was quite enjoying being able to catch up on her favourite shows while she worked. Some of the silly soaps she enjoyed were utterly deplorable, but at her age she wasn't going to feel remotely guilty about her 'guilty pleasures'.

'Afternoon, Dolly,' Cecelia Highton-Smith said as she walked into the room carrying a basketful of clean sheets. 'I could murder a cup of tea.'

'Hello, dear. I was about to pop the kettle on. Would you like a slice of hummingbird cake? Mrs Greening brought it over earlier. After Harold's trip to the doctor last week, she mentioned he's not supposed to be indulging in sweet treats, but you know Maggie – she can't help herself when it comes to baking.'

'That would be lovely,' Cecelia replied with a sigh, depositing the basket onto the end of the scrubbed-pine kitchen table before pushing the sleeves of her sky-blue shirt up over her elbows. 'I'm exhausted and the children aren't even here yet.'

'And a good thing they're not,' Highton Hall's resident housekeeper Mrs Shillingsworth said, as she walked into the room carrying another basket of clean clothes from the laundry. 'I've still got a list of jobs as long as my arm to get through.' The woman was, as always, dressed for business in a practical navy skirt and crisp white shirt with her grey hair pulled into a neat chignon.

'Shilly, you've done far too much already. You know the children won't notice if there's a speck of dust on the lampshades in the sitting room,' Cecelia tutted.

'No, but I will and besides, your mother will be here on the weekend and Valentina still scares the socks off me, even after all these years,' Shilly said.

Dolly chuckled and wiped her hands on her apron. She knew the feeling. Working for Cecelia Highton-Smith and her husband Hugh Kennington-Jones had been one of the joys of her life – the pair treated her and Shilly and everyone else in their employ at Highton Hall as family. And as for Alice-Miranda, Dolly loved the child more than she thought it possible to love anyone. Cecelia's mother, Valentina, was a wonderful woman too – but her exacting ways kept the staff on their toes.

'Well, at least let me help you,' Cecelia said.

'Only if you insist,' Shilly said, a glint in her eye.

'I insist,' Cecelia replied, filling the teapot with boiling water while Dolly cut three slices of cake and arranged them onto plates. Shilly fetched the teacups and saucers from the long oak dresser.

The three had just sat down to enjoy their afternoon tea when Dolly realised that, although the sound was muted, the television was still on.

'Sorry – I'll get rid of that nonsense,' she said, reaching for the remote control. She was about to switch it off when a news bulletin flashed across the screen.

'Hang on a tick. What's that about?' Cecelia asked. Dolly turned up the volume.

'In another act of Christmas Grinchdom, the villagers of Westbury have woken today to find that the town's entire Christmas display, including the decorated tree and extensive lighting, has been stolen. Last night, despite the dreary weather, the square had been a place of celebration as the annual ceremony to turn on the lights brought families out in their droves. This is the second Christmas robbery in as many days, following a brazen theft at Lord Littleton's Hollyford Estate where a dozen mid-sized Christmas trees and their decorations disappeared from the gardens. Police are perplexed and surprised that so far, no CCTV footage has been able to capture the thieves' activities. Authorities are appealing for the public to beware of offers of cheap lights or Christmas paraphernalia and to report any suspicious behaviour,' the newsreader announced.

'Good heavens, what's the world coming to – stealing Christmas decorations, for goodness sake?' Shilly said, shaking her head.

Dolly poured three cups of tea to which she added splashes of milk. 'What a bunch of miserable so-and-sos.'

Cecelia tapped her finger against her lip. 'I'll phone the warehouse and see if Highton's has anything suitable we can offer Westbury village to replace what they've lost.'

'That's a lovely idea,' Shilly said and sipped her tea.

'What about Lord Littleton?' Dolly said.

'I think he can afford to buy his own replacements,' Cecelia said. 'Though no one deserves to be robbed.'

'True.' Shilly nodded. 'It's understandable that not everyone's a fan of Christmas and I completely agree that people have their own beliefs but, if nothing else, isn't the festive season an opportunity to come together and celebrate with loved ones? To think about those less fortunate than ourselves and give the little ones something to look forward to? Stealing the village decorations is a terrible business.'

'I couldn't agree more,' Dolly said, stabbing a little piece of cake with her fork.

'I wonder if Highton Mill should employ some security at the Christmas Lights Celebration on

Friday evening,' Cecelia said. 'I'll ask Hugh if he can spare anyone.'

'I can't imagine it will be a problem, dear,' Shilly said. 'But then again one can never be too careful, apparently.'

The three women sipped their tea and ate their cake in silence, wondering what would possess anyone to want to ruin Christmas – especially for the children. It just wasn't right at all.

Chapter 3

Back in the senior boarding house at Winchesterfield-Downsfordvale, in the converted Caledonia Manor stables, Jacinta Headlington-Bear stuffed the last of her clothes into a small suitcase, then struggled to do up the zip. Usually, she left most of her things at school, given she and her mother lived in the village not five minutes away, but tomorrow she was headed straight to Highton Hall for Alice-Miranda's pre-Christmas celebrations. She realised she probably needed a few more things this time – although perhaps it would have been sensible to have her mother bring over a bigger bag. It was too late now. The woman had left on assignment two days ago.

Jacinta's mother was Ambrosia Headlington-Bear – pen name, Rosie Hunter. She had spent the past few years writing feature articles for fashion blogs and magazines, including for her friends, Cecelia and Charlotte Highton-Smith (Alice-Miranda's mother and aunt), and their glamorous department store chain, Highton's. Ambrosia had been booked to write a piece on the Christmas shopping habits of patrons at the company's flagship stores in New York, Paris and London, which required a whirlwind trip to visit each location in person.

At least now Jacinta would be able to spend time with her boyfriend, Lucas. His father, Lawrence Ridley, apart from being one of the most famous actors in the world, was married to Alice-Miranda's aunt, Charlotte. The couple had the most gorgeous twins, Imogen and Marcus, and they were all coming to Highton Hall for Christmas. This year, Lucas was spending the holidays with them. His mother, Kitty, was going to be close by as well, as her sister, Lily, and her husband, Heinrich, ran the farm on the property. It was lovely that Lucas's parents and step-parents had such convivial relationships. Unlike Jacinta's mother and father, who didn't speak at all anymore. Unfortunately, her father, Neville Headlington-Bear had proven himself again not long ago to be a dirty rotten scoundrel. Thankfully, Jacinta and her mother got on terrifically these days, so while she was sad that her father was no longer part of her life, she was relieved that her mother had escaped his clutches. The fact that Ambrosia had forged a fabulous career as a journalist was testament to her grit and determination. She really had changed for the better in every single way. Jacinta couldn't have been prouder.

She was in the middle of a lovely daydream when her thoughts were rudely interrupted by one of the other students barging into the room. The copper-haired girl made herself at home on the second bed, which this term belonged to Sloane Sykes.

'Are you leaving?' Caprice asked.

Jacinta turned to her and frowned. 'Aren't we all?'

'Only for a couple of weeks,' the girl replied. 'You look as if you've packed your whole life in there. Are you changing schools or something?'

'You wish,' Jacinta said with a grin. 'May I help you with something?'

'No,' Caprice said. 'I'm bored. And Mummy still hasn't called to tell me what time she's going to be here tomorrow. I hate that she always leaves everything to the last minute. It's typical of her.'

As the school's resident diva, there was no doubting Caprice's talents – especially for singing. She'd won the National Eisteddfod several years in a row, and she would happily tell everyone about her myriad other gifts too. Unfortunately, her constant boasting didn't do her any favours with her peers.

The fact that Caprice's mother was the famous television chef, Venetia Baldini, didn't help either. It only gave her something else to brag about – though the two seemed to have a somewhat strained relationship at times. The girls tried hard to be her friend, but Caprice didn't make it easy for them to like her.

'I thought you'd be busy packing for Tuscany?' Jacinta said. The girls had been hearing about this trip for weeks now.

'I'm almost finished,' Caprice said. 'You know we're –'

'Staying at your villa that's actually more like a castle.' Jacinta pre-empted the end of the girl's sentence.

'You don't have to be snippy about it. Just because you're stuck here in boring old Winchesterfield. Maybe your mother's asked Mrs Parker for Christmas dinner – wouldn't that be fun?' Caprice teased.

Jacinta shrugged. 'I wouldn't mind. Mr Parker is lovely and Mrs Parker is entertaining in an annoying way.'

Little did Caprice know that tomorrow Jacinta and her friends were heading for Alice-Miranda's place. No one had spilled the beans yet and it was a good thing as Caprice had a habit of turning up unexpectedly at their gatherings. This time there was no way she was going to spoil their fun. Tomorrow, Caprice would be on her way to Italy and the others would be on a minibus to Highton Hall for five days of festivities before returning to their own homes for Christmas.

'Don't you have to rehearse or something?' Jacinta asked. Come to think of it, she needed to organise her own outfit for the concert – which she was excited and terrified about.

'Why?' Caprice said. 'I'm a professional – there aren't too many people my age who've had the lead in a Hollywood film and definitely not a musical.'

'How could I ever forget?' Jacinta said. She really didn't feel like getting into a fight with the girl, but the longer Caprice stayed the more likely that would be the outcome.

Footsteps echoed outside in the hall.

'Jacinta, have you got that note Alice-Miranda gave us about what we're doing this week? I was wondering if I need something smart to wear,' Sloane asked as she walked through the door blissfully unaware of their visitor.

Jacinta made a cutting action across her neck, but it was too late.

Sloane grimaced then took a deep breath. She had a feeling that attack was going to be the best form of defence. 'Any particular reason you're lying on my bed, Caprice?'

Caprice sat up and glared at the girls. 'What are you talking about?' she demanded, narrowing her eyes.

'Nothing,' Sloane said.

'Are you going to Alice-Miranda's place?' Caprice asked.

Sloane and Jacinta looked at one another. It probably wasn't worth the additional grief if they lied to her.

Sloane raised her eyebrows and Jacinta nodded.

'Yes,' the pair replied in unison.

'When? Why? Who else is invited?' Caprice fired questions like bullets.

'Does it matter?' Sloane said. 'You're off to Tuscany tomorrow.'

'Well, it would have been nice to be asked – even if I couldn't go!' Caprice exclaimed. She slid off the bed and balled her fists like a three-year-old on the verge of a tantrum, then stomped out of the room.

Sloane sat down on the edge of her bed. 'She took that well.'

Jacinta bit her lip. 'You think? I only hope she doesn't say anything to Alice-Miranda.'

But it seemed that sentiment was already too late.

Caprice spotted Alice-Miranda, Millie and Britt coming through the doors into the boarding house.

They'd just shaken the water from their umbrellas and popped them into the stand in the entry way.

'Gosh, I wish this rain would stop,' Alice-Miranda said. 'I'm drowned.'

The three girls had walked from the main dining room at Winchesterfield Manor back to their boarding house. It wasn't terribly far, but the downpour was bordering on torrential – not to mention that the temperature had plummeted too.

Millie looked up and spotted Caprice charging towards them with a face like thunder.

'Uh-oh,' the girl said.

'I hear you're having a Christmas celebration, Alice-Miranda,' the copper-haired girl spat. 'Thanks so much for the invitation.'

Millie, Britt and Alice-Miranda looked at each other, eyes wide.

'Hello, Caprice,' Alice-Miranda replied. She had a horrible feeling that this wasn't going to be an easy conversation.

Millie walked over and stood in front of the girl. 'Why would you want to come? You don't even like us.'

'Who said I didn't like you?' Caprice snapped. 'And I bet it was you who told Alice-Miranda not to invite me. We all know she's too kind for her own good and *you* hate me.'

'It wasn't just me,' Millie said. 'We all agreed.'

Caprice slowly blinked her long lashes. It was as if she was rehearsing for a scene where she was about to burst into tears – except that she probably was.

'Please don't be upset, Caprice,' Alice-Miranda said.

'Of course, I'm upset – Millie hates me and you all believe everything she says about me – which is not true. At least, not most of the time,' Caprice said.

Millie's jaw dropped. 'Not true – are you kidding me? For a moment, while we were in Egypt and even afterwards, I let myself believe that you'd turned a corner – but the new Caprice didn't last long, did she? You left me to do all the work on our science project even though you knew I had the tennis tryouts coming up and I needed to practise.'

'I did not,' Caprice said. 'I was the one who came up with the idea – you just had to do a bit of research.'

'Like, all of it,' Millie said. 'And write the whole thing up!'

'As if that was so hard,' Caprice snapped. 'You're always blaming me for everything. Have you ever thought that I might not be the only person you rub the wrong way, Millie?'

Millie's hands balled into fists and her face turned red. 'I'm glad that Alice-Miranda didn't invite you because I, for one, want to have a fun Christmas,' she spat. Millie stared at Caprice whose lip was beginning to quiver. 'Oh, here it comes – the famous Caprice waterworks.'

Tears spilled from Caprice's sapphire-blue eyes.

'You're so . . . so . . . hateful,' Caprice blurted.

She wiped at the tears that were tumbling down her cheeks and for a moment no one said a word.

Millie's eyes brimmed with tears too, but Alice-Miranda knew her friend well enough to see she was determined not to cry.

'Millie, why don't you and Britt go and get ready for dinner? I'll be there soon,' Alice-Miranda suggested.

'Are you sure?' Millie asked. 'You're not going to do anything rash, are you?' The girl then cupped her hand and whispered in Alice-Miranda's ear. 'Like invite her?'

Alice-Miranda frowned and shook her head.

'Go on,' Alice-Miranda insisted. Britt took Millie's arm and gave her a nod. Reluctantly, Millie went with her down the hall.

The small sitting room near the entry was empty so Alice-Miranda manoeuvred Caprice inside.

Britt and Millie were intercepted by Sloane and Jacinta, who pulled the pair into their room eager to find out what was happening. The girls had been spying from a safe distance and wondered where their housemistress Mrs Clarkson was. She usually would have intervened by now.

Alice-Miranda suggested Caprice sit down. She pulled up a chair opposite and offered the girl the tissue box from the side table.

'Please don't blame Millie or anyone else for leaving you out, Caprice,' Alice-Miranda said. 'It was my decision in the end.'

Caprice glared from under her blunt fringe.

'So, you hate me too,' she sobbed.

Alice-Miranda shook her head. 'Of course, I don't. But to be perfectly honest, Caprice, it's tricky because even after it looked as if things were improving between you and Millie, you haven't exactly been fair to her. I should have told you how upset she was about that science project. You know as well as I do that she did almost all of the work – and you got a brilliant mark for it.'

'She didn't do it *all*,' Caprice said.

Alice-Miranda frowned. 'Are you sure? You were off rehearsing with Mr Trout every time Millie asked if you could help her.'

'Fine – I probably should have planned my time better,' Caprice said. 'So you think I'm mean and horrible too?'

'I don't want to but there are times when you don't help yourself,' Alice-Miranda said. She bit her lip. 'My granny always says you catch more flies with honey than vinegar.'

Caprice huffed. 'Well, I'm not very sweet, am I? Unlike my mother who *everyone* loves. You don't understand what it's like. People fawn all over her constantly and totally ignore me. It's as if I'm invisible when she's around, but I've got more talent in my little finger than she has in her whole body.'

This was even harder than Alice-Miranda had first imagined. Obviously, Caprice was completely oblivious to the things she said. If only she realised that people would like her a whole lot more if she didn't boast so much while at the same time playing the victim.

'Everyone knows you're talented, Caprice, but it might serve you better not to remind us of that all the time. Being humble is a quality to be admired,' Alice-Miranda said.

'But that's the problem. When I'm humble no one notices me. I have to remind them how good I am, or they might forget,' Caprice replied.

Alice-Miranda could see that she was being honest – which in itself was possibly part of the quandary.

'Have you ever thought of talking to someone about the way you feel – especially towards your mother?' Alice-Miranda said.

'What? Now you think I'm crazy and I need to see a psychiatrist or something,' Caprice replied.

Alice-Miranda took a deep breath. 'No, Caprice, I'm not for one second suggesting that. But I know that talking to someone can help.'

'You?' Caprice said, rolling her eyes. 'Little Miss Perfect?'

'I'm far from perfect, Caprice, and yes, sometimes there are things that I don't want to share with the girls so it's easier to speak to an adult – a professional. After my horse-riding accident, I struggled. Even though I got straight back onto Bony and I knew it wasn't his fault, I was secretly terrified. Miss Grimm made an appointment for me to talk to someone and it really helped,' Alice-Miranda explained.

'*You* were scared?' Caprice said.

Alice-Miranda nodded. 'I'm just like everyone else. I get scared and worried and nervous about things. Perhaps I'm better at hiding it at times but I promise you – it's true. In fact, the older I get, the less sure I am of everything. I can't believe how brash and confident I was when I was little. These days, I can't imagine I'd be quite so bold.'

Caprice blinked her long wet lashes. 'Would you have invited me to come if I wasn't going to Tuscany?'

Alice-Miranda shook her head. 'No. That wouldn't have been fair to Millie – at least not unless the two of you had made a truce.'

Caprice pulled a tissue from the box and blew her nose. She blinked her long lashes and screwed up her face. 'I don't want everyone to hate me. I want to have friends.'

'Daddy says that what other people think of you is really none of your business,' Alice-Miranda said.

Caprice frowned. 'That doesn't make any sense.'

'I promise you it does. It means you can't control what other people think about you – but you can control how you act and how you *react* to others.'

'Oh, I get it.' Caprice nodded. 'My mother says that too. You know lots of people love her show, but there are these awful trolls who say she's fat and she has wrinkles and she shouldn't eat so many of the things she bakes. And she says that the best way to deal with them is to ignore it. I'd sue if they were talking about me.'

Alice-Miranda's eyebrows jumped up. 'That's horrible. But I think your mother is right not to engage with them – it would probably only get worse.'

'Your uncle must get things like that as well,' Caprice said. 'He's one of the most famous movie stars in the whole world. I bet lots of people have opinions about him.'

'He's never said much,' Alice-Miranda replied. 'I suppose one of the downsides of being famous is unwanted attention.'

'But I *want* to be famous,' Caprice said. 'Ever since I can remember, that's all I've wanted. To sing and perform in front of millions of people and make the whole world fall in love with me.'

'That's just the point, Caprice – you can't make everyone love you, but we can all try to be more lovable,' Alice-Miranda said. 'I'm sure that you'll be a star – you're too talented not to be.'

Caprice bit her lip. 'I'm sorry. I really am. I want to have friends and I want to learn how to be a good friend.'

'It's not me you should apologise to, Caprice – I'm sure that Millie would appreciate the gesture,' Alice-Miranda said.

Caprice shrugged. 'All right. I'll think about it.'

And with that, the girl flounced out of the room and down the hall, leaving Alice-Miranda completely confused.

Chapter 4

Hoxton Manor was set to sparkle. The Christmas decorations began at the bottom of the mile-long drive, with a pair of giant wreaths attached to oversized iron gates, and continued with fairy lights winding through the avenue of beech trees up to the house. There, an enormous fir tree stood centre stage in the middle of the circular carriageway, dripping in shiny red and gold baubles. Inside the house was even more impressive. Sebastian Smote and his team of decorators had spent days perfecting this year's theme in anticipation of Elliot Turner's favourite celebration of the year – his annual Christmas party. The guest list was always interesting. Elliot was one of those people who could talk to anyone and frequently did – hence the diverse crowd that enjoyed his hospitality.

'I love those gold reindeer,' Elliot called to a smiling young woman who had just spent the past hour trying to decide which direction the pair should face.

'Thank you, sir,' she replied with a nod.

'Though I do hope you'll all be finished soon,' Elliot said loudly, immediately gaining the attention of the team of six.

A man with an impressive ginger coif, dressed in a purple suit and paisley pink waistcoat, rushed towards him. 'I can assure you, Mr Turner, we'll be out of your hair before the end of the day. We've got a huge wedding at Penberthy House to set up tomorrow and this lot are already exhausted.' He looked at Elliot and bit his lip. 'Well . . . what do you think?' Sebastian twitched nervously, fiddling with his gold pocket watch while awaiting the man's answer.

'It's . . .' Elliot tapped his foot and fanned his fingers under his chin. 'It's magnificent, Sebastian – I think this might be my favourite yet.'

Sebastian Smote clapped his hands and grinned widely. 'You say that every year, sir. But I do tend to agree, this does feel very special. And don't worry – the party will be fabulous as always.' The man turned and shimmied away, shouting to one of his decorators that the stars hanging from the banister rail weren't level. 'Get me a spirit level, someone – a spirit level – pronto!' he shouted.

Elliot grinned and felt a pang of hunger, realising that he'd quite forgotten to eat lunch. He'd head downstairs and make himself a sandwich. The labyrinth of rooms in the basement had several years ago been transformed into a kitchen complex any hotel, let alone private home, would be proud to have. He entered the main space to find his personal chef, Paloma, leaning against the giant marble-topped island bench, pen in hand, scribbling something into her notebook.

'How goes it?' Elliot asked. The woman looked up and gave him a dimpled smile. Her long dark hair was tied up in a ponytail and she was wearing her uniform of white chef's pants and a pinafore top. The only thing missing was her hat.

'Hello, Mr Turner,' the woman replied, then grimaced.

Her response didn't go unnoticed.

'Are you all right, P?' he asked, a note of concern in his voice.

She nodded. 'Probably something I ate,' she replied.

'I jolly well hope not,' the man said, pulling a face. 'How's the menu coming along?'

'Fabulously,' she said. 'I'm about to send the last of the orders through now.' He noticed her phone sitting on the bench beside the notebook.

'May I take a peek?' he asked.

Paloma shook her head. 'No,' she said firmly. 'You told me when I started here five years ago that you liked surprises – and I'm not going to spoil this one – it's the biggest of the year and your favourite.'

He rolled his eyes. 'Is it really five years since you came to drive me mad?'

'Five years and thirteen days,' she replied. 'Don't you remember I started a couple of weeks before the party? It was the worst. Sebastian Smote had no idea what he was doing and neither did I. Why I ever stayed is a complete mystery. Though I suppose you're not that bad a boss – at least not all the time.' She smiled, then grimaced again. 'And, thankfully, Sebastian and I have both come a long way since then.'

'True,' Elliot grinned his megawatt smile, his eyes creasing at the edges.

The man might have been nudging sixty-five, but he was still extremely handsome with a thick shock of salt and pepper hair and tanned complexion. Elliot looked after himself, working out with a personal trainer three times a week and playing regular games of golf. The man's choice in clothing was always elegant no matter the occasion and, today, dressed in a pair of beige pants with a dark green shirt and brown brogues, he was a picture of casual chic. Paloma often wondered why he hadn't remarried. He was a catch, that's for sure – though not her type (apart from the fact that he was old enough to be her father).

'Would you like something to eat?' she asked.

'I can get it,' Elliot said, walking to the bank of commercial refrigerators. 'I was just going to make a sandwich.'

'There's smoked salmon and cream cheese. I've got homemade mayo too,' she replied, then gasped. 'Ow, ow, oh gosh.' The woman was doubled over in pain. Beads of perspiration peppered her brow and her skin had turned an awful shade of grey.

'Paloma!' he rushed to her side, then shouted for help.

A woman in a black trouser suit hurried in from the hallway. 'What's the matter, sir?'

'We need an ambulance – now!' Elliot ordered. Delia Wickham pulled a phone from her pocket and dialled the emergency number.

Elliot helped the chef to her feet and onto one of the stools. She was clutching her side and looked as if she might throw up.

'I'm sorry. I don't know what the matter is,' Paloma said between gulps of air.

'It's okay – you're going to be fine. The ambulance will be here soon,' he said.

She sat still taking shallow breaths. He grabbed a glass and poured some water from the tap encouraging her to take small sips.

Elliot had found Paloma completely by accident when she was working in a restaurant in the south of France. He was staying in the village and had eaten at the same place several nights in a row, having found the food to be extraordinary. It hadn't been hard to lure her to his employ – the poor woman was slaving away six nights a week for terrible wages. It was funny – while they often bantered when he wandered into the kitchen, he realised right now that he barely knew anything about her. She was a private soul. He wondered whether he should offer to call someone – he couldn't help noticing a small tattoo on her wrist. *Familia*.

The word smashed into his skull like a freight train and for a few seconds he was back there. Like a movie reel on fast forward until he squeezed his eyes shut and pushed the thoughts from his mind. This wasn't like that. She would be fine. Paloma was not going to die on his watch.

Suddenly she clutched her side and screamed blue murder, then slumped down, unconscious, her head hitting the bench.

'Where's that darned ambulance?' Elliot called out. In the distance he could hear a siren.

The next ten minutes were a blur. There was a flurry of activity from the medics, then Paloma was loaded onto a gurney.

'I'll go with her, sir,' Delia said.

He nodded. 'Thank you. Please let me know as soon as you have any news.'

'Of course,' she said and disappeared, leaving Elliot Turner alone with his thoughts. He knew better than anyone that was a very bad place to be.

★

It was early evening when Elliot received an update on Paloma's condition. She'd been rushed into surgery with suspected appendicitis, which turned out to be far worse than first thought.

'I'm afraid that Paloma will be out of action for a while, sir,' Delia reported, having returned to the manor to pick up some things for the woman. 'She was in the early stages of peritonitis – thank heavens you came down to the kitchen. The doctor said, had she waited too much longer, her condition might have proved fatal.'

Elliot shook his head. 'Good grief. Will she make a full recovery?'

'Yes, she should be fine in a few weeks,' Delia replied. 'But we'll have to think about finding someone else for the party.'

In his anxious state, Elliot hadn't even thought of that. Paloma would want the show to go on, but to get someone who could do her menu justice wasn't going to be easy – not at this late stage.

'Do you have anyone in mind, Delia?' he asked.

The woman rattled off a list of names of people she'd already contacted and discovered were unavailable.

Elliot bit his lip. There was someone. He'd met her at an event a while back. Apart from being one of the best chefs in the country, she was completely mesmerising. The woman was renowned for her desserts – though he had attended a party where she'd been responsible for the entire menu, and it was superb.

'Are you all right, sir?' Delia asked, jolting the man back to reality.

'Yes. I have an idea, but I'll need to get moving on things right away,' he said.

The woman looked at her watch. 'I'm afraid that in all of the commotion earlier with Paloma, I'd quite forgotten that you're doing that interview this evening – with Mr Goodman from the *Financial Weekly*.'

Elliot sighed. He'd overlooked it too.

'I could cancel,' Delia said as the doorbell rang. It seemed she was too late.

Elliot swallowed hard. He hated talking about himself and the only reason he'd agreed this time was because he occasionally played golf with Raymond Agnew, the newspaper's editor. Ray promised that the guy he was sending was not your usual boring money market journo.

'Give me ten minutes, Delia,' Elliot said. 'Take our guest to the front sitting room and offer him some tea. I have something I need to do first.'

The woman nodded. 'Very well, sir. I'll wait until Mr Goodman is gone before I return to the hospital.'

'Thank you,' Elliot said and hurried away to make a call.

Chapter 5

As the dulcet tones of Bing Crosby's 'White Christmas' filled the school dining hall, Ophelia Grimm made her way to the podium. To honour the occasion, she had worn a pretty red-and-white Fair Isle jumper teamed with a dark-green wool skirt. Her hair was pulled back into a soft bun with a red bow.

Ophelia waited a moment in front of the microphone before clearing her throat and eyeballing Cornelius Trout, the school's music master, who was sitting by the sound system.

Several girls were now pointing and giggling.

'Mr Trout,' Miss Grimm whispered although given it was into the microphone the entire school could hear her.

But Cornelius was completely oblivious, singing along, lost in his own world.

'Oh, for goodness sake, will somebody please turn the music off? I have something to say,' the woman barked.

There was a chortle of laughter as Mr Trout very nearly fell off his chair and quickly switched off the sound system.

'Thank you, Mr Trout,' she muttered before pulling her shoulders back and smiling with all her teeth.

'Good evening, girls, staff and guests. We're delighted that you can be with us to celebrate Christmas and our annual Talent Show. Miss Reedy and Miss Wall tell me that we're in for a treat – and I know we're also in for a delicious feast, thanks to Mrs Smith and her team. Recently, Miss Reedy had a wonderful idea to host a Christmas writing competition which involved entrants creating a modern version of Clement Clarke Moore's classic poem, 'The Night Before Christmas'. I would now like to invite Francesca Compton-Halls to come and share her winning entry with us before dinner is served,' Ophelia Grimm announced to a burst of applause.

The woman's husband, Aldous, and young daughter, Aggie, were sitting at the table directly in front of her. Everyone giggled when the clapping died down and Aggie called out, 'I love you, Mummy.'

'Mummy loves you too, darling,' Ophelia replied to another volley of laughter. The girl couldn't have been any cuter in her red and green tartan dress with matching bows in her hair, red Mary Jane shoes and white tights.

'Why did I agree to do this again?' Chessie mumbled as she took a deep breath and stood up.

'You'll be fine,' Alice-Miranda mouthed, giving the girl a smile.

Chessie scampered to the podium, a crisp white page in her hand.

'Hello, everyone. Happy Christmas,' Chessie said into the microphone, which let out a horrible squeak.

'Stand back a little bit, dear,' the junior housemistress, Mrs Howard, suggested.

The girl cleared her throat.

'Twas the week before Christmas and all round
   the school,
The teachers were grumpy, one or two, even
   cruel;
Some said the cause was the horrible weather,
That if the rain didn't stop, we'd spend
   Christmas together . . .

'That was amazing,' Alice-Miranda said, getting to her feet while the audience clapped and cheered. 'Bravo!' Mrs Clinch called as Chessie reluctantly took a bow. By now the entire audience was standing. Chessie's cheeks were alight, but she couldn't stop smiling. It was something of a triumph, given how shy the girl had been when she first arrived. That probably had something to do with having been horribly bullied at her past school.

Miss Grimm only hoped that the girl's poem wasn't prophetic as she listened to the sound of the rain belting on the roof. That was the last thing she needed – for everyone to be stuck at school for the holidays. Ophelia had booked a surprise trip to Lapland to meet Santa and his reindeer, ostensibly for Aggie but even more so for Aldous, whose love of Christmas outstripped anyone she knew.

Chessie rejoined her table, where she was heartily congratulated by her friends as the food began to arrive. There were steaming platters laden with turkey, lamb and roast ham, plus baked potatoes, brussels sprouts and cauliflower cheese. Huge jugs of gravy and Yorkshire puddings were the last things to come out.

Ophelia Grimm stood up and asked that the girls pull their crackers. On a count of three, they'd all do it together – the degree of difficulty made harder by the fact that everyone was crossing their arms to pull two at once with the person either side of them. There were loud bangs and oohs and aahs followed by lots of bad dad jokes and donning of coloured paper hats.

'You can turn the music on again, please, Mr Trout,' the headmistress announced, but the man had abandoned his post. Miss Reedy hurried over to do it. This time, 'Jingle Bells' blasted momentarily until the woman got the volume under control.

'I think Mrs Smith has outdone herself tonight,' Britt said. 'This is superb.'

The others agreed, though Caprice was muttering about the baked potatoes being overcooked. She still hadn't said a word to Millie. Alice-Miranda was disappointed. If the girl really wanted to be accepted, then she had to take responsibility for her behaviour and, so far, it didn't seem that was ever going to happen.

A little while later, when pudding was being served, Alice-Miranda noticed Adalynn, one of the new GAP girls from America, tap Miss Grimm on the shoulder. The woman hastily exited the room and returned minutes later looking pale. It was obvious something was awry. Miss Grimm hurried over to Mrs Howard and whispered in the woman's ear.

The housemistress shook her head. Whatever Miss Grimm had asked her, the woman was most definitely saying no. Miss Grimm headed for Mrs Clarkson, who sighed deeply and pursed her lips.

Millie had also seen Miss Grimm leave and return looking rather too much like her namesake – grim.

She nudged Alice-Miranda. 'What do you think the matter is?'

'It might be the weather. Perhaps there's some flooding, although I spoke to Mummy earlier about the Kennington's thing and she said that conditions are supposed to improve tonight,' Alice-Miranda explained.

'Did she know what the grocery issue was?' Millie asked.

'Mummy said it was nothing to worry about,' Alice-Miranda replied. 'Some of the trucks had been delayed by the weather and, given everyone's been out shopping, that's why things would have been a bit bare. We both agreed that Mrs Parker was likely to have exaggerated the situation a little bit.'

'Of course, she would have. That woman loves a drama almost as much as Caprice does. I wonder if they're related,' Millie said.

Miss Reedy walked to the podium and asked that any girls who were performing finish their meal and head backstage to get ready. Alice-Miranda stood up and Jacinta did too, garnering several pairs of raised eyebrows.

'What are you doing?' Sloane asked.

'Can't tell you – it's a surprise,' Jacinta replied with a grin.

'At least you've got talent,' Millie said. 'Unlike me.'

Caprice was walking past right at the time the girl said it, but much to everyone's surprise she kept quiet.

'What did you say to her earlier?' Millie asked Alice-Miranda.

'I promised I'd keep that between the two of us, but I'm hoping she'll talk to you before we head home tomorrow,' the girl replied. 'I'd best get moving.'

'Maybe you're going to get an apology from Caprice for Christmas,' Sloane said.

'That would be a rare and unusual gift,' Millie said. 'And you know what? I'm in a very forgiving mood. I'd accept it in a heartbeat.'

Next door, in one of the old classrooms, the girls who were set to perform were busy getting ready. Caprice was in the corner warming up her voice with runs and trills – while a couple of younger students who were doing a gymnastics routine were busy stretching and practising the splits. Alice-Miranda was tapping out beats and making sure that Jacinta knew exactly when she was supposed to start her part, while over in the corner Miss Grimm, Mrs Clarkson and Mrs Parker looked to be having a very serious conversation.

Alice-Miranda noticed the threesome spent a lot of time glancing at Caprice, who was completely oblivious to their attentions.

Probably just as well because she was first up to perform. Miss Wall was standing by the door with her clipboard, reminding the girls of the program order. The first five acts would stay in the room until their performance, then return to their seats immediately afterwards, while girls in the last five acts were allowed to watch until Miss Wall called them back again. The room was quite literally buzzing with excitement, though that could also have had something to do with one of the acts, which was an interpretive dance about honeybees with requisite sound effects.

'Caprice, you're up,' Miss Wall called. 'Good luck.'

The girl flicked her long copper tresses and flounced towards the door.

'When have I ever needed luck on stage?' she replied.

'I'd say *you're* going to need some, Petunia, looking after that one for the next few days until her mother can get here,' Myrtle Parker said to Mrs Clarkson, *tsk*ing loudly.

Alice-Miranda frowned while Jacinta's eyebrows flew up.

Everyone in the room had just heard the woman – except Caprice, who had already exited.

'Mrs Parker, honestly, you have all the tact of a bull in a china shop,' Miss Grimm said, glaring.

'I'm sorry, Ophelia, did I say that out loud?' Myrtle said, a smirk on her lips. Though it was obvious that she wasn't sorry at all.

Chapter 6

Caprice's rendition of 'O Holy Night' brought many in the audience to tears and was followed by rapturous applause.

'That was stunning, Caprice,' Mr Trout called from his seat behind the piano. 'Bravo!' He wiped his eyes and gazed at the girl like a proud parent. The music teacher was renowned for his emotional responses, particularly where his star student, Caprice, was concerned.

'I just got the shivers,' Britt said. 'Her voice

is so beautiful.' The other girls could only agree and even Millie had to concede that Caprice was talented beyond the realm of mere mortals.

The girl took several more bows, then shushed the audience – a smile spreading across her lips. There was an obvious glint in her cobalt-blue eyes. 'That was such a success, Mr Trout – why don't I do another?'

The man looked out at the audience, hesitating for a moment before exclaiming, 'Oh, yes, let's.'

But Benitha Wall was having none of it. She strode onto the stage, her clipboard under one arm, and grabbed the microphone from the girl. This evening, the PE teacher and deputy head (alongside Miss Reedy who shared the role) had swapped her trademark navy tracksuit for a navy A-line skirt and cream jumper with a cowl neck. Her hair, which was rarely seen out of a ponytail, fell loosely around her shoulders. Despite her softer look, she was still a woman not to be trifled with.

'Thank you, Caprice. That was a wonderful performance as always and if we have any time left at the end, perhaps you can lead the school in some carols. But you need to vacate the stage for our next act,' the woman ordered, a steely look on her face.

Caprice's face went from picture-perfect to peeved in one fell swoop. She rolled her eyes. 'Sorry, everyone, prepare to be disappointed from here on in.'

Millie raised her eyebrows at Sloane who shrugged. 'I don't think you're going to get that apology after all. Not when her head's *that* big.'

Miss Wall cleared her throat before plastering a big smile on her face. 'Our second performers for this evening are Alice-Miranda Highton-Smith-Kennington-Jones and Jacinta Headlington-Bear – try saying that quickly ten times.' The audience chuckled as the curtain pulled back to reveal Alice-Miranda sitting at the drums and Jacinta standing off to the side in front of a microphone stand. She was holding a tambourine.

Alice-Miranda began quietly before Jacinta's voice rang out. 'Come they told me, par rum pum pum pum . . .' The pair's version of 'The Little Drummer Boy' was gorgeous – at least until the last few bars when an unholy wail started up in the back corner of the room.

'What?' Caprice screeched. 'I'm not staying here with Mrs Clarkson!'

The whole hall fell silent save for a final flourish

from Alice-Miranda. The boom-tish seemed a little blasé, all things considered.

'Oh, goodness,' Miss Grimm muttered from her seat near the stage. 'Who told her?'

But it seemed that honour had most likely gone to the girl's mother as Caprice was holding her phone, staring at the screen and ranting about how much she hated the woman. Given the rest of the school population generally adhered to the rules about no phones in class or the dining room, it would have been odd if it had been anyone else who'd sent the message. Venetia Baldini's timing was terrible.

Caprice stormed to the front of the room and stood beside the headmistress.

'What's this?' she waved the screen in front of the woman's face.

Ophelia Grimm stood up. Fortunately, she still towered over the girl and could be as intimidating as the next authority figure when she wanted to be.

'This is not the time or place, Caprice,' she hissed. 'And I'll take that, thank you.'

The headmistress held out her hand. Caprice's lips wrinkled and she shook her head.

'I'm not giving you my phone. It's holidays tomorrow and I have to take it with me,' Caprice said.

'Please tell me this isn't happening,' Millie mumbled, her head in her hands.

Ophelia eyeballed Caprice. 'Hand that over. We'll discuss this after the concert. Your mother promised she wouldn't contact you until later.'

'I hate her!' Caprice shouted. 'And where is she, anyway? Has she gone to Italy without me? You know we're going to Tuscany to –'

'Stay in your villa that's really more like a castle,' a chorus of voices echoed through the dining room. It seemed everyone in the school had been told about Caprice's upcoming adventure.

'Oh, shut up, you lot!' Caprice's pretty face was the colour of a Santa suit.

Aggie frowned at Caprice and waggled her finger at the girl.

'Naughty!' Aggie put her finger to her lips. She pointed at the stage where Alice-Miranda and Jacinta were waiting for this alternative show to finish before taking their bows.

'Don't tell me to shush, Aggie – you're just a baby!' Caprice snapped. She turned on her heel and stormed out the door with Miss Grimm hot on her heels. Thankfully, the stunned silence didn't last.

'Bravo!' Reginald Parker called out and began to clap. He was soon joined by the rest of the audience, aside from his wife who had charged out after the headmistress, claiming she was off to see if there was anything she could do to help. Millie thought it was more likely she couldn't bear not knowing exactly what was going on.

'Well done, girls,' Miss Reedy said. 'And for our next act we have . . .'

Alice-Miranda and Jacinta joined the girls at their table.

'That was amazing,' Sloane said. 'I thought you were going to wow us with one of your contortionist gymnastics routines, Jacinta. But now I know why you've been going to "visit your mother" every time Alice-Miranda had a drum lesson this past month.'

The girls grinned.

'But what are we going to do about that?' Britt said, motioning her head towards the door where Caprice and Miss Grimm had disappeared.

'We're not doing anything,' Millie said. She looked at Alice-Miranda. 'Are we?'

The girl bit her lip.

Alice-Miranda couldn't help feeling sorry for Caprice. Jacinta frowned and caught her eye – she was obviously troubled by the situation too. Surely there had to be a way of getting Caprice to her family tomorrow or maybe the girls would have no choice other than to take her with them to Highton Hall. Anything else would be too mean-spirited for words – especially at Christmas.

Chapter 7

'Please tell me you're not serious,' Millie said, wringing her hands together. After the concert, Alice-Miranda had called a meeting. Presently, she, Sloane, Millie, Jacinta, Chessie and Britt were gathered in Alice-Miranda and Millie's room, seated on beds, desk chairs and, in Britt's case, the floor, discussing Caprice's predicament.

'I agree with Alice-Miranda,' Jacinta said. 'I know – it's not ideal, but I've been there before and it was horrible. Don't you remember the bad old days when my mother and father used to go away on those glamorous trips and leave me here with Howie and, even worse, with Shaker before she retired? Fortunately, Mummy has proven that everyone can change but let's not even talk about my father.'

Millie sighed. 'But we don't know how long her mother's going to be away for – it might only be a day or two. And why can't Mr Radford come and get her?'

'I think we should talk to Caprice,' Alice-Miranda said. 'See what she'd like to do. And for the record, Millie, I know she wants to be better. I just don't think she knows how to go about it.'

'That would be fair,' Britt said. 'I mean, she may prefer to stay here with Mrs Clarkson rather than come with us – given she knows we'd all agreed not to invite her.'

Millie was perched on the edge of Sloane's bed. 'Oh, she'll want to come. Believe me. That girl has the worst FOMO ever.'

'I'll go and get her,' Jacinta offered.

The others nodded.

Millie picked up a cushion from her bed and began fiddling with the tassel. 'I can't believe that Jacinta caved too.'

'Why?' Britt said. 'Jacinta is lovely – she's such a caring and considerate girl.'

'Who used to be known as the school's second-best tantrum thrower,' Millie replied.

Britt's eyebrows jumped up. She couldn't imagine it. 'Really?'

'That was a long time ago, Millie,' Alice-Miranda said. 'Everyone can change. Jacinta's living proof of that – and like she said a minute ago – look at her mother. Ambrosia's a different person since she split up with Neville Headlington-Bear.'

'I know,' Millie said and folded her arms in front of her. 'You're right. I'm a horrible sceptic when it comes to Caprice.'

'I suppose if things get tricky, I could always take Caprice home with me,' Chessie offered. Her mother and stepfather lived not far across the fields from Alice-Miranda in a mansion called Bedford Manor. 'Although I think Mummy has a pretty full house right up to the weekend.'

Having inherited the country pile and a title to boot, Lord Tavistock had soon realised that there was no *pile of cash* to run the place. His creative new wife Jemima, Chessie's mother, had opened the Manor as a high-end bed and breakfast. She'd been surprised by how much she enjoyed the hospitality business and soon found the place booked up for months.

'I'm sure it won't come to that,' Alice-Miranda said.

For a few minutes, a stony silence fell over the group. Each of the girls seemed to be lost in their own thoughts.

There were footsteps in the hall and the room's door slid open. Jacinta reappeared with Caprice in tow.

'I thought you said you wanted to give me a present,' Caprice said, arching her left eyebrow. 'What's all this?'

Alice-Miranda slid off her bed and stood in front of the girl.

'How are you feeling?' she asked.

'Why do you care?' Caprice said. 'You're all going on holiday tomorrow and now I'm stuck here with Mrs Clarkson until Mummy finishes a job that was "too good to refuse". Whatever.'

'What about your father?' Jacinta asked. She looked at Millie, whose face brightened in anticipation of the answer.

'He and my brothers are already in Tuscany and Mummy says that he can't leave them to come and get me because they have some deadline to meet – who knows what that's about?' Caprice said. 'She says it's only for a few days but I'm not sure that I believe her.'

Jacinta looked at Britt, who glanced at Sloane, who peeked at Chessie, who turned to Alice-Miranda, who eyeballed Millie.

'Fine,' Millie said. 'But if there's one outburst, one mean word, one conceited comment, one –'

'We get it.' Jacinta cut her off.

Caprice frowned. 'What are you saying? Are you asking me to come to Alice-Miranda's?'

Alice-Miranda nodded. 'You shouldn't have to stay here on your own. It's not right.'

'Are you serious?' Caprice's eyes began to fill with tears. 'Do you really mean it?'

The girls all nodded. Even Millie, though it was grudging.

'I promise to be good. I really do. And Millie, I'm sorry for being so mean all the time and I know you did most of the work on our project. I'm a horrible human being. I think there's something wrong with me,' Caprice said.

'Well, duh.' Millie grimaced. She quickly followed it up with a grin. 'Apology accepted – I really don't want to spend the rest of my life fighting with you either, Caprice. But you have to stop pushing my buttons and setting me up. I don't like who I am around you, either.'

Then Caprice did a most unexpected thing. She grabbed Millie and hugged her so tightly she had to wriggle from her embrace.

'Sorry, it's just you don't know what this means to me.' Caprice sniffled.

Alice-Miranda passed her a tissue. 'Caprice, we're glad that you're going to join us and I really appreciate that you've apologised to Millie, but you need to understand that everything Millie said before still stands. One sniff of trouble and I'll ask Mummy to send you back to Mrs Clarkson. We're going to have a wonderful pre-Christmas celebration and I can assure you there will be some terrific surprises, but we don't want any drama. Is that understood?' Alice-Miranda's brown eyes gazed steadfastly into Caprice's blue ones. 'And no flirting with the boys either. Lucas is coming and Sep and Neville Nordstrom – you know he's on exchange at Fayle this term like Britt.'

Caprice nodded. 'Wow – everyone was going except me, but I promise. No drama, no batting my eyelashes at the boys and if I'm mean at any time, I'm heading straight back to school.'

Millie stared at the girl. 'Seriously, who are you and what have you done with the real Caprice?'

Caprice frowned and then realised it was a joke.

'Oh, funny,' she said.

Jacinta turned to Caprice. 'Do you know what this amazing job is that your mother has been asked to do?'

Caprice shook her head. 'She said it's confidential – so that's usually code for she's working for someone really important or super-rich. I hope it's worth it.'

Britt frowned. 'Surely your mother does well out of her show.'

Caprice shrugged. 'I suppose so.' But she knew that times were turbulent. Caprice was on an academic scholarship at Winchesterfield-Downsfordvale – something her parents were very pleased about – particularly as she'd applied for it herself.

Since *Sweet Things* had taken off, her mother's business had expanded considerably but she'd recently overheard her parents talking about their new restaurant chain being in trouble. Then, last time she'd been home, she'd seen something about the ratings for her mother's show being much lower than expected. There was just so much competition out there – and most recently there was a woman who seemed to have modelled her entire persona on Venetia, though she was much younger and even prettier. It seems the life of a celebrity chef wasn't always cupcakes and sprinkles, and Venetia Baldini had had more than her fair share of flops. Hopefully, whoever her mother was working for this time was paying very well – otherwise what was the point of Venetia messing up her family's Christmas plans?

'Well, that settles things. Mummy's sending Mr Greening over tomorrow morning to collect us and the boys. We should probably get to bed,' Alice-Miranda said. 'Have a good night, everyone.'

And with that the girls drifted to their rooms, excited about what the week would bring.

Chapter 8

Elliot Turner was feeling very pleased with himself. The woman had been a little difficult to convince at first, but Elliot had ways and means of ensuring that people did what he wanted. He was surprised at how quickly she capitulated when he mentioned the fee he was prepared to pay.

He strode into the front sitting room. It was decorated in a pretty mint-green with overstuffed floral couches, antique side tables and huge landscapes in gilded frames.

'Sorry to have kept you waiting, Mr Goodman,' Elliot said as the fellow stood up and the pair shook hands.

'Call me Lewis,' the man said.

Elliot couldn't help thinking Lewis looked as though he had barely finished high school, let alone completed university. Dressed in a pair of skinny jeans, trendy multi-coloured trainers and a T-shirt bearing the name of some ghastly heavy metal band, he was hardly a picture of professionalism. Ray was right when he said that the guy was different – but different in a good way was yet to be proven.

'Would you like some more tea?' Elliot asked.

A tray bearing a stout floral teapot and matching teacups and saucers with a milk jug and sugar bowl sat on the coffee table alongside some of Paloma's homemade biscuits.

Lewis Goodman shook his head. 'No, thanks. Can't really stand the stuff. I could go some kombucha if you've got any?'

Elliot gritted his teeth and plastered a smile. 'Sorry – no. Now, I'm afraid we'll need to make this brief. One of my staff members has taken ill and I need to get to the hospital to see her.'

Lewis sat down and pulled a phone from his

pocket, which he fiddled with for a second. Elliot poured himself a cup of tea to which he added a splash of milk.

'Do you mind if I record this?' Lewis asked.

Elliot did mind but in the interests of getting rid of him as quickly as possible, he agreed to the use of the device.

'So, I presume you're aware I'm doing a profile piece on you for the *Financial Weekly*,' Lewis said. 'But I'm keen to get beyond the stuff that everyone knows already. Your rags-to-riches background – that you worked in the back office of a merchant bank, then rose through the ranks as a trader before you bought the company the day after your thirtieth birthday. I mean, it's admirable the way you managed to escape from council housing to all this.' He waved his right arm and looked around the room. 'But that's old news.'

Elliot narrowed his eyes. He had a bad feeling. 'What exactly do you want to know then, Mr Goodman?'

'The deaths of your wife and daughter – well, especially your wife – it was suspicious, wasn't it – though no one was ever charged?' he asked, staring straight into the man's eyes.

Elliot recoiled. 'What?'

But Lewis Goodman was a young man on a mission.

'I read all the reports. It must have been harrowing – and then your little girl died so soon afterwards,' the man said. 'Is it true she was poorly from birth? You've never really said anything publicly about that.'

Elliot felt the thrum of blood in his left temple. He stood up. If he didn't know that it would end up in the papers the next day, he would have taken a swing at the guy. 'Do not mention my wife or daughter again, Mr Goodman. If you wish to profile me for a business piece then I'm happy for that to take place, but as per the conditions of the interview, my family is not up for discussion.'

'But I know the public would be keen to hear from you about what happened,' Lewis said.

Elliot walked to the door and rang the buzzer on the wall. Moments later, Delia Wickham appeared.

'Sir?' she said.

'Show Mr Goodman out and get me Ray Agnew's direct line,' he said quietly.

The woman nodded.

'Why do you want to speak to Ray?' Lewis asked. He had good hearing. 'You know this was his idea. If you think he's going to sack me, you're wrong. He loves my work – says I'm amazing. I'm, like, the youngest person ever to have interviewed the Prime Minister – and you know what a tricky git he can be.'

Elliot turned around. 'I wasn't going to ask for your employment to be terminated – that would be far too easy.'

Lewis looked at the man. 'What are you saying?'

'I was just going to ask that Ray gives you some new challenges,' Elliot said.

Lewis Goodman frowned. 'How do you mean?'

Elliot was stunned that he had the gall to still be sitting on the couch.

'Have you ever considered what it would be like to work as a foreign correspondent – perhaps in Africa or the Middle East?' Elliot asked.

'No way – not my thing at all. I can't stand hot weather. They'd be the last places on earth I'd want to go,' Lewis replied.

'Oh, that's a pity,' Elliot said. The boy was even wetter around the ears than he'd first thought.

Raymond Agnew should have known better. His wife and daughter were off limits then, now and forever. Elliot had always liked Ray – thought he did a good job running the *Financial Weekly* for the most part. But before the start of business tomorrow, he'd ensure that Ray's career was over and Lewis was on the first plane to his new posting – preferably one of the hottest, most godforsaken places on earth.

Chapter 9

'Hello, Mr Greening!' Alice-Miranda called. She rushed towards the man as he hopped out of the black minivan.

'Look at you, darling girl!' he exclaimed as she hugged him tightly around the middle. He stepped back. 'I think you've grown at least half an inch.'

'Have I really?' Alice-Miranda's eyebrows jumped up.

'Definitely,' he replied with a grin.

'Well, it's about time – though I think you might be overstating the fact. How's Mrs Greening and gorgeous Betsy? I can't wait to see them.'

'They're very well,' he said. 'Morning, girls,' he called to the rest of the group who were milling about nearby with their luggage.

Everyone said hello, and Alice-Miranda introduced Caprice and Britt who had both never been to Highton Hall before. The children then took turns helping to load their bags into the back of the van.

'Mrs Greening's been baking for days – all your favourites and some new recipes she's been dying for you and your friends to try,' Harold Greening said.

Alice-Miranda smiled. 'I can't wait – as long as there's Heaven cake, you know I'll be happy.'

The man struggled to pick up the last suitcase, which was twice as big as all the others.

'Good heavens – are you hiding a body in here, Caprice?' he joked.

'Sorry, I can take that,' Caprice offered. 'I'm a late inclusion and I wasn't sure what to pack. I'm going straight to Italy after this.'

'Well, you're a lucky one,' the man said.

'Yes, I am, aren't I?' Caprice replied.

Millie was standing beside her. She stared at the girl. 'Seriously – again, who are you and what have you done with the real Caprice Radford?'

Caprice shrugged. 'I know I deserve that, Millie, but I meant what I said last night. I promise.'

Millie still wasn't entirely convinced but she was prepared to give the girl the benefit of the doubt – for now.

'What did your mother say about you coming to Alice-Miranda's place?' Jacinta asked as the girls piled on board.

'Nothing,' Caprice replied, taking a seat in the second-last row.

Alice-Miranda and Millie were in front of her.

'Well, I'm glad that she was happy about it,' the tiny girl said.

Caprice nodded. The reason her mother hadn't said anything was because Caprice hadn't actually called her. Mrs Clarkson had been thrilled to find out that she wasn't going to be looking after Caprice for the next few days, so what did it matter if her mother knew or not. Caprice would send Venetia a message sometime – but for now she was just going to enjoy the festivities with the girls. And if her mother had to drive a little bit out of her way to collect her, then that was a small price for yet again choosing work over her family.

★

Venetia Baldini pulled into a parking space at the rear of the mansion as per the instructions she'd received on her phone. That had also included the access codes, which allowed her to get through the gate – though she had a feeling she was being watched the entire way. She peered through the windscreen marvelling at the sheer size of the place.

It was enormous – not to her taste, but she didn't have to live there. At least not past Sunday, when her contract would be over and she'd pocket enough money to ensure that the restaurants would be solvent for at least another year. There hadn't been time to find out much about her employer – but now that she was here, she'd have a poke around.

When Venetia had taken the call about the job, she'd initially refused. But the man was persuasive and, ultimately, she couldn't say no. There was too much at stake. Her husband and sons were at their villa in Italy, preparing it for sale. Not that Caprice knew anything about that. Venetia rather hoped that would give them a last-minute reprieve because, with the restaurants on the brink of collapse, they had to get a capital injection from somewhere.

Venetia straightened her jacket and checked her hair in the mirror before reapplying her signature cherry lipstick. Then she hopped out of the car and grabbed her suitcase and knife bag from the boot.

It was a short walk to the back door where she rang the bell. A cool breeze sent a shiver down the woman's spine and she wondered whether she should try to call Caprice again. The girl was angry – and rightly so – but they needed the money and that was that. Hopefully she wasn't giving poor Mrs Clarkson as bad a time as Venetia knew her daughter was more than capable of.

The door swung open.

A smiling woman with stylish cropped silver hair greeted her.

'Hello Miss Baldini, please come in,' she said. 'We're terribly excited that you're here.'

Venetia smiled. 'Thank you for the opportunity.'

Chapter 10

Ellie Higgins wrenched open the cupboard doors, giving the contents nothing more than a cursory glance before slamming them shut again.

'Did you find him?' her mother called from the next room where she was searching too.

'No,' Ellie shouted. The girl caught a glance of her reflection in the mirror and rubbed at a smudge of black kohl that had escaped the perfect line on top of her left eyelid.

'Have you looked under the bed?' her mother, Juliette, yelled.

'No,' Ellie mumbled.

'What was that?'

Ellie spun around. Her mother – all five foot nothing and thin as a rail – was standing in the doorway with her hands on her hips. 'Did you look under the bed?' she asked again.

'Yes,' Ellie hissed, rolling her eyes while simultaneously flicking a long dark braid over her shoulder. It was a skill. Though not one her teachers or mother generally appreciated.

'Are you sure about that?' Juliette said, frowning.

Ellie glared at the woman – her lips pressed into a tight line. 'Do you think I'm lying?'

The woman shook her head. 'Of course not.' She paused. 'I just wonder why everything has to be a fight these days.'

'Because I'm a teenager and that's what we do,' the girl replied with a smirk. 'Tell me why we have to do that stupid elf on the shelf thing anyway.'

'Your brother loves it,' Juliette replied, tucking a tendril of light brown hair behind her ear.

'No, he doesn't,' Ellie said. '*You* love it, Mum. Myles loves shiny Christmas ornaments – that's his thing.'

From a young age, Myles had been different to other children. He talked a lot – and he remembered everything – all the small details. If someone gave him a present, he could tell you when (including the time of day) and where it happened. He never said whether he liked something or not. He had a laser focus – which was impressive but totally annoying sometimes when Ellie wanted to watch something different on the television or read him a different book. Myles loved a cuddle, but only on his terms.

He collected things too. For the past few years, it was Christmas ornaments – the shinier and prettier, the better. He'd spend hours arranging them on his bed, running his fingers over them and staring, completely mesmerised. Then he would pack them away into their tin box – but they had to go in a particular order and no one was allowed to help. It was tricky when they went out – especially during the festive season as Myles was always on the lookout to add to his collection, and sometimes that meant he would take things that didn't belong to him. That was a worry – the last thing they needed was for someone to report him for shoplifting.

Juliette rubbed her arms and shivered.

'And yes, Mum, why *is* it so cold in here? Oh, that's right. Because there's no money for firewood, because we're broke – as usual,' Ellie said. Her accusatory tone stung like a bee.

'Just put another jumper on, darling,' Juliette said. 'Your father will be back soon and then everything will be better. I promise.'

'He's not *my* father,' Ellie snapped, her eyes going to the ceiling. Bronson was Myles's dad. Ellie had never met her own father. He'd disappeared years ago. 'And you know he's not coming back, right?'

'No, Ellie, we don't know that for sure – there has to be a good reason Bronson hasn't been in touch, but I'm not giving up on him,' Juliette said. 'The extra money that appears in my account each month must come from somewhere. I know Bronson loves his family. He's probably working somewhere remote and communications are tricky.'

'Well, you're a bigger fool than I ever took you for, Mum,' Ellie retorted.

Bronson Byers had always been away more than he was ever at home. From what Ellie knew, he'd had a whole lot of different jobs over the years – from working on oil rigs in the North Sea to mining in the outback of Australia to captaining tour buses on the continent. And then just over a year ago, he'd left and they hadn't heard from him since.

Her mother said that he sent money – but did he?

Juliette pushed her shoulders back and stood up taller – perhaps she was trying to rise above it all. 'Anyway, then it's Christmas,' the woman added cheerfully.

It was exactly like her mother to change the subject. As if that would suddenly make everything better.

Ellie hated the holidays. They were just another reminder of what they didn't have and that elf on the shelf had only made things worse as far as she was concerned. Her little brother would be disappointed all over again.

But what could Ellie do? She was a fourteen-year-old schoolgirl – and unless her mother suddenly won the lottery, nothing was going to change anytime soon.

Though one day it would. Ellie was determined and smart – and despite having moved schools more times than she could count on two hands, she'd always been a good student. Ellie could read before she started prep. The one constant in her life had always been a library card. She glanced at the book lying open on the end of her bed. It wasn't a life changer, but the story was entertaining, nonetheless. Though not enough to make her want to stay home right now.

'I'm going out,' Ellie said.

Her mother looked at her. 'Really? What happened to asking?'

'I'm not a kid anymore, Mum. I have friends. We're just hanging out.'

'And I'm still your mother,' Juliette said. 'Where are you going?'

'Hazel's place. Don't worry, Mum. Hazel has a perfect family – and a beautiful warm house, which is huge by the way – two parents who actually like each other and turn up each night, and she gets on well with her brothers,' Ellie said. 'Would you like me to go on?'

Juliette picked up a stray sock from the floor and exhaled loudly. 'I don't like you going over there all the time – it's not fair to her parents and I'd really like to meet Hazel. Why don't you ask her to come here?'

Ellie scoffed. 'Are you kidding?'

'I'm sorry that our home embarrasses you so much. At least meet me for a milkshake after work one day with her,' Juliette said.

There was no way that was going to happen either. Juliette worked shifts in the local supermarket. Hazel's mother spent a lot of time at the gym and going out for lunch with her friends. Her clothes were all high-end designer – even her active wear looked as if it cost a small fortune. Hazel's father was the manager of a national freight company and she had two brothers – her twin, Jake, and Kane who was older and worked for a local courier service delivering parcels. Hazel said that was only until he saved up enough to take a gap year to America. The girls had only been friends for a few months since Ellie and her mother and brother had moved to the village.

'You and your brother get along too.'

'It's different, Mum – and you know it,' Ellie said. She narrowed her eyes. It's true she loved Myles more than anything, but it wasn't easy. Some days he was a lot to deal with.

'I'm sorry that life's so disappointing for you, Ellie,' Juliette said. 'I promise this wasn't what I had in mind when I was your age either.'

Ellie grabbed her bag from her bed. 'Whatever,' the girl said and pushed past her mother down the hall to the front door where she didn't dare turn around. Her mother was not going to see her cry today.

Chapter 11

Ellie linked arms with Hazel as they spilled from the forest trail onto the narrow country road half a mile from the village.

'Where are we going?' Ellie shouted to Hazel's twin brother Jake and his friend Liam, who were ahead of the pair.

'You'll see,' Jake said, waving his arm and motioning them forwards.

Ellie had gone to see Hazel at home, but soon enough Jake and Liam had asked the girls if they wanted to join them for a walk in the forest. Ellie hadn't been that fussed given it was cold and dreary, but Hazel seemed keen. She was regretting her decision not to take Hazel up on her offer to raid the biscuit barrel before they left – and even more than that, she wished she had a warmer coat and a scarf and hat.

'What are you doing for Christmas?' Hazel asked.

Ellie felt her stomach tighten. 'Staying home.'

'Lucky you. We have to go to our grandparents' place. It's mega boring. And the food – you'd think Granny was cooking for the whole village. There's always ham and turkey and pork and roast vegetables and green vegetables and at least three puddings. Honestly, I can't eat anything for a week afterwards,' Hazel said.

Ellie thought it sounded amazing, but she wasn't about to say so. She could only dream about a Christmas table heaving with treats and gifts piled high around the tree. Hazel, on the other hand, seemed to have it all.

A black minivan with tinted windows drove past as the group neared the entrance to an estate called Hoxton Manor.

The boys stopped and stared at the gates, which were adorned with two enormous wreaths.

'This is it,' Liam said.

'This is what?' Ellie asked.

Jake looked at his sister and ran a hand through his dark blond hair. 'I thought you said you'd told her?'

Hazel shook her head. 'No, but Ellie's cool.'

The boys stood in a huddle, whispering in hushed tones.

Liam cast Ellie a glare. 'We hardly know her.'

'What are you talking about?' Ellie asked.

The boys continued their inaudible discussions and called Hazel over to join them.

'We should give her a test – see if she can be trusted,' Jake said. But this time Ellie had heard him.

'What about tonight?' Liam said.

'We can do that on our own with Kane,' Jake said.

'But anything bigger is going to be tricky,' Liam added. 'We'll need help.'

The gnawing feeling in Ellie's stomach was getting worse. Maybe she should make an excuse that she had to get home, but she didn't want to disappoint Hazel. The girl was the first friend Ellie had made in years.

When her mother said she'd found a house they could afford in a village called Highton Mill (which Ellie had never heard of), she was angry – not because she was going to miss her friends (she didn't have any), but because she hated being the weird new kid all the time. It was funny, but the one place her mother said she knew was Hoxton Manor – because her aunt had worked there. The woman died when Ellie was a baby, but they could never drive past the place without Juliette mentioning it.

They'd moved because her mother had a job at a boutique supermarket that Kennington's was trialling to see if it could work in other villages. At least the prep school where Myles was going had a special support unit for kids who were neurodiverse – which made life a bit easier for everyone.

For some reason though, Highton Mill felt different to all the other places they'd lived before. Almost as if they belonged – which made no sense at all. She'd never been there, as far as she could remember.

'Hey,' Jake said, getting Ellie's attention.

She walked over to the group.

'Hazel says you're cool – but we want to know if that's true so you're going to have to prove it,' Liam said.

Ellie frowned and bit her lip. She didn't like the sound of this at all.

'How?' she asked.

'You know on the counter at Kennington's they have that donations box,' Liam explained. 'The one that people put their spare change in for the poor kids. We need it.'

'What for?' Ellie asked.

Liam tilted his head and looked at her. A strand of greasy hair fell across his pimply forehead. 'For the poor kids, of course.'

'But isn't that what Kennington's do – give the money to the needy?' Ellie asked.

Liam rolled his eyes and scowled. 'Yeah, right – as if they do anything for anyone other than themselves. Corporate fat cats – that's what they are.'

'Yeah, they're evil – like the guy who owns this place and half the people in this village who don't care about anyone other than themselves and their bulging wallets,' Hazel said. 'It can't go on – people are starving, you know – there are kids who don't even get presents at Christmas.'

Ellie was well aware of that, having been one of those kids herself, but it seemed a strange argument coming from this lot.

'But what if I get caught?' Ellie asked. It felt as if her stomach was being pulled at either end and tied in a knot like a shoelace.

'That's the whole point. You don't,' Liam said. 'Unless of course you're not interested in helping the poor kids.'

Ellie didn't know anything about Liam, but she was pretty sure Hazel and Jake weren't poor – certainly not in the 'I haven't eaten all day and the blanket on my bed is threadbare' kind of way. Maybe they thought that if you didn't get an overseas holiday every year that counted as being destitute. Ellie could attest to that not being the case. She'd only ever been on holiday once in her entire life – to stay in a caravan by the sea that was owned by someone her mother knew. It was tiny but she'd loved it and would give anything to get the chance to do something like that again.

'So why do I have to prove myself to you? What's that about?' Ellie asked.

'All in good time, Princess, all in good time,' Jake replied, mysteriously.

Ellie swallowed hard. She wasn't a thief. But if she didn't do what they asked then that was it – she'd be on her own again.

'So when do you want it?' Ellie asked. The late afternoon air was bone chilling, but so was the thought of what they'd asked her to do.

'Let's meet up again the day after tomorrow. If you've got the box, then we'll let you know what the mission entails,' Liam said, flicking his stringy hair over his shoulder.

'Okay, James Bond, can't wait to hear what you're up to,' Ellie said. She tried to sound tough, but her insides were turning to jelly.

Ellie looked at Hazel, her eyes pleading. She wanted the girl to throw her head back and laugh and say that it was all just a joke, but she didn't.

'You can do it, El – I know you can,' Hazel said.

But that wasn't how she felt at all.

Chapter 12

Having collected Sep, Lucas and Neville from Fayle School for Boys on the other side of the village, the children were soon on the road to Highton Mill. The weather had improved considerably, although the forecast for the next few days wasn't terribly good. There was plenty to do, regardless. Cecelia had promised Alice-Miranda some surprises too.

'Has anyone got anything special they'd like to add to the plans for the next few days?' Alice-Miranda asked from her seat behind Mr Greening.

'Shopping, please,' Millie said. 'I still have quite a few gifts I need to get.'

'Perfect,' Alice-Miranda said. 'I've got to buy a few things myself.'

There was a murmur of agreement from the others.

Jacinta opened a bag of jelly snakes and passed them to Lucas, who handed them back to Sep and Neville behind them. 'So what's everyone getting for Christmas?' Lucas asked.

'I'm hoping for a new mountain bike,' Neville said.

'Cool, me too,' Sep said with a nod.

'Awesome! We can go riding together,' Neville replied. He and his parents lived quite close to the Sykes's villa in the northern suburbs of Barcelona (their parents were in business together – the Sykes's developing properties and the Nordstroms in earthmoving), so the boys and Sloane often got to hang out in the holidays. Sloane thought Neville's parents were adorable, unlike her own mother who spent most of her time sunbathing and recovering from minor cosmetic surgery procedures.

'Are you getting a bike as well, Sloane?' Neville asked the girl.

She shook her head. 'I was hoping for a surfboard.'

'That sounds like fun,' Alice-Miranda said. 'What about you, Jacinta?'

'Mummy said that she's planning to take me to Fashion Week in Paris next year, so I haven't really asked her for anything because I know that's going to be expensive,' the girl replied. 'It would be amazing to see it again – maybe without all the drama that we had last time.'

A while back, the children, as members of the Winchester-Fayle Singers, travelled to Paris to take part in one of the fashion shows – though the trip turned out to have more twists and turns than a rollercoaster.

'What about you, Caprice?' Jacinta asked.

The girl took a deep breath. 'Well . . . I've got quite a long list. A gold pendant and matching earrings for a start, and there's this dress I've had my eye on for ages which will be perfect for next year's National Eisteddfod, and makeup – proper stage makeup for my performances – and a voucher to go to the nail salon in Downsfordvale during term time and . . .' She stopped and realised Millie was staring. Caprice took a deep breath.

'Truly, I don't mind what I get. What about you, Millie?'

'A new tennis racquet,' she said. 'And some trainers.'

'All I want for Christmas is my family and friends to be together having a wonderful time,' Alice-Miranda said.

'Sure thing, little Miss Perfect,' Lucas scoffed. 'What do you really want?'

'Nothing,' the girl shook her head.

'Not buying it,' Lucas retorted. 'There must be something you'd like.'

Alice-Miranda grinned. 'I suppose there is one thing I've thought would be nice.'

There was a pregnant pause.

'Out with it,' Millie demanded as the bag of snakes made its way back to the front of the bus and Mr Greening helped himself to the last one.

'I'd like a book,' Alice-Miranda said.

'A book? That sounds boring,' Sloane quipped.

'Which book?' Millie asked.

'I'm not sure, really – just something special that I haven't read before,' Alice-Miranda said, then promptly changed the subject. 'Oh look, we're almost home.'

The bus was approaching Hoxton Manor, a stately pile owned by a businessman called Elliot Turner, which was not terribly far from Highton Hall. He and Alice-Miranda's parents were friends, but she'd only ever met him on a handful of occasions.

Alice-Miranda noticed a group of teens about the same age as her friends walking along the side of the road. There were two girls and two boys. All of them were wearing heavy coats and boots, except for one of the girls with long dark hair who looked as if she could have done with a warmer coat along with a scarf and hat.

'Look at those wreaths on the gates!' Britt said as they passed the entrance to the driveway. 'They're gorgeous.'

'Mummy says that Hoxton Manor is one of the most beautiful homes she's ever seen,' Alice-Miranda replied.

'It must be stunning then, because yours isn't too shabby either,' Jacinta said.

'I haven't seen it in person, but perhaps one day I'll be lucky enough to get an invitation,' Alice-Miranda said.

Britt Fox was excited to see Alice-Miranda's family home. The girls had told her a lot about the estate, but she couldn't quite imagine the size of it or the grandeur.

The bus continued past another set of gates – but these were modern, made of thick black steel. There was no seeing what was behind them. Security cameras perched on top of the posts.

'Who lives there?' Millie asked, pointing.

'I'm not sure. Mummy and Daddy said that the house was only finished a year or so ago and it's all a bit mysterious. They've never met the owners,' Alice-Miranda said. 'It's called Loff's Folly, but we don't know who Loff is or why it's their folly.'

'I guess some people just like their privacy,' Lucas said.

'Maybe they're famous like your father,' Sloane said. 'And sick of being stalked by the paparazzi.'

'Or they're criminal masterminds and up to something really dodgy and that's their hideout,' Neville added.

'Listen to all of you crime writers in the making,' Millie said with a chuckle.

A little further along, they drove by a row of tiny, terraced houses on the opposite side of the road. The dwellings all looked as if they'd seen better days.

'I thought your village was supposed to be one of the best kept in the country,' Caprice said, wrinkling her nose as they passed the sign that announced they'd arrived on the outskirts of Highton Mill. 'Those places need a bulldozer through them.'

It was true that the row of semi-detached houses wasn't in the best state. Some of the slates on the rooves were missing and there was plenty of peeling paint.

'Yes, you'd think that, wouldn't you, Caprice?' Mr Greening said. He was enjoying listening to the children's banter, but her comment had raised his hackles a little. 'Except that then there'd be a whole lot of families that would have nowhere to live.'

'But can't they renovate?' the girl said. 'And get rid of all that junk. It looks so . . . ugly – compared to everything else.'

'Not everyone has the money,' Millie said. 'Renovations cost a fortune – I know because my parents did some a while back and they're still complaining about the cost.'

'What about your parents, Alice-Miranda? Couldn't they pay to fix them up? They're rich,' Caprice said.

The minivan slowed down to turn left into the gates at Highton Hall.

Alice-Miranda bit her lip. Maybe she could ask her parents if they could do something.

Mr Greening intervened. 'Hugh and Cecelia are very generous to the community here – and they have always known that with great privilege comes great responsibility,' the man said. 'But they can't fix everything. People are proud too and rightly so.'

Still, Caprice's comment had got Alice-Miranda thinking.

'Isn't that your house, Mr Greening?' Sloane asked as they drove past the gatehouse at the entrance to the property.

'It's tiny,' Caprice said, then added as an afterthought. 'But cute.'

'Aye, I was born in the front room,' the man said. 'Mrs Greening and I raised four sons in that house and we got on just fine,' the man replied. 'It's not the size of the house that matters but the people inside of it.'

'Are the boys coming home for Christmas?' Alice-Miranda asked. The Greenings' sons were all grown up these days and had families of their own. But none of them lived close – in fact three of them were overseas.

'Not this year – it's the in-laws' turns. Mrs Greening and I are looking forward to a quiet time at home – though I suspect your mother will have something to say about that.'

Alice-Miranda grinned. 'I know she will. If anyone is here at Christmas, then they're at our dinner table – no arguments.'

Harold Greening steered the van through another set of ornate gates along a broad avenue of oaks. In the distance, the chimney pots of Highton Hall stood tall against the grey sky.

'Wow!' Britt gasped. Caprice did too. It was the first time she'd been to Highton Hall as well.

'Are you sure you're not actually a princess?' Britt asked, giving her friend a smile.

Alice-Miranda shook her head. 'You know I'm not. Look – there's Shilly and Mrs Greening and Mrs Oliver.'

The three women were standing on the steps by the side entrance. Dolly Oliver, with her helmet of brown curls, had a tea towel slung over her shoulder. She looked as if she'd just abandoned the washing-up to meet them.

'I still can't believe how much Mrs Oliver looks like Aunty Gee,' Millie said. 'Or vice versa.'

Alice-Miranda grinned at her friend. 'Although I'm sure you wouldn't get the two of them mixed up these days.'

'Don't remind me,' Millie said. 'I can't believe that I mistook the queen for Mrs Oliver's sister – what a twit.'

'Oh, I think that's one of the reasons Aunty Gee loves you a lot, Millie – you've always treated her like a regular person, which she much prefers to being fussed over,' Alice-Miranda said.

The vehicle had barely come to a stop before Alice-Miranda was out the door. After hugging all three women, Cecelia Highton-Smith appeared, apologising for just having got off the phone.

'Hello, my darling,' the woman said, lifting her daughter into the air and spinning her around. She peppered the child's face with kisses. 'I'm so glad you're home.'

'Hello, Mummy,' Alice-Miranda said, then realised that she'd left everyone in the van. 'Oops, I've quite forgotten my manners.'

She held her mother's hand and rushed back

onto the driveway where Mr Greening had already begun to unload the suitcases.

'You know everyone, Mummy, but Caprice and Britt – this is Mrs Greening and Mrs Oliver and Mrs Shillingsworth,' the child said to the girls.

'Lovely to meet you,' Mrs Oliver said. Her thoughts were echoed by the others who were impressed with both girls' manners.

'I've got fresh banana bread just out of the oven and hot chocolate for your afternoon tea, so come along, everyone – let's get in out of the cold,' Dolly Oliver decreed to much excitement from the young guests.

Millie was keeping an eye on Caprice. So far, apart from her rather extensive list of Christmas wants and slightly snobby attitude towards the run-down houses, the girl hadn't put a foot wrong. Unfortunately, Millie also knew that there was still time.

'Where's Daddy?' Alice-Miranda asked.

Cecelia Highton-Smith's brow tightened. 'He's on a work call. He won't be long.'

But there was something about the look on her mother's face that didn't sit well with the girl. She'd seen if before and it usually meant trouble.

Alice-Miranda's Pre-Christmas Celebration Planner

Wednesday
Travel home by minivan with Mr Greening
Settle in
Surprise activities

Thursday
Decorate Christmas tree
Gingerbread-house building
Christmas charades and other games
Visit Poppy and Jasper – decorate the cubby for Christmas

Friday
Shopping
Gift-wrapping
Make Christmas stockings
Hide-and-seek
Village Christmas light ceremony

Saturday
Build snow families (snow permitting)
Sledding (snow permitting)
Ice-skating
Baking

Sunday
Aunt Charlotte, Uncle Lawrence, Imogen and Marcus arrive
Granny Valentina arrives
Family day of games and exchanging presents

Monday
Guests travel home for Christmas

Chapter 13

Following a delicious afternoon tea, the children were soon settled into their allocated bedrooms along the hallway from Alice-Miranda, who was sharing her room with Millie. The girls often slept beside each other in Alice-Miranda's giant four-poster bed and this week would be no different.

The guest rooms at Highton Hall were all beautifully appointed with antique furniture and rare artwork. Alice-Miranda's was one of the most stunning though, with its huge doll's house – an exact replica of Highton Hall that had been made by Mr Greening's father for Cecelia and her sister Charlotte when they were girls. Surprisingly, it wasn't only to be looked at – Alice-Miranda had always been encouraged to use her imagination and play with it and thankfully so, as it helped her and Millie locate Aunty Gee after the woman had been kidnapped and held hostage a few years back.

Another favourite piece was a giant white rocking horse, which had also seen plenty of action over the years. Hugh and Cecelia knew that while in many ways Highton Hall resembled a museum, they never wanted it to feel like one. It was first and foremost their home, so there was no point being precious about things – even if many of the things in it were quite precious.

'Do you think everyone will have finished unpacking by now?' Alice-Miranda asked Millie, who had just hung the last of her clothes in the wardrobe.

'Why? What have you got planned?' the girl asked.

Alice-Miranda had a glint in her eye. 'I asked Shilly if she could set up the banister challenge.'

'Yes!' Millie clenched her fists and shouted. 'I'm in!'

'Shall we get the others?' Alice-Miranda said. Sloane and Chessie were next door with direct access to a Jack-and-Jill-style bathroom with Alice-Miranda's room. Jacinta volunteered to be with Caprice and Britt in the Blue Room down the hall. Since it was largely her idea to bring Caprice along in the first place, she thought it only fair that she bunk in with the girl. Besides, Britt was so much like Alice-Miranda, Jacinta thought she'd know all the right things to say if Caprice started to go off the rails. Not that there had been any signs of trouble yet.

The boys were sharing the Yellow Room together. Cecelia had reconfigured it with three single beds, so it was perfect for the lads.

'Let's go,' Millie said as the pair charged out of Alice-Miranda's room and along the hall, knocking and calling for the others to hurry up.

'What's happening?' Lucas asked as he opened the door.

Alice-Miranda could see around him inside the room and was surprised that everything had been put away and Neville and Sep were laying on their beds reading. She wondered if they were always so neat.

'Are you boys up for the banister challenge?' she asked.

Lucas's eyes were wide. 'Yes!' he shouted. 'I was disappointed not to see that on the program, but I knew you'd have some surprises up your sleeve.'

'Meet us at the top of the stairs in five minutes,' Alice-Miranda said.

Millie had already told the girls, who were excited too – though Britt and Caprice weren't exactly sure about the details.

Alice-Miranda ran along the hallway to the top of the giant staircase.

At the bottom, Mr Greening had just finished strategically placing several large gym mats while Shilly was madly polishing the banister rail.

'Extra slick,' the child said. 'Exactly the way I like it.'

'Well, I knew you'd want to give everyone a *flying* chance,' Shilly said with a grin.

Riding the Highton Hall rollercoaster had been a family tradition for years. And while most parents would fret about their tiny child throwing themselves backwards down a sweeping staircase rather much larger and longer than you'd find in your average home, in the Highton-Smith-Kennington-Jones household it was a regular event.

'Have you got your stopwatch, Shilly?' the girl asked.

The woman trotted down the stairs and put the polish onto one of the side tables before picking up a clipboard.

'Very official,' Millie said as the other children appeared at the top of the landing.

'The banister record is a hotly contested sport in this family,' Shilly said. 'Now make sure that none of you fall off, please, as we really don't want any trips to the hospital before Christmas.'

Millie frowned and bit her lip. She wished the woman hadn't said anything about accidents.

'So, who's up first?' Alice-Miranda said.

'I'll go,' Lucas offered. He was keen to improve on his last time of just over nine seconds. Since he'd joined the family, the times had steadily got faster and faster. The boy threw his leg over the rail and rubbed his hands together before wriggling his bottom.

'I'll count you down, Lucas,' Mrs Shillingsworth said. She had always been the official timer for these events and revelled in her role as the keeper of the clock.

'On your mark, get set, go!' Shilly clicked the stopwatch and the children cheered as Lucas sped down the rail as if he was on a rollercoaster.

He leapt off at the bottom and fell backwards onto the mats that Mr Greening had brought in.

'Whoa, that was awesome,' he said, dusting himself off and getting to his feet.

Mrs Shillingsworth arched her eyebrow at the lad. 'Not bad, Master Lucas, not bad.'

'What was my time?' he asked.

'I think I'm going to keep that a secret until everyone has had their turn,' the woman replied to the others' groans.

'Please don't, Shilly – it's more fun knowing the time to beat,' Millie said.

Upstairs on the top landing, Britt was leaping about excitedly, volunteering to go next. Caprice, on the other hand, was strangely silent.

'Are you all right?' Millie asked.

Caprice nodded. 'Fine.'

But Millie wasn't convinced. 'You know you don't have to do it if you don't want to,' the girl said.

'Who said I didn't want to?' Caprice snapped.

'You just look a bit . . . I don't know . . . nervous,' Millie said. 'I don't blame you. It's a big staircase. I was a bit terrified the first time I did it too.'

'I'm not scared,' Caprice said, rolling her eyes.

Mrs Shillingsworth tapped her clipboard and looked up at the children. 'Millie, you're next and the time to beat is 8.5 seconds, which I do believe, Master Lucas, is a new household record.'

Lucas punched the air and gave a yelp of excitement.

'Calm down, Lucas,' Millie said. 'You haven't seen me in action yet.'

'Okay, Millie – whatever,' Lucas replied with a grin.

The girl climbed onto the rail and got into position. Millie had an idea. She was going to start like the runners in the bobsled races to give herself some extra propulsion. As Mrs Shillingsworth counted her down, Millie pushed herself up and down the banister trying to gain some extra oomph. On the shout of 'go', the girl flew down the polished timber rail, leaping off at the bottom and somehow managing to stay on her feet.

'That was incredible!' Alice-Miranda yelled. Everyone agreed and when Shilly announced that Millie had shaved a tenth of a second off Lucas's time, no one was surprised. Lucas grumbled and said that he should be allowed to have another go – he wanted to try Millie's start routine, which he hadn't thought of himself.

The fun continued with Sep and Neville both falling slightly short of Millie's new record. Jacinta, however, was determined she could do it and her run was greeted with rousing applause. Shilly announced that the new time to beat was 8.3 seconds. Britt was fast but careful, as was Chessie, and Alice-Miranda's time of 8.9 seconds was a new personal best for her. Last up was Caprice.

'Are you sure you want to do it?' Millie asked.

'Of course, I'm sure,' the girl retorted.

'You don't have to if you'd rather not,' Alice-Miranda called, then sprinted back to the top of the stairs.

'Yeah, you don't have to,' Millie echoed.

'And let you lot make me look bad?' the girl said with a scowl, then swallowed her words. 'I didn't mean it to come out like that – but I'm fine – just watch me.'

'Okay, Caprice,' Mrs Shillingsworth said. 'On your mark, get set, go!'

The rest of the children watched from the ground floor as the girl absolutely flew down the banister rail. Perhaps it was the fabric of the pants she was wearing or the fact that the other children had polished the timber even slicker than before, but the rest of them stood with their mouths agape.

'Whoa!' Lucas gasped.

Caprice was on track for a new record when suddenly, only a metre or so from the end, she lost her balance and flew over the side hitting the floor with a thud.

'Caprice!' Alice-Miranda shouted as she ran to her.

Everyone held their breaths waiting for the inevitable screams, but surprisingly there was just a small gasp.

'Oh, heavens!' Mrs Shillingsworth declared and hurried over to see what damage had been done. 'I knew I shouldn't have made that comment about a hospital trip. Talk about Murphy's Law. Caprice dear, are you all right?'

Millie was just thinking the same thing – about Murphy's Law, that is.

The girl was lying facedown on one of the large oriental rugs, which thankfully would have cushioned her fall somewhat.

'Caprice, can you hear me?' Alice-Miranda asked urgently.

'Uh-huh,' the girl whimpered.

'Where does it hurt?' Alice-Miranda asked.

A muffled reply sounded like 'my face', but it was hard to tell exactly what she'd said.

The children watched as a pool of blood began to spread out across the silk mat like red ink – it had been hard to see until the liquid escaped the edges of the red flowers in the pattern.

'Look at all that blood!' Millie exclaimed.

Sloane gave Millie a nudge and whispered. 'Don't say that. She'll freak out.'

'I think I'm okay,' Caprice said and rolled over. 'I'm fine.'

The others had formed a circle around her.

'Eww!' they gasped in unison.

Caprice's aquiline nose was beginning to swell and was dripping like a tap.

'What's wrong?' Caprice sat up and felt her face throbbing.

By now, Jacinta had run to get Mrs Oliver,

who had brought the first-aid kit and a huge box of tissues.

'Oh, dear me, I think someone is going to have to take a trip to the A and E,' Shilly said, garnering a nod from Dolly Oliver.

'I'll get Mummy,' Alice-Miranda said and hurried away to find the woman, who was working in her study.

'Have I got a cut?' Caprice whimpered.

'Don't worry – I think it's just a nosebleed,' Britt said.

When Mrs Oliver tried to stem the flow, touching Caprice ever so gently, the girl almost hit the roof.

'Ow! Is it broken? I can't have a broken nose. My nose is lovely. What if I'm not pretty anymore?' Caprice cried. Fat tears spilled down her cheeks.

'Of course you will be,' Millie replied, rolling her eyes.

'What's that supposed to mean?' Caprice demanded. 'You've always been jealous that I'm pretty and you're not, Millie.'

Jacinta and Sloane looked at Caprice, eyebrows raised. Caprice had promised no outbursts and this wasn't a good sign.

'I never said you weren't pretty! Why do you have to be so mean? Seriously, I knew this wouldn't last – because underneath all that rubbish about being better, well, you're still YOU!' Millie shouted, then sprinted away up the stairs and into Alice-Miranda's bedroom.

'I'll go after her,' Britt said.

The other children stood in silence, staring.

'Don't look at me like that,' Caprice said. 'Millie was being sarcastic – she rolled her eyes. She was being mean to me – not the other way around – and now I've got a smashed nose and the only reason I even rode that silly banister is that she made me feel like I had to. This is *all* her fault.'

Alice-Miranda arrived with Cecelia in tow. Mr Greening had already brought the car around to the side entrance by the kitchen. A bloody trail of tissues littered the floor and Caprice's white jumper was streaked red. It looked like a murder scene and could well have been if Millie hadn't left. Caprice managed to get to her feet, aided by Lucas and Jacinta.

Cecelia Highton-Smith had an icepack wrapped in a tea towel, which she placed gently on Caprice's cheek. 'You poor thing – but don't worry, Caprice – I'm sure that it looks much worse than it really is,' Cecelia said. 'I've broken my nose a couple of times and the doctor has always managed to straighten it up. I'll call your mother on the way to the hospital.'

'No,' Caprice said, shaking her head. 'I don't want her to come. She's busy.'

Cecelia frowned. 'At least let me tell her what's happened.'

'Afterwards,' the girl said. 'Or she'll be too worried and I'm not sure where she is at the moment. She could be in Siberia for all I know.'

Cecelia nodded, though she didn't like it. If it was Alice-Miranda who was injured, she'd want to know right away.

'Where's Millie?' Alice-Miranda asked, looking around.

Sloane motioned towards the second floor.

'Is everything all right?'

'No – Millie was horrible to me,' Caprice said.

Alice-Miranda frowned and caught sight of Jacinta, who surreptitiously shook her head. Something had obviously happened when she'd left the room but now was not the time to find out.

'Come on then, let's go,' Cecelia said. 'Could someone let Hugh know what's happened? I think he's in his study.'

Shilly nodded sheepishly. 'Of course, ma'am, and Dolly and I'll organise dinner and some board games. I think I must have put too much polish on that rail.'

'No, you didn't,' Alice-Miranda said. 'I'm sure that Caprice doesn't blame you. It was an accident.'

Caprice began to wail. 'It's hurting.'

'Come on, then,' Cecelia said and wrapped her arm around Caprice's shoulder. 'The doctor will give you something for the pain and then I'm sure you'll feel much better.'

Minutes later, Caprice was in the car with Alice-Miranda and Cecelia heading for the hospital.

Chapter 14

Griffin Hendrix removed his glasses and rubbed his tired eyes. He'd been staring at the screen for the past hour or so and could feel the heat rising up his neck. There were at least seven lorries running way too late. He needed them to get back to the warehouse and stocked up in time to leave first thing in the morning, or the schedule would be impossible. He chewed his blistered bottom lip and tried to think about something other than the message that was on his phone this morning. He'd ignored the call – knowing that in doing so, there would be consequences. He just couldn't deal with anything else at the moment.

The door opened silently behind him and a hoarse voice asked, 'What are those blue blips on there?'

The question almost startled Griff from his chair. He spun around. 'Have you ever heard of knocking, Trevor?'

The man stood behind him, staring at the screen.

'There's no one else here,' Trevor said. 'So what are they?'

'Nothing to do with you,' Griff replied. 'Haven't you got paperwork to collect?'

Griff pointed towards the bays down below the glass control room where at least twenty lorries were in the process of being loaded. The drivers would be in the break room or taking showers to freshen up before a long night ahead.

'I've done it all,' the man said. 'I came to ask if you've thought anymore about putting my son on.'

Griff turned around. 'I told you already – there's nothing for Dorian at the moment. I'll let you know as soon as something comes up.'

'That's what you said last year – just before you hired that fellow Bobby – the one who reminds me of a labrador,' Trevor said.

'Well, I'm sorry, mate, but that's the way it is. Dorian might have to keep grave digging for a while yet,' Griff said. Truth be told he would never give that deadbeat kid of Trevor's a job. And if he could get rid of Trevor, he would. Problem was he was vaguely related by marriage to the family who owned the company and the last thing Griff needed was for them to start questioning his judgement.

But Griff was sure that Trevor was right about Bobby – at least that's what he hoped. He needed someone to expand the business and he seemed like just the guy. Bobby didn't ask questions and went about his work without a complaint. Not one squeak when he had to drive two weeks without a rest day either – unlike others who were always having a whinge. He had a good feeling that things were back on track. They'd better be. There were people relying on him – people he couldn't afford to upset. Not least of which was his wife and children. And even more so, the man at the top.

Chapter 15

Cecelia Highton-Smith pulled up in the driveway at Accident and Emergency. A single length of silver tinsel surrounded the entrance doors to the hospital with a piece of plastic holly taped up above. Alice-Miranda helped Caprice out of the car and the two girls walked into the waiting room while her mother found a parking spot. Fortunately, there was only a couple of other people inside; an older chap with a nasty hacking cough and a pregnant woman who seemed quite fine, though her partner was panting like a dog.

A sad-looking Christmas tree adorned with a handful of silver baubles stood in one corner. Alice-Miranda decided that next year their local hospital should be in line to receive some of the Highton's ex-display decorations. Perhaps she and her mother could come and help put it all together. No one wanted to be in hospital at Christmas – the least they could do would be to make the place feel more festive.

Caprice was a gruesome sight with patches of dried blood all over her face. Her jumper and jeans hadn't escaped the drenching either. Fortunately, the tide had stopped flowing although there was still the odd clot dribbling from her nose. Alice-Miranda was carrying a box of tissues and collecting the used ones in a plastic bag.

A kindly nurse with a bright smile walked out from behind the reception desk to greet the pair.

'Hello, girls,' she said, then turned her attention to Caprice. 'You look as if you've been in the wars.'

'You should see the other guy,' Alice-Miranda said with a grin.

The woman chuckled then considered Caprice's face. 'Is it just your nose, dear?' she asked.

Caprice nodded. 'I think so.'

'Oh, I've quite forgotten my manners,' Alice-Miranda said. 'I'm Alice-Miranda Highton-Smith-Kennington-Jones and this is my friend Caprice Radford,' she said, offering her hand.

The nurse took it, then smiled and exclaimed, 'You're Cecelia's little girl! I'm Dotti. It's lovely to see you. I was your mother's home-care nurse after you were born. You were such a darling baby. I don't think I've ever met another with quite your temperament. Born with a smile on your wee face and barely a whimper in all the times I saw you. I ran into your mother in the village a while back and she said that you were practically grown up and at boarding school. And here you are – just look at you.'

Caprice tapped her foot. 'Excuse me – hello?' she said pointedly.

'Sorry, dear. I'll get you into one of the examination suites,' Dotti said. 'You can come too, Alice-Miranda, although is there an adult with you? I'll need to get the paperwork sorted once the doctor comes.'

'Mummy's parking the car,' the child replied as Cecelia Highton-Smith walked through the automatic doors.

'Hello, hello,' Dotti greeted the woman.

The pair hugged and Caprice tapped her foot again. 'Sorry to break up another lovely reunion,' she said, 'but I'm still here – with my broken face.'

The women parted and Dotti led Caprice with Alice-Miranda and her mother in tow down the corridor to a small examination area.

'Dr Babbage will be with you in a minute,' she said, dragging the curtain around the bed. She hurried out to take care of a mother who had just arrived with a screaming baby.

Caprice hadn't yet seen herself in a mirror. She'd realised there was one in the room and was about to take a look when the doctor interrupted her.

A tall woman wearing beige trousers, a sensible blue shirt and a white coat appeared through the gap in the curtains and announced herself.

'Now, who do we have here?' she asked.

Alice-Miranda's mother took care of the introductions and said that she was acting in the capacity of Caprice's guardian.

'And what have you done to yourself?' The woman bent down to peer at Caprice's face.

Alice-Miranda explained about the banister challenge and that Caprice was clearly going to break the record when the mishap occurred. But the doctor wanted to hear it from Caprice and suggested Alice-Miranda might like to go and get herself a hot chocolate from the cafeteria.

It was probably a good thing, given that the minute she left and Dr Babbage touched Caprice's nose all hell broke loose.

Alice-Miranda trotted down the corridor. She made a left turn as directed and followed the signs down another long hallway past several wards. A male orderly with arms like Christmas hams effortlessly pushed an empty bed past her and there were several nurses darting in and out of rooms, answering patient calls. It was such a busy place. Alice-Miranda remembered her own time in the children's hospital after her horse-riding accident and how kind everyone had been. Ever since then, she'd been thinking about whether she might become a doctor one day – although she'd have to study extremely hard to win a place at university.

She arrived at the cafeteria to find it almost empty. Alice-Miranda ordered herself a hot chocolate and sat down at one of the tables. There was an elderly lady with a mop of curly white hair and a middle-aged man who looked like he could have been her son, having a hushed conversation in one corner of the glassed-in room. Another well-dressed man with salt and pepper hair was sitting at the table beside her, nursing a mug in both hands.

He looked up and smiled and it was then that Alice-Miranda realised that she vaguely knew him.

'Excuse me, sir, are you Mr Turner?' the girl asked.

He tilted his head to the side questioningly. 'Yes, I'm Elliot Turner but to whom do I have the pleasure of making my acquaintance?'

Alice-Miranda introduced herself in the usual way.

'Of course,' he said. 'We've met a couple of times before, haven't we?'

The girl nodded. 'I think you came to Mummy's garden party a few years ago. But I have grown since then. Are you visiting someone?'

'Yes, one of my employees. She had an emergency appendectomy yesterday. Gave us all quite a fright. But she's going to be fine. I just stepped out while the doctor was doing his rounds,' the man explained. 'What about you?'

'One of my friends is in A and E with Mummy. She fell off the banister rail at home – we were having a time-trial race,' the child said. 'Caprice was the last one. She was going to win but then she lost her balance and fell and hit her nose.'

Elliot Turner's eyes widened. 'Goodness, that sounds drastic,' he said. 'And quite good fun too – apart from the fall.'

Alice-Miranda grinned. 'It's the best. I think Caprice will be fine, though I suspect her nose might be broken and she's rather attached to it the way it is. I don't blame her – it's a very nice nose. I don't think I've ever seen so much blood in my life although my best friend Millie said that there was a river when I fell off my naughty Bonaparte and hit my head – I was unconscious, so I didn't see it. Head injuries are like that, aren't they?'

Elliot Turner seemed to shudder. 'Yes,' he said vaguely, as if remembering something horribly unpleasant.

Alice-Miranda didn't want to pry. 'We drove past your gates today on the way home from school. Your Christmas wreaths are gorgeous. I don't think I've ever seen any more beautiful.'

Elliot smiled. 'Why, thank you. Sebastian and his team have done an incredible job this year. I'm thrilled to bits.'

'Do you mean Mr Smote?' Alice-Miranda asked. 'Mummy had him do the decorations for Granny's birthday last year after he was recommended by Lady Clarissa Appleby from Penberthy House Hotel. I think he used to specialise in weddings, but now he's doing lots of other parties too. He's fun.'

'Indeed, he is,' Elliot said, smiling at the child.

'We're decorating the tree at home tomorrow, then on Friday I'm very excited to be taking all my friends to the Christmas light ceremony in Highton Mill,' the child explained. 'I love it when the whole village comes together – it's especially fun seeing all the little children. My cousins are due to arrive soon; they love everything about Christmas – except mince pies.'

There was suddenly a faraway look in Elliot's eyes. 'Yes, you're right. Christmas is always lovelier with children.'

'Do you have grandchildren, Mr Turner?' the child asked.

Elliot's face fell as if he had just plummeted back to earth. 'No.'

Alice-Miranda realised she had probably said too much. 'I'm sorry – that's none of my business. I tend to ask far too many questions. I hope I'm not turning into Mrs Parker – she's working in the office at my school at the moment and she's a bit nosy. I really need to think before I open my mouth – it's a problem.'

Elliot's smile returned. 'Please don't be too hard on yourself. You're only how old?'

'I'll be twelve in a few months,' she said. 'But most of my friends are turning fifteen or more. I've always been a bit old for my years – though it's funny because the older I get, the less sure I am about so many things. It's easy to see the world in black and white when you're young. But then you realise that it's really so many shades of grey. Everyone sees things from a different perspective, and I know that mine is a very privileged one.'

'Goodness – are you sure you're not actually an elderly woman inhabiting the body of a nearly twelve-year-old?' the man replied with a chuckle.

Alice-Miranda shrugged, then sipped her hot chocolate that had cooled considerably since the start of their discussion.

There was a dull buzzing and Alice-Miranda realised it was a telephone ringing.

'I think that must be yours,' she said, pointing at his jacket when he hadn't responded.

'Oh,' the man pulled a phone out of his pocket and looked at the screen. 'I'll call them back.'

'Feel free to take it. I don't want to hold you up and I probably should get going,' the girl said. 'Have a very happy Christmas, Mr Turner. It was lovely to see you,' the child said and skipped away down the hall.

Elliot Turner stared at Alice-Miranda as she disappeared around the corner at the end of the hall, then brushed a tear from his eye. But she'd got him thinking. Sebastian Smote might have assumed he was done working on the Highton Hall decorations, but Elliot had other ideas.

Chapter 16

Alice-Miranda, Cecelia and Caprice were on their way home by eight. Thankfully, Caprice's nose wasn't broken – just badly bruised. The doctor said that when the swelling went down she'd be as lovely as ever, which seemed to improve the girl's mood exponentially.

'I must call your mother and let her know that you're okay,' Cecelia said.

'No, please don't worry. I'll speak to her,' Caprice said. She pulled out her phone and dialled the number, telling the woman what had happened before hanging up rather quickly.

'Is everything all right?' Cecelia asked, glancing at the girl in the rear-vision mirror. 'Would you like me to follow up and have a longer chat with Venetia?'

'No,' Caprice snapped, then softened. 'She's very busy with work – that's why she couldn't really talk, but she's not worried. She knows I'm fine. You shouldn't bother her. She gets very stressed. She doesn't need to be thinking about me on top of everything else.'

Alice-Miranda had a strange feeling about Caprice's conversation. The other night at school she'd been so upset that her mother had to work and now, even after a trip to the hospital, she didn't appear to be bothered at all. Something didn't sit right, but for the moment Alice-Miranda was keen to get home and find Millie. The last thing she wanted was for her friend to be upset.

Cecelia pulled into the portico outside the side entrance to the kitchen.

'Now, Caprice, you need to go straight up and have a shower and then hop into bed. Leave your clothes in the bathroom and we'll soak them overnight. Shilly will no doubt have something magic to get rid of the blood stains. I'll bring supper for you – probably just soup, I think. How does that sound?' Cecelia asked.

Caprice nodded. 'Lovely, thank you.'

'Are you okay to go up on your own?' Alice-Miranda asked.

The girl nodded.

'Oh, hello ladies,' Mrs Oliver chirped from around the corner where she was packing the dishwasher. 'The children are in the lounge playing charades. Everyone was pleased to hear you're all right, Caprice.'

'I'll bet not *everyone* was,' Caprice mumbled, then headed for the back stairs.

Cecelia and Alice-Miranda both heard her.

'You'll have to get Millie and Caprice together, darling,' Cecelia said. 'It's not in the spirit of Christmas for them to be fighting.'

Alice-Miranda nodded. 'I'll do my best but I'm afraid they can both be stubborn. If Caprice has played a role in the upset, then I suspect she'll apologise. I was very clear about her not being unkind to anyone while she's here, although I don't think

I could stand to send her back to school to be on her own. It doesn't seem fair.'

'I'm sure that it won't come to that,' Cecelia said. 'Besides, your friends are only staying for five days and then everyone will be headed home for Christmas.'

'As long as the weather they're forecasting doesn't eventuate,' Mrs Oliver said. The television was on in the corner of the kitchen with the sound muted. 'I've been listening to the news and apparently there's a system on its way that's likely to blanket the country from top to bottom in the thickest snow we'll have seen in years. It will make for some lovely pictures but will definitely put a dent in everyone's travel plans.'

Dolly ladled thick pumpkin soup from the stove into a bowl and set it down on a tray next to a crusty bread roll and a knob of butter. She placed a chocolate brownie on another plate beside it, along with a glass of iced water with lemon and mint.

'I'll take that, Dolly,' Cecelia said. 'Have you seen Hugh? He's been practically invisible since the children arrived.'

'Mr Kennington-Jones left a few hours ago,' Dolly explained. 'He said that he had some urgent business to attend to at the office, but that he shouldn't be long.'

'What's the matter, Mummy?' Alice-Miranda asked.

Cecelia shook her head. 'I'm not sure. I'll give him a call once I've delivered Caprice's dinner. Why don't you head off and find the others, then come back and have something to eat too?'

Alice-Miranda agreed. She was feeling a bit hungry, but she really wanted to see Millie first.

'Are you happy with soup, darling girl?' Mrs Oliver asked. 'I can make you something else if you'd prefer, but I'm afraid your friends devoured the ham and salad I made. I'm not used to feeding hungry teenagers – especially those boys. They must all have hollow legs.'

'Soup is perfect, thank you,' Alice-Miranda replied.

And with that, she hurried away to find the others. Sloane was standing in the middle of the room acting something out that looked as if she may have been on the toilet, but it was hard to tell.

'You're back!' Jacinta yelled, ruining Sloane's turn at charades, which turned out to be toasting marshmallows around a campfire.

'How's Caprice?' Lucas asked. He was sitting on the couch beside Jacinta, while Sep and Chessie were looking quite cosy. Neville was perched on the floor.

'She's going to be fine. Nothing broken – just some swelling. It should settle down in a few days,' Alice-Miranda explained.

Millie was slouched on the couch on the other side of the room on her own. 'I'm not apologising to her. I didn't do anything wrong.'

'She's convinced you were mocking her,' Alice-Miranda said.

'Well, I wasn't,' Millie said. 'She's so sensitive.'

An uncomfortable silence fell over the room.

'What?' Millie eyeballed her friends one at a time.

'You can be a bit sensitive too sometimes, Millie,' Lucas said. Jacinta grabbed his arm and gave it a squeeze, knowing that the comment would not go down well with the girl.

'What?' Millie barked. 'Are you kidding? Caprice is horrible. She always tries to blame me for everything and now you're taking her side. I can't believe it. You all know what she's like and then she put on this big fake act, so we'd let her come along, and now her true colours have come out already.'

Millie's face was almost the same shade as her red hair.

'Calm down, Millie,' Sloane said.

Millie had always been known for her somewhat fiery temper – she was once in terrible trouble at school for dumping her dessert over Sloane's head (admittedly the girl probably deserved it), but lately Millie had been crosser than usual. Sloane and Jacinta had discussed it and Chessie had mentioned that it didn't take much to get her back up.

Alice-Miranda was worried. Maybe it was hormones and the fact that they were all growing up, but it didn't make life easy. Walking on eggshells around Caprice was bad enough – they didn't want to have to do it with Millie too.

'Millie, can we talk – upstairs?' Alice-Miranda asked. She thought it was probably a better idea if they continued their discussion in private.

Millie stood up. 'Fine,' she said and thundered out of the room towards the staircase.

Alice-Miranda could feel everyone's eyes on them, but she didn't turn around.

The two girls made their way to Alice-Miranda's room.

Millie jumped up onto the bed but before Alice-Miranda could say another word she started to cry. Great big gulping sobs.

'Oh, Millie, whatever's the matter?' Alice-Miranda hopped up beside her and put her arm around the girl. 'This isn't like you at all.'

There was no stopping Millie for the next few minutes. Alice-Miranda decided the only thing she could do was hug her friend as tightly as possible and hope that she started to feel better. A good hearty cry often had that effect.

After a time, Millie's racking sobs began to subside.

'Is this about Caprice?' Alice-Miranda asked.

'I'm sorry. That was ridiculous,' Millie said.

Alice-Miranda shook her head. 'No, it wasn't. We all get upset about things from time to time. But was that about Caprice?'

'Not exactly. I hate that I've become so difficult – I know I get mad about things at times, but am I really that bad?' Millie asked.

Alice-Miranda bit her lip. 'Sometimes. But is it just that?'

Millie shook her head. 'Grandpa has to go to hospital to have some tests tomorrow. Mrs Oliver mentioned it earlier and then realised that I didn't know. She asked me not to say anything to anyone. So between Caprice and what everyone said before, and the idea that Grandpa could be sick, I lost it.'

'You have every right to,' Alice-Miranda said. 'Is it serious?'

'I don't know. When I asked Mrs Oliver, she clammed up. You know when grown-ups tell you half of something and then you know there's more going on. I don't want to ask my parents, because Mrs Oliver thought they'd told me and when she realised they hadn't then she was feeling bad too – as if she'd betrayed a secret.'

Dolly Oliver had been married to Millie's grandfather's best friend Dougal for many years before he sadly passed away. In recent times, Ambrose and Dolly had grown close – often going on outings together and generally enjoying each other's company. The man only lived a couple of miles away. Millie had wondered if perhaps the pair would get married one day, but it didn't seem likely as they were both getting on in years and hadn't made any progress in that department.

'Why don't you give your grandfather a call?'

Alice-Miranda suggested. 'You can use the phone in Mummy's study. No one will be there.'

Millie nodded. 'I will,' she said, wiping her face with the back of her sleeve before plucking a tissue from the box on the bedside table and blowing her nose.

'And I'll make peace with the beast – I mean Caprice,' Millie said. 'I promise I wasn't mocking her, but I suppose I can see how she thought that. I meant it when I said that she'd always be beautiful and I suppose when she said that I'd never be, it stung. She's right, though. I'll always be the ugly duckling of our group and I have to learn to be okay with it.'

Alice-Miranda frowned at her friend. 'There is nothing ugly about you, Millie. You're lovely – on the inside and out.'

'You're just trying to make me feel better, but I'll never be the girl who gets the boy. I mean you had Sep and Neville fighting over you in Egypt and you didn't even realise. Now I think Sep likes Chessie,' Millie said with a sigh.

Alice-Miranda bit her lip. 'Do *you* like Sep?' She slid off the side of her bed onto the floor and turned around, looking back at her friend who was propped up against the mountain of pillows.

Millie rolled her eyes and grinned. 'I don't know how you've missed that, but yes. Trouble is, he doesn't even know I'm alive.'

Alice-Miranda giggled. 'I'm sorry, Millie – when it comes to matters of the heart, I'm totally clueless. Except for Jacinta and Lucas, but that's because they're practically an old married couple.'

'Anyway, I need to go and call Grandpa, and hopefully he's okay, then I'll see Caprice and I promise there won't be any fireworks. I'll be my usual charming self and prove to everyone that the old cliché about redheads and fiery tempers is absolutely not true,' Millie said, hopping down off the bed.

Alice-Miranda reached out and hugged her. 'I meant what I said about you being beautiful, Millie – one day you'll see.'

Millie smiled back. 'How did I ever get lucky enough to have you as my best friend?'

Alice-Miranda bit her lip. 'I'm the lucky one,' she replied as Millie turned and headed out the door and down the hall to Cecelia's study.

Chapter 17

Ellie rolled over and pulled the duvet up around her frozen ears. She could feel the cold quite literally leaching through the walls, but that was only one of the reasons she had no desire to get out of bed. No doubt her mother would be at the door soon, telling her to hurry up.

Sleep hadn't come easily and, when it finally did, Ellie had the most frightful nightmares. Something about being caught stealing. Perhaps it wasn't a dream, but a prophecy.

She'd stayed at Hazel's for an hour or so after they walked back from the mansion gates. The boys headed to Liam's house and Ellie was glad they left. There was something about Liam that made her think of a weasel or an otter. Maybe it was his greasy hair and whiskery face – he didn't have a proper beard or anything, just a horrible fuzz that happened to pubescent boys of a certain age.

When Ellie had tried to talk to Hazel about the moneybox, the girl parroted everything the boys had said about rich people having all the money and power, and poor people having nothing. That it wasn't right. Ellie didn't disagree, but stealing wasn't right either. She'd turned the idea over and over in her mind last night for hours and despite feeling sick at the thought, there was something about Hazel that made her determined to do it anyway. The girl was the kind of friend Ellie had dreamed of for years. Besides, Ellie knew better than any of them what it was like to be properly poor.

A sharp knock on the door interrupted her thoughts.

'Ellie, you have to get up. You'll be late for school,' her mother said.

'Coming,' the girl called back. It was better

to shout, or her mother would come in. Ellie had been tossing up when to go to Kennington's. She could do it before school on the way to the bus stop or afterwards when she got home. That would probably be safer. Her mother was working the late shift, which might be helpful. If she got caught, she could probably talk her way out of it – say that the box had fallen off the counter into her bag or something like that. Juliette wouldn't be happy, but she wouldn't call the police.

Despite having let her mother know she was awake, the door opened anyway and Juliette poked her head around. 'Morning, honey.'

'I said I was coming,' Ellie snapped.

Juliette opened her mouth, then paused and swallowed whatever it was she was going to say. 'I bet you're happy there's only a couple more days of school left.' She waited for a reply but when she didn't get one, she added, 'I've got bacon for breakfast.'

'How come? Did some poor unfortunate piggy wander into the kitchen?' Ellie said and pushed back the covers, gasping as the cold air seeped straight through her cotton pyjamas.

'Mr Withers let me buy a packet that was past its use-by date – half price,' her mother replied.

'He made you buy it,' Ellie said sarcastically. 'He should have given it to you.'

'He can't do that. He's just the manager,' Juliette said.

'Wouldn't we be better off spending what little money we have on some heat? You know we could quite literally freeze to death in this place,' Ellie said.

'I'm getting it sorted,' her mother replied. 'I promise. The landlord's coming to take a look at the boiler tonight and maybe after school you and Myles could go to the woods and collect some pine cones for the fire.'

'It's been raining for weeks, Mum. Everything's soaked,' Ellie said. 'We need a proper load of timber – and I'm not taking care of Myles. He's always the neediest after school. You promised when we came here that I wouldn't have to do that anymore.'

Her mother nodded. 'I'm trying, Ellie – please. Things will get better. I can't afford to have him in after-school care every day – not yet.'

Ellie let out a deep breath that almost turned to ice in front of her. She grabbed the towel that was hanging over the bed rail. It was still damp from yesterday.

'Is there hot water?' Ellie demanded.

'I didn't have a shower,' her mother replied, then bit her lip. 'But your brother's been in.'

Ellie's shoulders slumped. If she didn't get to the bathroom before Myles, then she knew the outcome – unless by some miracle the water heater had suddenly increased to twice the size. Her brother would stay in the shower for exactly ten minutes – Myles had this stupid timer and no matter how hard she or her mother tried to convince him that three minutes would suffice, he was not to be deterred. They weren't even sure where the ten-minute obsession had come from, but it was just another of Myles's quirks. Ellie loved her brother – but there were times that she would happily have traded him for a cat.

'Go and see. The boiler might have warmed up again,' Juliette said.

'Seriously, Mum – there's really more chance of you actually slaughtering a pig.'

Juliette reached out to touch her daughter, but Ellie pushed past her and ran down the hall.

'I hate you, Myles,' Ellie shouted as she wrenched the taps on and felt the gush of freezing water.

Chapter 18

The children were seated around the kitchen table enjoying a hearty breakfast of eggs, sausages, bacon, hash browns, tomatoes and toast. Outside, a fierce wind whipped through the trees and whistled along the verandas, but at least the rain that had come down in buckets last night had stopped for now. Mrs Oliver was regaling them with a tale of another brazen robbery of Christmas decorations she'd heard on the early morning news. This time from the village hall at Penberthy Floss – which was just a couple of miles away. 'It's a nasty business,' the woman said as she spooned another batch of scrambled eggs into a bowl to replace the one that was now empty. 'Stealing Christmas decorations – what a miserable lot those thieves must be.'

'Either that or their house will have the best Christmas display in town,' Alice-Miranda said. She glanced over at Millie, who was sitting opposite Caprice. Thankfully, the pair had made their peace last night. Millie had told her all about it when she came to bed. After speaking to her grandfather, which turned out to be far less worrisome than first thought, Millie had gone to Caprice's room where she found the girl in a bit of a mess – quite literally. Caprice had accidentally up-ended her bowl of soup on the duvet and the floor and there was a little bit on her pillow too, and she was desperately trying to clean it up. Millie told Alice-Miranda that Caprice thought Mrs Shillingsworth would be cross. Millie tried to convince her that a half a bowl of spilled soup would be the least of Shilly's worries. She offered to help her and the pair sorted their differences over a mop and bucket and a change of sheets. As Millie had predicted, Shilly wasn't upset at all and, on the contrary, was most impressed with their efforts.

Alice-Miranda was pleased to hear that although Millie still had misgivings, she was determined to give Caprice the benefit of the doubt. Caprice admitted that she may have misread the situation when she had her accident, which Alice-Miranda thought was a big breakthrough. Self-awareness wasn't one of the girl's stronger suits. Millie said that she'd apologised if she'd sounded sarcastic, which she hadn't meant to be.

All round it was a good result and there was more positive news about Millie's grandfather too. Apparently, he'd been having some tummy troubles and was booked in for a top and tail – a colonoscopy and gastroscopy. Millie said that her grandfather admitted he shouldn't have been so mysterious about things when he was talking to Mrs Oliver, but he didn't like the idea of having a camera poking about in his bottom. Understandable, really, and no point worrying until he had the results.

Cecelia and Hugh were yet to join the group. Alice-Miranda hadn't seen her father for more than five minutes since she'd arrived, but this morning she was planning to pin him down. They were all supposed to be trimming the tree together after breakfast then, depending on the weather, Alice-Miranda thought they could go for a walk to the village for a spot of Christmas shopping.

'More bacon, anyone?' Dolly asked, as she transferred rashers from the frypan to the plate in the middle of the table.

'Yes, please,' Neville said, as he tucked in. 'Your bacon is the best, Mrs Oliver.'

Hands swooped in from all directions and seconds later, the entire lot was gone. 'Thank you, Neville, but I'm sure it's no better than what you get at school these days,' the woman said.

Lucas swallowed the piece of egg on his fork and looked up. 'Are you kidding? Our cook is a nightmare. I'm not sure where Professor Winterbottom dug her up.'

'Dug her up is right,' Sep said. 'I think she's older than our step-granny, and Henrietta is getting on a bit. She suggested that we might like to have an offal night – for fun.'

'That sounds absolutely offal,' Jacinta said in an American accent causing a collective groan around the table.

'I don't believe that for a second,' Dolly said with a chuckle.

'It's true,' Neville said. 'I was there. She said that lamb's fry and bacon was her favourite, closely followed by liver. I'm told liver's tasty, but I think we've all been rather spoilt when it comes to food – I really can't stand the idea of it. It's funny but my grandad eats all those things too.'

'It's definitely generational,' Dolly said.

'What is?' Hugh Kennington-Jones asked as he came through the door.

'Daddy!' Alice-Miranda exclaimed as she jumped up to give her father a hug.

'Offal,' Dolly replied.

'Oh, I love it,' Hugh said. 'And the gorier the better as far as I'm concerned. Chicken feet in China, haggis in the Hebrides, kat-a-kat in Karachi.'

'What's that?' Sloane asked.

'It's sort of like a hash of kidney, brain, heart, liver and testicles usually of goats or sheep – it's delicious,' Hugh replied.

'Gross . . .' a chorus sprung up around the table.

'I'm sorry I asked,' Sloane said. 'But is there any more bacon?'

'Changing the subject, Daddy,' Alice-Miranda said. 'Where have you been? We've hardly seen you at all and you said that you'd be home the whole time we were here.'

Hugh smiled at his daughter. 'Sorry, darling – there've been a few supply chain issues at work and I've had to hop in and do some investigating.'

'Is that why Mrs Parker said that the Kennington's at Downsfordvale didn't have any Christmas stock?' Millie asked.

'I'm still getting to the bottom of that one,' Hugh said. 'And it seems a whole lot of others.'

Alice-Miranda looked at the man. 'Can we help?'

Hugh shook his head. 'You're not spending your Christmas holidays working, young lady. And haven't we got a tree to trim? I've just called Mr Greening and asked him to bring a couple of extra ladders around.'

Cecelia arrived in the room. She was dressed for work in a pair of dark jeans and a crisply ironed white-collared shirt with the sleeves rolled up. Alice-Miranda often joked that was her mother's uniform – tailored shirts and jeans with short leather boots.

'Good morning, all,' the woman said. 'How are you feeling, Caprice?'

'Much better, thank you,' the girl replied. 'My nose is swollen but it's not nearly as bad as I thought it might be.'

'Don't worry, Caprice, you're still beautiful,' Neville said, earning himself several surprised stares.

'Why, thank you, Neville,' Caprice said. It looked suspiciously like she batted her eyelashes at the boy, whose cheeks turned puce.

'I meant that purely as an observation,' the boy squeaked. 'It's just that I know a beautiful girl when I see one . . . I think I'll be quiet now.'

Everyone laughed as Caprice flicked her copper-coloured tresses over her shoulder.

'Have you spoken to your mother today, Caprice?' Cecelia asked.

Caprice nodded. 'Oh yes, Mummy's very busy. She asked that I not call her again until the end of the week – she really needs to concentrate on this job. Though I still don't know where it is or who she's working for. It's all a bit of a mystery.'

'Oh – well, as long as she's fine with everything,' Cecelia said, though it was clear she still felt uneasy about the situation. 'Right, I'd better have my porridge and then we can get on with the tree.'

The children finished their breakfast and drifted away upstairs to brush teeth and tidy rooms.

After a while it was only Alice-Miranda and her parents who were left.

'Are you sure there's nothing wrong?' the child asked. She looked at her mother and then at her father, who seemed to be avoiding her gaze.

'Yes, everything's perfect, darling – especially now that you and your friends are here,' Cecelia said. 'And Charlotte and the twins will be here on Sunday with Lawrence and Granny. We'll have a full house.'

Cecelia Highton-Smith bit her lip and inspected her fingernails, a worried look on her face while Dolly poured the woman a cup of tea from a china pot. Except that the pour looked more like a fountain spraying everywhere.

'I think you've sprung a leak, Dolly,' Hugh said.

'Oh, heavens,' the woman said, grabbing a cloth to wipe up the mess. 'That's new. There must be a crack in the spout.'

Alice-Miranda looked at the pot. 'It's such a

lovely one.' The teapot had a pretty pattern of blue flowers with birds and other foliage.

Dolly frowned and looked at the offending split which was possibly worse than first thought. 'This is my favourite. I'll have to see if Mr Greening can fix it.'

Hugh Kennington-Jones's phone rang. He pulled it out of his pocket and looked at the screen then stood up. 'I'd better take this.'

The man walked into the small side sitting room off the kitchen.

'What do you mean it's gone?' Alice-Miranda heard him say. 'Again! That much stock just can't disappear in a puff of smoke. It has to be somewhere.'

'Everything's *fine*, Mummy?' Alice-Miranda said. 'That doesn't sound very fine to me.'

Hugh reappeared. 'Sorry, ladies, I've got to go – small problem at the office.'

'Daddy, what's the matter?' Alice-Miranda demanded. 'You're not going anywhere until you tell me.'

The man looked at his only daughter. He could barely get away with things when she was a five-year-old and now she was more than double that he had no chance.

'In the past month or so, we seem to be missing a large amount of Christmas stock. It's leaving the warehouses but not arriving at the destinations. Trucks are going out full and turning up half empty. Everything that's missing is Christmas-related,' Hugh explained.

'So it's not supply-chain issues then,' Alice-Miranda said.

'No,' Hugh said. 'We have a gang of thieves and we have no idea where the stock is going or how it's getting there. But honestly, darling – you shouldn't worry. It won't kill us – at least not in the short-term – but it's not good for our reputation that's for sure, or for the shoppers who rely on us.'

'Have you got cameras in the trucks?' Alice-Miranda asked.

Her father nodded. 'Yes – in the trailers and the cabins. But so far, there's nothing out of the ordinary. It's as if somehow the stock disappears into thin air. Anyway, I've got to get going.'

Alice-Miranda picked at a piece of leftover bacon on her plate. 'There has to be a logical explanation. Things don't just vanish.'

Hugh reached for his coffee mug and took a large swig before setting it back down.

'Here, sir,' Dolly handed the man a paper bag. 'I've made you an egg and bacon buttie – to take with you.'

The man took it and gave the cook an unexpected kiss on the cheek. 'You're a darling, Dolly.'

'Oh, Hugh – get away with you,' the woman replied, her cheeks blushing.

He then kissed Cecelia and Alice-Miranda.

'I'll be back as soon as I can,' he called as he rushed out the door.

'Come on, darling, your father will get everything sorted – we have a tree to decorate,' Cecelia said. She placed her teacup on the saucer, folded her napkin and stood up.

But Alice-Miranda couldn't help thinking that she'd like to help in some way. Surely there had to be something she could do.

Chapter 19

Venetia Baldini sat at the kitchen bench scanning the menu she'd just finished writing. Her employer was keen to try a wide variety of dishes before deciding on the final selections for his party. The man was exacting, that's for sure. Venetia's feet hurt and her back ached. She rubbed her temples and hoped that the headache that had been threatening for a week now stayed away. The last thing she needed was a migraine. They could put her out of action for days.

Venetia pulled her phone from her pocket. She'd try and get hold of Caprice again. The girl was clearly upset about having to stay at school but, honestly, Venetia would rather suffer the wrath of her youngest child than lose the business she'd spent years creating. Anyway, she was fairly certain that her daughter rather enjoyed her holidays in Italy and the other trappings that had come with Venetia's success. To have it all disappear overnight would be difficult for everyone. Thankfully, Caprice was on a scholarship so that was one less thing to worry about. But having her ferried around to all of the singing competitions she was keen on wasn't an inexpensive exercise either.

She dialled the number and listened to it ring before going to voicemail yet again.

'Hello, darling, Mummy here. Just checking in to see that you're okay. Give me a call when you can, though I'm sure that Mrs Clarkson is keeping you busy. I'm sorry about having to leave you at school, but I promise I'll explain all when I see you. Love you,' the woman said and hung up. Perhaps she should try Mrs Clarkson but, truthfully, she was reluctant to phone the woman given she'd probably ruined her pre-Christmas plans. She'd organised to have a hamper sent to thank her.

'Excuse me, Miss Baldini. Sir would like to see you upstairs,' the woman in black said.

Venetia tried not to let out the sigh she was holding in.

'I'll be right there,' she said, reaching across to her handbag and the packet of pills that she hoped would put an end to the throbbing in her skull.

Delia Wickham rubbed her neck. She hadn't been sleeping well at all in the past few weeks – waking up every morning just after four with her mind racing. Only yesterday, she'd received a letter from her sister's solicitor asking that she attend the reading of the woman's will. It wasn't likely there was anything left in her estate after the years of care Maggie had received, but the man said it was important she be there, and her daughter too, if the girl could be located.

The last private detective Delia had consulted to try and find her niece had come to the conclusion that Aster had most likely left the country and made a new life for herself overseas. But Delia wasn't convinced about that – she'd only been fifteen when she ran away. At that age, she didn't believe the girl would have had the resources nor the wherewithal to obtain a passport and get to another country. Delia had always imagined her niece was probably pulling beers in some country pub.

When she called another company this week, she was stunned by how much higher their fees were these days. She could scarcely afford to engage them and while Delia hated the idea of asking for her employer's help, she might have to if she really wanted to get anywhere. But this week, Elliot Turner had other things to think about. She'd wait until after Christmas to discuss it with him.

Chapter 20

Ellie had been feeling sick all day. Not helped by the conflicting voices in her head – one telling her that she wasn't a thief and asking why she'd take such a stupid risk, and the other the voice of someone who wanted desperately to keep Hazel's friendship and prove that she was in fact 'cool' enough to be part of something. Ellie had never been part of anything before – at least nothing worth remembering.

She stared out the window at the bare limbs of the oak tree that sat in the middle of the quadrangle.

A square patch of dirt surrounded the majestic trunk while beyond that the entire yard was concrete. But at least the buildings here were well kept. There were flowerboxes outside the office and playing fields with grass – unlike most of the schools she'd attended up to now. She could imagine how pretty the oak tree would be in spring and summer.

It was the last class of the day and Ellie wasn't remotely thinking about the novel they were currently reading – even though she quite liked it.

'And who can tell me how Tegan felt when she betrayed her best friend?' the teacher asked. She looked around the room at a sea of blank faces. 'Ellie?'

The girl was still staring out the window.

'E-llie – anyone h-o-me?' Mrs Lewis sang to chuckles from her classmates.

The girl looked up and blinked, then realised that the teacher had been speaking to her. 'Sorry, Mrs Lewis, what did you say?'

The woman sighed and glanced at her watch.

She was about to repeat herself when the shrill ringing of the bell infiltrated the building. Immediately, chairs scraped backwards and books were gathered as the students began to leave.

'Well, that was fortunate,' Mrs Lewis said, pushing a strand of mouse-brown hair behind her ear. 'See you all tomorrow — and just because it's the last day before the Christmas break doesn't mean that I won't be collecting homework.'

There was a collective groan from her charges.

Ellie stood up and gathered her things. Hazel didn't take the advanced English class and would be waiting for her at the lockers.

'Ellie, are you all right?' The teacher intercepted the girl on her way out, standing in front of the doorway. Mrs Lewis had kind blue eyes and a soothing voice, and Ellie had felt a connection with her from the moment she'd set foot in the woman's class. She always wore interesting shoes too. Today they had cat faces on them.

'Yes, I'm fine,' Ellie replied.

'I know it's tough starting at a new school, but you're a clever girl. Your writing is some of the finest I've ever seen from a student your age, but . . .'

Ellie had a feeling the woman wanted to ask if there was anything wrong at home — thankfully she didn't. Ellie would have loved to tell her exactly how things were — we don't have enough food, there's no heat, Mum can barely pay the bills, my stepfather has been missing in action for over a year and my little brother is prone to taking shiny things that don't belong to him. Other than that, life is tickety-boo. But she didn't.

Ellie bit her lip and cast her eyes to the floor, hoping that Mrs Lewis hadn't noticed the holes in her coat or that her shoes were a half size too small. Her mother said that she'd get her new ones as soon as she could afford it.

'Ellie, if there's anything I can do to make life here easier, please let me know,' Mrs Lewis said with an understanding smile.

'Thanks,' the girl mumbled and hurried out the door and down the hall where Hazel was standing by the lockers waiting for her.

'What took you so long?' Hazel asked, as she stuffed a pile of books into her locker.

'We still have homework,' Ellie said with a frown as she worked out what she needed to take home with her.

'Seriously? You're not going to do it, are you? It's almost Christmas,' Hazel said.

Ellie shrugged. Of course, she would. If she was going to get a scholarship to university and become something, she had no choice – because there was no way she was going to end up in the same situation as her mother.

'So, are you going to Kennington's?' Hazel asked.

'Sure,' Ellie said as she slung her bag over her shoulder and felt the knot in her stomach tighten.

Alice-Miranda and her friends had spent most of the morning and another hour after lunchtime decorating the Christmas tree. Not that everyone had worked on it the whole time. Millie and Sloane had drifted away to the kitchen to help Mrs Oliver cook sheets of gingerbread, which they were going to use later that evening to make gingerbread houses. It was one of the activities on Alice-Miranda's schedule, which also included sledding if there was any snow, ice skating on the frozen pond (again this was dependent on conditions, but there was always the ice rink a few villages away as a backup), various games including hide-and-seek, which, given the size of Highton Hall, could take at least half a day, and other crafty pursuits – to name but some of what she had planned.

Neville and Chessie busied themselves adorning the entrance hall with fairy lights and other decorations while Lucas, Jacinta and Sep were seconded by Mr Greening, who decided that the outside of the house needed some additional festive charm. He'd found a stash of giant-coloured baubles in one of the sheds – left over from when the family had held the Highton's Christmas party onsite some years before. He thought they could make a perfect display in the garden and he even had some fake snow to add in the absence of the real thing arriving yet. There were some life-sized wire reindeer, as well.

Caprice stuck with Alice-Miranda and was surprisingly helpful sorting the decorations and pointing out spaces where things might go. During the day the swelling on her nose had gone down a bit but she still had two dark circles under her eyes, so it would be a few days before her face would be completely back to normal. Caprice didn't seem too worried, which was somewhat surprising.

Alice-Miranda had been up and down the ladder more times than she could count, much to her mother's concern. One trip to the hospital this week had been quite enough.

Mrs Shillingsworth wandered through the lounge with a feather duster in hand, having spent much of the day finishing her jobs before the rest of the family descended over the weekend.

'That's looking splendid,' Shilly said.

'We need everyone for this last part,' Millie said, as she handed Alice-Miranda the oversized star. She and Sloane had returned from the kitchen while the last of the gingerbread was in the oven.

Lucas, Sep and Jacinta thundered through from the hallway. 'You should see outside,' Lucas panted. 'The garden looks amazing, and yum,' he inhaled a deep breath. 'Something smells delicious.'

The children gathered around the tree with Cecelia, Shilly and Mrs Oliver while Alice-Miranda scampered back up the ladder for the last time.

She reached out and placed the star at the very top. 'Tah-dah!' she exclaimed.

The others clapped and cheered and proclaimed that it was the best-decorated Christmas tree they'd ever seen. Even Cecelia had to admit that it looked every bit as good as the ones in the stores and they were put together by teams of professional Christmas decorators.

'Well done, darlings,' Cecelia said. 'What a marvellous job. I hate to think we've got to take it all down again in a couple of weeks.'

'True – but putting it up was fun,' Alice-Miranda said.

'It was, wasn't it?' Caprice said. 'Thank you for letting me help.'

'Bravo, everyone,' Dolly said. 'But I'm afraid we have a small problem.'

The children looked at her.

'I was just getting the sweets out for the gingerbread decorating later and realised that we only have half as much as we need, and I know I bought at least double the amount that's there.' She glared at Lucas, who raised his hands in protest.

'Don't look at me,' he said – pointing at Sep and Neville. 'I didn't eat them all.'

'Oi – it wasn't us either,' Neville said. 'We didn't take them – though we might have helped eat them.'

Sloane sighed. 'It was me. I thought we needed some extra sugar while we were playing charades last night. I'm sorry, Mrs Oliver. I didn't realise they were for the gingerbread houses.'

'Sloane Sykes, I might have known,' Dolly said, shaking her head.

The girl bit her lip. 'I'm so sorry – really, I am.' Her eyes filled with tears and Dolly suddenly looked horrified.

'Oh, dear girl, I was only having a laugh. You're not in trouble. Goodness me – if Alice-Miranda had been here last night I doubt there would have been any left at all.'

'Excuse me!' the girl said, putting her hands on her hips. 'You know I would have left the liquorice. Yuck.'

The others laughed.

'So you're not really cross?' Sloane said.

'No, of course not,' Dolly said and hugged Sloane around her shoulders. 'But you can take yourselves for a walk to the village and buy some more sweets. I won't have those gingerbread houses looking underdone,' she said, then handed the girl some money. 'Why don't you each buy what you want?'

'Is it a competition?' Caprice asked. 'The decorating.'

Dolly looked at her, then at the other children. 'Always. But I was thinking this year we'd have three categories – best overall, most interesting, and potential tastiest.'

'I'm in,' Lucas said.

There were murmurs of agreement from everyone else.

'Although the one I made last year when I was with Dad and Charlotte and the twins in LA was pretty terrible,' Lucas added.

'All right – let's ask Mrs Greening to do a blind judging,' Shilly said.

Caprice grinned.

'Why do you look like the cat who got the cream?' Millie asked.

'Because my mother isn't the only one in the family who has talent when it comes to sweet things,' the girl said, raising her eyebrows then grimacing. 'Ow – I shouldn't do that.' She clutched at her nose.

The others all looked at each other, then at Caprice.

'Game on,' Lucas said.

Chapter 21

Ellie had just turned the corner onto the high street. She could feel the beads of perspiration dripping down her back – which was ridiculous given it was barely five degrees and she'd shivered through most of the day. Now the closer she got to her destination, the hotter she felt.

Hazel hadn't offered to come with her and Ellie was glad of it. While Ellie might have grown up poor, she'd never once resorted to stealing and though she didn't disagree with the ideology of sharing the wealth (everyone knew the story of Robin Hood and his Merry Men) – actually being one of the Merry Men wasn't proving so easy.

Ellie reached the entrance to Kennington's. There was no sign of her mother, who she hoped was working behind the scenes at the supermarket today. She spied the small donations box sitting atop the service counter. It didn't look as if it was attached to a security cable. Surely it wouldn't have that much money in it anyway. Was it even stealing if the contents were going to people who really needed it? At least that's what the voice in her head kept telling her.

The checkouts were empty, save for one pimply teen, who was serving a woman dressed in brown from head to toe. Ellie thought she recognised her and realised that she was one of the teachers at Myles's school. Fabulous. There was no one at the self-service check-outs.

Ellie took off her coat and draped it over her arm, then walked to the counter and stood right by the donation box. It wasn't very big. The plan was to use her coat to cover the box then slide it off the counter into her backpack. It seemed the best idea – at least until she spotted a small girl with chocolate curls holding a basket full of sweets heading for one of the self-serve check-outs. Ellie needed to move fast. She placed her coat over the box. Below it on the floor her backpack sat open, wide enough for it to drop inside. Trouble was, the next time she looked up, the girl with the curls was surrounded by a group of chattering kids. From the looks of their baskets, they were buying half the confectionery aisle.

Ellie swallowed hard. She was waiting too long and she knew it. Before she could blink, the girl with the chocolate curls had finished her transaction and was standing right beside her.

'Hello, do you need some assistance? I could get someone if you like,' she said.

Ellie shook her head. 'No, I'm fine. I'm, um . . . waiting for my mum.'

Ellie's fingers were wrapped around the box under her coat. She couldn't move now, or the girl would know what she was up to.

The girl looked down at Ellie's open bag. 'Oh, don't you just love that book? *A Little Princess* is one of my all-time favourites.'

Ellie could feel her face flushing. How embarrassing. She'd been meaning to drop it into the returns chute at the library on her way and completely forgotten.

'Do you like reading?' the girl asked. 'I'd read all day and half the night if I could.'

Ellie nodded. '*The Hundred Dresses* is better.' She wished she hadn't said it, but the words were out of her mouth before she had time to stop them.

The girl bit her lip. 'I've never heard of that one. Is it by the same author?'

Ellie shook her head, wondering why she'd said anything. *The Hundred Dresses* was her favourite book, but she didn't need to share that fact.

'Goodness, how rude. I haven't even introduced myself,' the girl said. 'I'm Alice-Miranda Highton-Smith-Kennington-Jones and I'm very pleased to meet you.'

Ellie baulked as the girl thrust out her hand. Thankfully, they were interrupted by Ellie's mother who appeared through a side door, which Ellie knew led to an office further back.

'Hello, sweetheart. I didn't realise you were here,' the woman said.

Ellie swallowed hard. This was even worse than she imagined. 'I . . . I was just on my way home and thought I'd say hello.'

'Really? You hardly ever visit me at work,' Juliette said, giving her daughter a grin. 'Who's your friend?'

'No, she's not . . .' Ellie started but was cut off.

'I'm Alice-Miranda,' the girl said.

There was a flicker of recognition on Juliette's face. 'Oh, you're Hugh and Cecelia's daughter,' she said. 'It's good to meet you. I'm Juliette and this is my daughter, Ellie.'

Ellie suddenly realised that in that ridiculously long surname there was a Kennington. This was the girl whose parents owned the grocery store – not just this one – there were about a zillion others across the country too. Her mother had told her that the family lived on the edge of the village in some mansion.

'It's very nice to meet you,' Alice-Miranda replied. 'Have you worked here long?'

'Just a few months – I started when the store opened,' Juliette said. 'It's lovely.'

'I think it's definitely one of Daddy's best,' Alice-Miranda said. 'I like that it's so much smaller than the regular supermarkets. You know it was a bit controversial with some of the locals to begin with, but when Daddy promised to keep the integrity of the high street shops, making sure that the butcher and baker, greengrocer and coffee shop all stayed pretty much as they were with the supermarket in behind, people came around to the idea. And all of the shopkeepers who wanted to retire were able to and some work here now instead. Even Mrs Bottomley told Mummy the other day that she thought it was a triumph – which, if you know her, is huge praise.'

Juliette smiled. 'Oh, I've met her. She works at my son's school.'

'Do you live in the village?' Alice-Miranda asked.

'Yes, we moved for my job. It's a gorgeous place and I think we're especially fortunate that your parents live close by. Your father often drops in to talk to the staff and check that everything's running smoothly.'

'And is it?' Alice-Miranda asked, a crease on her forehead. 'You haven't had any trouble with missing Christmas stock, have you?'

Juliette shook her head. 'Not that I'm aware of.'

'Oh, that's a relief,' the child replied.

Juliette frowned, wondering if she'd missed something. Just as she was about to ask,

Alice-Miranda was joined by the rest of the youngsters who'd been at the self-service check-outs. Several of the children were holding cloth bags full to the brim with their purchases.

One of the boys jostled another of the lads, who bumped into Ellie. Her coat fell to the ground but fortunately, as it did, her hand took the box with it underneath. She let it drop into her bag.

'These are my friends – we're having five days of pre-Christmas celebrations – our school's finished a few days earlier than most,' Alice-Miranda said. She then proceeded to introduce everyone; the names punctuated by a staccato chorus of hellos. 'We're making gingerbread houses when we get home. That's why we've bought bags and bags of sweets. Anyway, it was lovely to meet you, Juliette and Ellie. Hope we see you at the Christmas light ceremony on Friday. It's one of my favourite events of the year. We'll all be there and everyone else from home. We wouldn't miss it.'

And with that, the children spilled out the door and onto the street where spits of rain had begun to fall.

Juliette gave a wave. 'Well, she's adorable,' the woman said.

'If you like that sort of kid,' Ellie muttered.

Her mother frowned. 'Why, what sort of kid is she?'

'A spoilt brat,' Ellie said.

A look of disappointment spread across Juliette's face. 'I'm sorry, but she didn't seem like one to me. You know it's a stereotype, Ellie – the idea that because she comes from a wealthy family, she must be a certain type of person. If you didn't know who her parents were, I'm sure you would think she was a lovely girl. Just because you're rich doesn't automatically make you mean and horrible.'

Ellie rolled her eyes. 'And you'd know, Mum – because we're friends with so many rich people. I've got to go,' she said and quickly zipped up her backpack and threw her coat back on.

'I know life might not seem fair, Ellie, but Alice-Miranda's parents are always doing things for other people, and they're very well loved in this village. They gave me a job and last time Hugh was in here, he asked if I might be interested in doing a management course. That would really change things for us, El. Anyway, I'd better get back to work. I'll see you at home in a little while,' Juliette said.

Ellie shook her head. 'I'm going to Hazel's.'

'But I thought you said that you were on your way home,' Juliette replied. 'If I'd known you were coming, I wouldn't have booked Myles into that extra day at after-school care.'

'I told you I'm not looking after him anymore, Mum. I'm fourteen – I need a life,' Ellie said.

'Please don't speak to me like that,' Juliette whispered. She could see several customers looking their way and the last thing she needed was a scene with her daughter. 'I'll see you at home.'

'After I go to Hazel's. I've got to talk to her about something important,' Ellie said. 'And you know – if I had a phone, I could call her, but seeing that we're always broke and I'm just supposed to suck that up . . .'

'Ellie – I'm doing my best,' the woman said with a sigh.

'Seriously? Fine, whatever,' Ellie said as she charged out the door into the rain that was now coming down hard.

Chapter 22

'Run!' Millie shouted as the rain pelted down.

'I told you we should have brought umbrellas with us,' Caprice said. The children took off, dodging puddles and charging through the rear gates of Highton Hall along the back driveway towards the row of sheds near the farm.

'I'm freezing,' Jacinta wailed as Lucas put his arm around her and they ran along beside each other.

At least they were all wearing rain jackets and

wellington boots so would only be soaked from the neck up.

'The shed!' Alice-Miranda yelled above the hammering of the raindrops. 'We can wait it out in there.'

The children ran after her and spilled into the near-empty building, their eyes soon adjusting to the low light.

Neville shook his head like a dog, splattering the others with water and earning himself a telling off from Sloane. Then Sep did it too and Sloane punched him hard on the arm.

'Ow!' the boy griped. 'You're so mean, Sloane.'

'Yup,' the girl replied with a grin.

'Are you okay, Sep?' Millie asked.

He rubbed his shoulder and pouted. 'I suppose I'll live.'

Caprice ran her hands down her copper tresses and wrung the water out, letting it drip onto the concrete floor.

'I know this place,' Chessie said. 'It was one of my hideouts when I ran away from Bodlington and was trying to get home to Mummy.'

Britt looked at the girl. 'You ran away?'

'It was a spur of the moment decision. I actually

have Millie's cousin Madagascar to thank for it,' Chessie said.

'Urgh, please don't mention her name,' Millie said.

'I agree,' Caprice echoed. 'She's the meanest person I've ever met in my life. For a while she had me fooled, but then I realised – she wasn't funny, she was horrible.'

Millie looked at the girl, glad to hear it. Caprice and Madagascar had fallen out during the Queen's Colours trip to Egypt, where the pair had first seemed destined to be best friends. Cracks had started to appear when Madagascar said all manner of mean things about almost everyone and Caprice, it seemed, had grown a conscience. In the end, the two had a spectacular fight that ended the relationship on the spot.

Sloane and Chessie found some old crates, which they dragged into a circle. They dumped their shopping bags in the centre. Outside, the rain was even heavier now – the sound of it on the roof so loud that they had to shout to be heard above it.

'Anyone hungry?' Alice-Miranda asked, pointing to the bags.

'Are you sure?' Britt called back. 'I thought they were for the gingerbread houses?'

'One packet won't hurt,' Alice-Miranda said. 'Have some of these.' The girl reached into her bag. Alice-Miranda had bought chocolate freckles and marshmallows as well as musk sticks and peppermint leaves but in among the purchases there was something else. She peered inside and saw the donations box from the Kennington's counter.

'How did you get in here?' Alice-Miranda said, pulling it out and holding it up for her friends to see.

'Alice-Miranda – you little thief,' Lucas teased. 'Stealing the donations box from your parents' own supermarket chain. Shame on you.'

'Ha ha, Lucas,' the girl said. She was trying to think how on earth she came to have it when she realised that Ellie had been standing by the counter with her coat draped over the top. She'd seemed nervous, but why would she take the box?

Alice-Miranda wasn't about to accuse the girl without any proof – that wasn't fair.

'It must have fallen off into my bag and I didn't notice,' the girl said. 'I'll give it to Mummy when we get home.'

But the mystery was weighing on her mind – along with who was stealing from Kennington's and taking the decorations from the villages. It was all very strange indeed.

Chapter 23

Bronson Byers was looking forward to finally getting home. It had been a very long time and in truth he had no idea what the place was even like. He did know that Juliette had moved again. Keeping tabs on her with the life he currently led wasn't easy. His head of command required full immersion. It was lucky he still had a mate in the force who made a point of knowing where she and the kids were. Sending money was easy – but he couldn't pass on too much.

He never knew who might be watching.

And when he did make it home, would Juliette simply take him back? Ellie would be angry. He expected that. She was twelve and a half the last time he'd seen her and now what was she? Fourteen. Not the most forgiving of ages. And Myles – he missed that boy with an ache in his heart that some days made him wonder if he wasn't having a coronary occlusion.

In the early days, Juliette hadn't been worried that his work often took him away for months at a time. But that was because the jobs were relatively short. He'd never been involved in anything longer than six months – until this one. Thankfully, the end was in sight.

Bronson had been driving lorries for over a year now and, while it was tiring, he'd seen more of the country than he ever imagined and met some good people. He'd met some very dubious folks too. But his job wasn't to ask questions – it was to make deliveries and get back to the depot in the allotted timeframe. He'd recently changed companies – the new one offered more money – a lot more when it came down to it. And it took him closer to the top. The switch had come at a time he wasn't expecting.

Bronson stretched his arms over his head and arched his back. Despite the many hours he spent sitting, he was still fit. He had to be. It was a long drive tonight to a warehouse he'd never been to before. The paperwork said that he was to drop off one trailer and pick up another, and he'd receive instructions about his next destination. He'd sleep in the cabin of the lorry – like usual. But come the weekend, he was heading home. His boss had promised him it would be all over by then. That reminded him, once everything was done and dusted he needed to stop by the shops . . .

Bronson turned on the radio and began to sing along to an old rock song that reminded him of the days when he was young and the world was something to be embraced instead of feared. Being an adult had a habit of beating the joy out of life. He laughed to himself at the crazy ambitions he'd once had. Bronson had wanted to sell cars – expensive ones like Aston Martins and Porsches. He used to walk past the dealership at the end of the high street on his way to and from school. The bloke who ran the place always looked like a million bucks and the cars around him would have cost more than Bronson could make in twenty years.

These days, cars like that still turned his head – there'd been one assignment where he thought he might have ended up in the motor business, but that turned out to be a dead end.

Bronson's dad, Brian, had been a drunk who laughed himself stupid when Bronson said he wanted to sell Ferraris and the like. Brian told him he'd more likely be stealing them. But that was never going to happen. Bronson might have been a lot of things, but he had a conscience – unlike his old man, who'd had several brushes with the law for receiving stolen goods and breaking into houses. Bronson decided when he was just a kid that he wouldn't ever touch a drop of alcohol and he wasn't going to hang around with bad people who engaged in the sort of behaviour that could see you go to prison. For the most part, he'd managed to stay true to his word. Though his father probably wouldn't believe what he actually did now – at least his life wasn't boring. Far from it.

Chapter 24

Ellie raced through the rain to Hazel's house, where she stood on the veranda shivering. She reached out to ring the bell, her hand shaking uncontrollably.

It took a few minutes before Hazel's mother answered the door.

'Hello, Ellie, darlin',' the woman said, peering out into the street. 'You must be frozen to the bone. What were you thinking running around without an umbrella? Gosh, that coat of yours is far too light for this dreadful weather.'

Ellie nodded. Her teeth were chattering, and her fingers and toes were numb. She tried to speak, but the words wouldn't come out.

'Hazel's in her room, but let's get you inside and into the shower first,' the woman said. Keeley Hendrix was dressed in what seemed to be something of a uniform – black leggings and a pale-pink puffer vest over a matching long-sleeved top. She must have had just about every colour combination, from what Ellie had seen of the woman. Her long blonde hair was pulled up into a high ponytail.

Keeley directed Ellie to the downstairs bathroom, which was off the hallway beside the guest room. There were warm towels on the rack and underfloor heating.

'You hop in and I'll organise some of Hazel's clothes for you, darlin',' the woman said.

'Th-th-thank – you – Miss-ss-uss – Hendrix,' Ellie said, her teeth still chattering.

'Oh sweetie – if I've told you once, I've told you a hundred times, call me Keeley. Mrs Hendrix is my husband's mother and I wouldn't want to be mistaken for that old battle axe. Even though my husband thinks the sun shines out of her – Griffin's easily fooled.'

Ellie nodded and headed into the bathroom where she locked the door and stripped off her wet uniform. She placed her bra and underpants on the heated towel rail, hoping they'd dry enough for her to be able to put them back on. Then Ellie turned the shower mixer and waited until the water was steaming hot before she stepped inside. The spray prickled her skin and she felt as if she was quite literally thawing from the inside out like a frozen chicken defrosting in the microwave.

She couldn't remember how long she'd been standing there when suddenly the thought occurred to her that she was probably using all her friends' hot water. That wouldn't go down well — she knew how much she hated it when Myles ran theirs out. Ellie turned off the taps and stepped out onto the bath mat. She could feel the warmth of the underfloor heating on her toes. It was heavenly. She'd dried herself off and wrapped a towel around her when there was knock on the door.

'Hey, Ellie. I've got some clothes for you,' Hazel said. 'I hope you've got something for me too.'

Ellie swallowed hard. She'd done what the boys had asked. Surely now they'd trust her. She turned the lock and opened the door just enough for Hazel to pass the things around.

'Thanks,' Ellie said. 'I won't be long.'

'Come up to my room,' Hazel said.

It was lucky the two girls were more or less the same size – although Ellie had less meat on her bones. Missing meals could do that – sometimes when food was short she'd give her dinner to Myles. He was always hungry and not eating put him in a tricky mood. Ellie picked up her bra and undies, which she was surprised to find were almost dry.

She quickly threw on the jeans and sweater Hazel had brought for her and found a brush in the cupboard, which she ran through her long hair. She was tempted to look for a hair dryer, but Hazel was waiting.

Ellie grabbed her backpack (which was also soaked through) and opened the door. Her shoes and socks were still wet – she'd leave them on the floor and see if they were dry by the time she was ready to leave. She would have preferred to leave her backpack too, but it had something inside that she needed.

She headed out into the hall past the spare room towards the back stairs. Hazel's house was a total rabbit warren with a front and back staircase. Apparently, it used to be an old vicarage and Mrs Hendrix had once told Ellie she'd spent two years and close to a million pounds renovating the place. While it was lovely, Ellie thought the decor a bit garish. It was all patterned wallpapers and shiny light fittings, animal print cushions and shag pile rugs. Not really in keeping with the historical features of the house – at least, according to all the house renovation shows Ellie quite enjoyed watching.

She headed up and looked around, wondering where Hazel's bedroom was, then realised that she was in a part of the house she'd not seen before. Maybe there were three staircases? Now that she thought about it, the last time she and Hazel had used the one other than in the front hall, they'd ended up in the kitchen and this staircase was off the front hall at the end of the corridor near the guest room.

Ellie stood on a landing and was about to turn back when she heard a noise. A voice – almost like a yelp. And it was coming from behind a dark timber door. Ellie knocked, but there was no reply. She turned the handle and peeked her head around. The room wasn't very big and looked like an office. There was no one inside but there was a radio on the desk – that must have been what she heard.

Ellie was about to head back out when a crackle of static sent her skywards. She walked towards the desk and realised it wasn't a regular radio – this was a CB – like the ones they have in lorries and the like. It stood to reason, given Hazel's dad ran a transport company, that he might have one at home. Hazel said that he worked all the time.

There was more static, then a voice. 'They're onto me,' it said. 'Griff's just a pawn . . . he's dispens–' and then the line went dead.

Ellie's heart was racing. The person sounded scared. And Griff – did they mean Hazel's dad, Griffin? It wasn't a very common name. What did it mean that he was a pawn? A player in a game? Maybe it was someone having a laugh. Surely that was it.

Her eyes scanned the desk, falling upon a pile of what looked look bills. Ellie knew they were none of her business, but she couldn't help herself. She quickly thumbed through them and realised that they weren't regular monthly accounts. They were final notices and letters of demand. All addressed to Griffin Hendrix. There were lottery tickets too – not just a couple but a huge stack. And then there were invoices – they were all for a company called Freightliners. That must have been who Mr Hendrix worked for.

If the family was in financial trouble, Ellie had a horrible feeling that Hazel and her mother were completely in the dark. All they talked about was going shopping and taking holidays – which required money – and the way Hazel spoke made it seem she thought they had an endless supply.

Ellie put everything back and slipped out through the door then bolted down the stairs where Hazel met her at the bottom. 'What were you doing up there?' Hazel asked.

'I got lost,' Ellie said, avoiding eye contact with her friend. 'Your house is so big I didn't realise there was a third set of stairs.'

'Seriously – it's not that big compared to some of the places around here. And it's just Dad's study up there – nothing to see,' Hazel said. 'He hates it if we go near the place – says it's got lots of important work things. He even cleans it himself. And it's usually locked anyway.'

Ellie didn't wonder, given what she'd seen. 'Sorry – I didn't go in,' Ellie lied. Now she couldn't say anything even if she wanted to.

Hazel walked through the hallway with Ellie following.

'How come you were soaked when you got here?' the girl asked.

'It's wet out there if you haven't noticed,' Ellie said, clutching her backpack as she followed Hazel upstairs. 'Is Jake home?'

Hazel shook her head. 'He and Liam are out doing some jobs for Dad.'

Ellie wondered what sort of jobs those were. Her head was spinning.

Hazel plonked down on her bed and invited Ellie to sit down opposite.

'Would you girls like some hot chocolate?' Keeley called to them.

'No, thanks, Mum,' Hazel said. 'Do you want something, Ellie?'

Ellie was going to say no, but then she thought better of it. 'I'd love a hot chocolate if it's not too much trouble.'

'Ellie wants one,' Hazel shouted.

'Won't be long,' the woman called back.

'Your mum's lovely,' Ellie said.

Hazel nodded. 'Yeah, I know – I want to be just like her when I grow up.'

Ellie frowned. 'What did she do before she had Kane and you and Jake?'

Hazel shrugged. 'A bit of modelling for product launches and that sort of thing, but as soon as she got pregnant with Kane she stopped, and she's stayed home ever since. She and Dad have been together since they were in high school. I'm going to get married as young as I can.'

'Really?' Ellie said.

'Why not? Then I wouldn't have to do some boring job,' Hazel said. 'As long as the guy's rich. Which he will be because I'm not marrying a loser.'

Ellie hadn't ever talked to her friend about their life ambitions before. It was a bit of a surprise that Hazel didn't really have any. Ellie wanted to be a barrister – she was determined to make it and there was no way she was going to rely on a man to provide for her. Her mother had let herself fall for that trap and it hadn't exactly turned out well.

'Don't you want to go to university and make something of yourself?' Ellie asked.

Hazel wrinkled her nose. 'Why? I hate studying. Mum's the happiest person I know and Dad said that he's going to retire in the next few years, and they'll probably buy a place in Spain and live there for half the year. I could go with them.'

Keeley Hendrix tapped on the door and poked her head around. She had a tray with two mugs of hot chocolate, even though Hazel had rejected the offer, and a plate of choc-chip cookies.

The sweet smell of their drinks was almost overwhelming. Ellie felt her stomach twist.

'Thanks Mrs . . . I mean, Keeley,' Ellie said.

'Have you warmed up now, love?' she asked as she set the tray down on Hazel's desk.

Ellie nodded.

'I might have a coat you can take home too,' the woman said. 'It's one of Hazel's from last season. I've been meaning to take it to the charity shop but haven't got around to it. It's in the back of the car.'

'Oh, no,' Ellie said. 'My coat's fine.'

'It's not and we both know it,' the woman said. 'Anyway, I'm sure that Hazel would rather you have it.'

Hazel frowned. 'Are you sure, Mum? You know I always like my clothes going to people who really need them.'

Ellie could feel her cheeks getting warmer. Hazel had no idea that she was one of those 'properly poor' people and she didn't want her to either.

'Oh well, you can discuss it,' Keeley said, but Ellie felt as if the woman was definitely more clued in than her daughter. 'Give me a shout if you'd like another drink or anything. I'll be downstairs reading. My new copy of *Gloss and Goss* just arrived and there's a huge story on Lawrence Ridley and his gorgeous wife, Charlotte Highton-Smith. You know her sister lives on the edge of the village with her husband and their daughter. She's quite the cute little thing.'

'Mum – why do you care about those people? They're so rich, it's disgusting, and I bet the kid is super stuck-up,' Hazel said.

'I think they sound like a lovely family and you know they do a lot for people around here,' Keeley said. 'You listen to your father too much. Always banging on about rich people and how life's not fair. He does all right. I don't think he's got much to complain about. We're not exactly on the bones of our backsides.'

Hazel rolled her eyes. 'Whatever.'

And with that, Keeley Hendrix left the girls alone.

Ellie bit her lip. Clearly, Mrs Hendrix knew nothing of the family's money worries. Maybe if she did, she'd get a job.

'I thought she was never going to leave,' Hazel said. 'I mean she's a great mum and everything, and she is my best friend other than you . . .'

Ellie smiled to herself. 'I'm your best friend?'

'Well, duh,' Hazel said. 'I used to be besties with Ally and before that it was Lara, but never mind. They're both so fake and they don't care about the stuff I care about.'

Ellie had wondered why Hazel had taken to her so quickly. She was curious about what had gone on with the other girls but decided not to ask. Ellie had never had a best friend before. And she liked it.

'So did you get it?' Hazel asked, taking a sip of her hot chocolate.

Ellie nodded. 'It was a bit tricky, but it's in my bag.'

She patted the top and started to undo the zip.

Ellie reached inside. She could feel the book she'd borrowed from the library and her science folder. She stared at the bag and frowned. 'I don't understand.'

'What's the problem?' Hazel asked.

Ellie tipped the entire contents on the floor. There were her books and the folder, a pencil case and a couple of scrunched-up muesli bar wrappers but no charity box.

'So what happened to it?' Hazel said, her eyebrows high. 'Did it fall out when you were coming here?'

Ellie shook her head. 'I zipped up the bag as soon as I dropped it inside . . . unless . . .'

She was thinking about the way she'd done it. Those boys were playing around, and she had her coat over her bag, and then there was that kid – Alice-Miranda. She had a shopping bag and she was standing right next to her. They all were.

'Surely not,' Ellie said, thinking out loud.

'What?' Hazel said.

'I think it must have fallen into someone else's bag,' she said, then explained about the girl she'd met and her friends.

'Now she's going to know that I was trying to take it,' Ellie said.

'Seriously, Ellie – the boys are never going to believe that. I don't believe that,' Hazel said. 'You didn't do it, did you?'

'I did. I promise,' Ellie said. Her heart was pounding and she could feel the beads of perspiration forming on her brow.

The sound of running feet on the stairs distracted the girls. Suddenly the door flew open and Jake and Liam burst into the room.

'Mum said that you were here,' Jake blurted as he swiped a cookie from the plate and plonked down on Ellie's desk chair. Liam grabbed one too and glared at Ellie.

'Did you get it?' Liam demanded.

Ellie swallowed hard.

She opened her mouth to say something when Hazel hurriedly regaled the boys with the whole sorry tale.

'What a load of twaddle,' Liam scoffed. He picked up another cookie and stuffed it into his mouth.

'It's true. I swear,' Ellie said. She could feel the tears pricking her eyes. She hurriedly wiped them away. 'I'll get it back.'

She had no idea how, but . . . Ellie wanted to belong – to something. Even if it didn't exactly sit right with her. She was Hazel's best friend.

Jake had been sitting quietly munching away when suddenly his face lit up.

'This is perfect,' he said.

The others frowned at him.

'What are you talking about?' Liam said. 'She's hopeless.'

Jake grinned. There was a chocolate chip caught in his front teeth, which his sister quickly pointed out.

'Ellie needs to get the donation box – which is with the Highton-Smith whatever-her-name-is kid – at their mansion,' Jake said.

Liam looked at his friend and a grin began to form on his lips. 'They're on the list. Kane said that he saw these huge baubles in the garden when he was delivering some parcels there this afternoon.'

'So while Ellie is getting the donations box, we can help ourselves to the stuff outside,' Jake said.

'Um, I think you're forgetting something,' Hazel said. 'Like, they would have security, and there's probably always someone around. They have staff, don't they?'

Ellie could feel the hot chocolate she'd enjoyed so much sitting like a stagnant pond in the bottom of her stomach.

'Why do you want their Christmas decorations?' Ellie asked.

Jake and Liam grinned at each other.

'Because we're the Bauble Bandits,' Liam said proudly.

Ellie frowned. 'I don't understand. What? You get a kick out of stealing Christmas decorations – and then what do you do with them?'

The boy sighed. 'We go and decorate people's houses – the ones who don't have any Christmas cheer at all.'

'But won't people know that it was you? I mean if our garden suddenly looked like a celebration we'd call the police,' Ellie said.

'Would you? Imagine that you have a little brother and he goes outside and realises that Santa's elves have been round and made the house look beautiful for Christmas. You'd call the cops and let them take it away?' Jake said.

'I do have a little brother and, no, I wouldn't call the police because he'd love it,' Ellie said.

'Right – so you understand then. We're just spreading the Christmas cheer to the people who need it the most,' Liam said. 'And rich people like the Highton-Smith whatever-whatevers have more than they need or deserve. Like that bloke from Hoxton Manor and that other old toff, Lord Littleton.'

Ellie remembered seeing something about the Christmas decorations being stolen from several of the villages around the place and a couple of private houses.

'So it's you?' she asked. 'The one who's been taking all those decorations?'

Liam grinned. 'And Jake and Kane and Hazel and a couple of Kane's mates when we need them. We're doing a community service, that's all.'

Jake looked at the boy and thumped him on the arm.

'Ow! Whatcha do that for?' Liam moaned.

'You just told her that we've been stealing, you daft git,' Jake said.

Liam ran a hand through his straggle of greasy hair. 'So what? Now she has to help – or . . .'

'Or what?' Ellie asked, horrified by what she was hearing.

'Or we set you up to take the fall,' Jake said.

Ellie's eyes widened and her stomach dropped.

'Are you in?' Hazel asked, a grin on her lips. 'Bestie?'

Ellie could hardly breathe. Either way, this wasn't going to end well for her. And a criminal record was the last thing she needed if she was going to get into law school.

'She said that they'd all be at the village Christmas light ceremony tomorrow night,' Ellie said.

'Who?' Hazel asked.

Ellie swallowed hard. 'Alice-Miranda.'

Liam and Jake grinned at each other. 'Looks like we're off to Highton Hall and then on Saturday, Hoxton Manor won't know what's hit it.'

Ellie shuddered. The idea of stealing the donations box was bad enough. What they were about to do next was on a whole other level.

Chapter 25

Alice-Miranda and her friends had arrived back at the house wringing wet after the worst of the rain had passed. Now, having showered and changed, they were all gathered around the kitchen table, with gingerbread houses under construction. It was something akin to a military exercise, with the sweets divided into bowls and placed in the centre, and the gingerbread sheets in front of each child. There was even a set of plans pinned up on the kitchen chalkboard for reference. There were piping bags with royal icing too, which they'd use to glue everything together.

Fortunately, they had a couple of hours before dinner to perfect their masterpieces.

After they'd returned, Alice-Miranda had left the donations box in her room – she'd talk to her mother about it later but there had to be a rational explanation. It must have simply fallen off the counter.

'Where's Mummy and Daddy?' she asked Mrs Oliver and Mrs Shillingsworth, who had both begun their houses along with the children.

'Your mother was on the phone to Charlotte,' Dolly replied, 'and I haven't seen your father all day. I think he's at the office.'

Alice-Miranda frowned. Her parents were usually the most enthusiastic gingerbread builders of all. It was something of a competitive sport in their household – although her father often ate his own body weight in sweets by the end of the activity and complained about having a stomach-ache for the rest of the night. Mrs Greening was coming around to judge the best houses after dinner before taking the rest of them to one of the local care homes tomorrow for the residents to enjoy. The winning three houses would remain as centrepieces for the table for the children's final celebratory dinner before everyone headed home on Monday morning to be with their own families for Christmas.

Caprice cast her eyes around the room, sizing up how everyone was getting along.

'I wonder whose house is going to be the most beautiful,' she said, then pulled a face at Neville's, which seemed to be leaning heavily to one side.

'Probably yours if you've had any coaching from your mother,' Sep said. 'And definitely not mine.' His roof had just fallen off.

'Probably,' Caprice agreed.

Millie rolled her eyes and grinned at the girl.

'What have I done now?' Caprice asked.

'I wish I had your confidence,' Millie said.

'More like overconfidence,' Caprice replied. 'I know it's not a very attractive trait – yes, Alice-Miranda, I did listen to what you said to me the other day.'

Millie turned to Alice-Miranda and raised her eyebrows.

'She really is trying, isn't she?' Millie whispered and Alice-Miranda gave a nod.

Sep was using one of the piping bags to try and stick his roof back on. 'You never know – I could win the most interesting, which I'm sure must be code for the ugliest,' the boy said.

Lucas was eating his third musk stick.

'You'll have nothing left for the decorations, Master Lucas,' Dolly admonished as he reached for a fourth.

'Sorry,' the boy said, taking his hand back. 'They're just so delicious I can't help myself.'

The group chatted amiably as the houses began to take shape.

'Mine's super wonky,' Jacinta complained as her walls began to collapse again. To everyone's surprise, it was Caprice who came to her rescue.

The girl stood up and walked around to show her how to angle things so that there was enough time for the icing to set.

'Thank you,' Jacinta said with a smile. Across the table, Lucas gave her a wink.

'I saw that, Lucas,' Caprice said. 'You know I'm not always as horrible as you think.'

The others grinned.

A knock on the back door startled everyone.

Dolly Oliver bustled away to open it and was surprised to see a young lad.

'I have a delivery for Miss Alice-Miranda Highton-Smith-Kennington-Jones,' he said.

On hearing her name, the girl slid out of her seat and ran to the door, where he passed over a large white envelope embossed in the most beautiful red and green edging and tied with a giant red ribbon.

'I wonder what it is,' Dolly said and walked back to help Neville, who was in a world of bother with his house.

'Thank you,' Alice-Miranda said with a smile. 'I hope you haven't had to travel far in this awful weather.'

'I've been running some errands for Mr Turner,' the young man replied. 'You're the last on my list. I'm off home now. My mum's got soup on the stove.'

Alice-Miranda held her hand up. 'Please wait a moment,' she said and ran back into the larder off the kitchen, returning a minute later with a brown paper bag. 'Please take some of Mrs Oliver's homemade bread rolls. She's baked dozens and they'll go well with your soup.'

'Thank you, miss,' the lad said. 'Much appreciated. Merry Christmas.'

Alice-Miranda waved him off and took the envelope back to the table, where she slid her nail under the flap and pulled out the most beautiful invitation.

'What is it?' Millie asked to a chorus echoing her words.

She scanned the text and smiled.

'It's an invitation – for all of us. To Mr Turner's Christmas party. Mummy and Daddy are already going, aren't they?'

'Oh, yes, your parents wouldn't miss it. It's one of the social highlights of the year,' Dolly replied.

'Can you read it out?' Jacinta asked.

Mr Elliot Turner would be delighted to have the company of Miss Alice-Miranda Highton-Smith-Kennington-Jones and her friends, Millie, Jacinta, Chessie, Britt, Sloane, Caprice, Lucas, Sep and Neville at his annual Christmas party to be held on Saturday, 21 December, at Hoxton Manor. Dress up and sparkle as we celebrate the magic of the season.

'How did he know our names?' Caprice asked. Alice-Miranda looked at Mrs Oliver, who shook her head. 'He must have called your mother, I imagine.'

'But what are we going to wear?' Jacinta asked. 'We're all too big to raid Alice-Miranda's wardrobe.'

'Speak for yourself,' Millie said with a grin.

Alice-Miranda tapped her cheek. 'I have some ideas,' she said coyly. You could almost see her brain ticking over.

Cecelia Highton-Smith arrived in the room only to be greeted by a flood of excitement about the upcoming party.

Alice-Miranda showed her the invitation and whispered something to her mother, which caused a smile to spread across the woman's face.

'What are you two conspiring about?' Jacinta asked. But the pair simply shook their heads. She had an idea, though. Cecelia had come to their rescue once before and her choices had been perfect.

'Where's Daddy?' Alice-Miranda asked her mother. 'He's usually the first one to make his gingerbread house and you're late as well.'

'I'm sorry, but your father's a bit busy at the moment,' Cecelia replied.

Alice-Miranda frowned. 'Is there more stock missing?'

Cecelia nodded. 'Unfortunately, yes, and apparently, it's not just us who've been losing things. Your father's been speaking to the owners of several other supermarket chains and they're having problems, too. Though it sounds like they've had small amounts of things going missing for months on end – and lots of small quantities add up to large quantities for everyone.'

'Surely there's a way to track the goods when they leave the warehouse?' Alice-Miranda said.

'I know you can track the lorries,' Sep said. 'We were watching a program at school for one of our technology classes and it was all about one of the freight companies and how they keep account of their vehicles. It was sort of like air traffic control except for heavy transport.'

'I'm never going to run my own business – it's a nightmare,' Caprice said, absently, while she was gluing mint leaves to the roof of her house to look like shingles.

The others looked over at the girl who continued with her job, not missing a beat.

'Why do you say that, Caprice?' Jacinta asked.

The girl stopped what she was doing and looked up, as if realising that she'd almost said too much.

'Are your parents having a hard time with their business?' Neville asked.

Caprice shook her head. 'No, of course not. *Sweet Things* is as popular as ever and the restaurants are packed every night. Mummy says they're booked out for months and months.'

'So why wouldn't you want to have your own business then – it sounds like your parents are doing fantastically well?' Sep asked.

'Who wants to do all that paperwork?' Caprice said and turned her attention back to the gingerbread house.

'Yes, well, you're right about there being a lot of it, Caprice,' Cecelia said with a tight smile. 'Anyway, I'm sure that Hugh will sort out the Kennington's problems. He is nothing if not determined.'

But Alice-Miranda was still concerned. 'Has the company lost a lot of money?' she asked.

Cecelia shook her head though from the look on her face, Alice-Miranda wasn't convinced her mother was being entirely honest.

'Anyway, that's quite enough talk of business,' Cecelia said. 'We've got gingerbread houses to make. And aren't they looking fabulous?' The woman cast her eyes across the table. Fabulous probably wasn't the right word for all of them, but encouragement was important in her books.

Alice-Miranda grabbed a handful of chocolate buttons and picked up the piping bag. They would make perfect wall decorations. But even though she was trying hard to concentrate on what she was doing, she couldn't help thinking about Ellie and the donations box and what was happening with her father. Life was never quite as straightforward as one might hope – not even at Christmas.

Chapter 26

The gingerbread houses had been a triumph – despite some wonky rooves, angled walls and missing sweets. (When Lucas declared he had a stomach-ache, absolutely no one was surprised.) As predicted, Mrs Greening had chosen Caprice's as the most beautiful (it truly was), while Neville's was the most interesting and Chessie's was judged the tastiest (to look at – they wouldn't know for sure until after the houses had done their job as centrepieces and then they'd be eaten). The trio unwrapped their prizes of ugly Christmas sweaters – Neville's with reindeer antlers, Caprice's with a Christmas tree with real lights and Chessie's had a huge gold bow around a present. Alice-Miranda had a feeling they'd all have one before the weekend was out.

The group was sitting in the playroom, having eaten yet another hearty breakfast – this time it was American-style pancakes with maple syrup and crispy bacon. Though Millie and Caprice had both enjoyed theirs with lemon and sugar instead.

Sep and Neville were in the middle of an intense game of chequers, while Chessie was knitting a scarf for her stepfather for Christmas. She'd only started it a week ago and everyone was impressed by how fancy it was – a Fair Isle in lovely shades of blue and cream. The girl's former housemistress at Bodlington, Mrs Fairbanks, had taught her how to knit and Chessie had used the activity as a distraction from Madagascar and her incessant bullying. Caprice, Sloane and Millie were playing cards without so much as a cross word – yet.

Caprice's face was looking a bit worse today with the bruises going through a green and yellow phase, although Alice-Miranda had told her that probably meant she'd turned a corner and would be much improved by the end of the week. Caprice was worried about the party on Saturday night at Mr Turner's place, but Cecelia promised that she'd help her cover any residual colour with makeup.

Alice-Miranda and Britt were playing gin rummy while Lucas was sitting on the couch with Jacinta in front of him on the floor while he brushed her hair.

'So who's up for a spot of Christmas shopping this morning?' Alice-Miranda asked. She'd been hoping to do some yesterday, but they'd only made it as far as the grocery shop for sweets.

There was a cacophony of yeses from her guests.

'I've still got to get a present for my grandpa and dad,' Millie said. 'Though what to get either of them is a complete mystery.'

'I haven't bought anything yet,' Sloane said. 'If anyone has ideas for what I can get my mother, please feel free to share. But don't worry about Sep – he never buys me anything.'

'Not true, little sister,' the boy replied. 'For your information I have a present for you, and you know Mum always loves makeup or a magazine subscription. I've got Dad a book – he was banging on about some old fellow from the television who's written a biography he was keen on.'

'I knew I should have ordered that when he mentioned it,' Sloane said. 'Now you'll be his favourite again.'

'You can come in with me,' Sep said. 'I don't mind.'

'Really?' Sloane asked.

'Yeah, of course,' Sep said. 'As long as you promise not to randomly hit me anymore.'

'I'll try,' Sloane replied.

The others chuckled. Sep had always been the sweetest boy, but Sloane could be prickly. It was nice to see the siblings getting on better these days.

The weather had improved considerably since the previous afternoon's downpour. With it confirmed that everyone was keen to head to the village, the group decided to leave at half ten. The shops would all be open by then. Alice-Miranda had a list to get through, but there were a few people she was still struggling to think what to get. Dolly being one of them. Shilly had mentioned something about a new sewing case.

'And what are we going to wear to the party on Saturday night?' Caprice asked. 'Do we need to look for something while we're out?'

Cecelia Highton-Smith had just poked her head in the doorway. 'No, Caprice,' the woman said. 'I've got some things being sent up this afternoon for you all to try. The last thing any of your parents need is the expense of new party dresses and suits at Christmas time. And especially not when I have access to rather a lot of things at Highton's.'

'Wow!' Chessie's eyes lit up. 'That's fantastic.'

'I knew it,' Jacinta said. 'Though I didn't want to be presumptuous, I saw you and Alice-Miranda whispering last night.'

Cecelia smiled. 'It'll be fun – we can have a fashion parade and see what everyone likes best.'

'I can't believe that Mr Turner invited us all to his party,' Alice-Miranda said. She jumped up. 'Oh, that reminds me, I have to RSVP. Should I write to him, or would it be better if I call?'

'I think at this late stage it might be better if you phone and let Miss Wickham know,' the woman said. 'She's Elliot's housekeeper and a lovely woman at that.'

Alice-Miranda nodded and scampered off to the kitchen where she'd left the invitation sitting on the sideboard. She'd call from the pantry.

'Thank goodness she's gone,' Caprice said, garnering some surprised stares from her fellow guests. 'Oh, don't look at me like that, Neville – you know as well as I do that we've been trying to get Cecelia on her own to talk about what we get little Miss Prim for Christmas.'

Jacinta and Millie both raised their eyebrows.

'Come on – I'm kidding,' Caprice said. 'Cecelia, you know I'm joking, right?'

Cecelia smiled. 'You wouldn't be the first person to refer to my daughter in that way and I'm sure you won't be the last.'

'See?' Caprice said. 'Anyway, forget that I said it. We have a question, Cecelia. We all want to pool our funds and buy something special for Alice-Miranda for Christmas. It wasn't my idea – it was Millie's – but we have to take the bull by the horns and organise something or else it won't happen.'

Millie nodded.

'Oh, gosh, that's hard,' Cecelia said. 'Her father and I can never think of what to get her. Even when she was little, she never asked for anything for herself. We used to wonder if there was something wrong with her.'

'Of course, there is,' Caprice said. 'She's not like a normal child. I mean, I used to take the toy catalogue when I went for my Santa photo and I had everything circled that I wanted – sometimes it ran to more than twenty pages.'

Jacinta grinned. 'Oh, I did that too.'

'Guilty,' Sloane said, raising her hand.

'Well, I didn't take a catalogue, but I had a list as long as my arm,' Millie said.

The boys all confessed to some sort of strategy as well.

'So, given Alice-Miranda is a total weirdo, we'd like to do something really special for her,' Caprice said.

The others were more than a little surprised. Who knew that Caprice could be so generous? Especially given that the trip hadn't exactly started off well.

'All right, I'll have a good think,' Cecelia said.

'She mentioned something about wanting a book,' Millie said. 'When we were on the bus. Do you have any idea what sort of book she was thinking about? Is there a first edition of something that she loves – I know she's a huge fan of *Anne of Green Gables* and *The Secret Garden*.'

Cecelia bit her lip and frowned. 'She's got copies of those.'

Britt hadn't said anything and had been thinking hard. 'Perhaps it's a modern book that she's after. Does she have any favourites?'

The children all thought for a moment.

'She loves those spy stories,' Jacinta said. 'Remember when we were in the outback, we watched that movie about Kensy and Max? Alice-Miranda is totally addicted. Maybe we could get in touch with the author and she could send us a note to put inside the collection.'

'That's pretty late notice,' Lucas said. 'She's probably busy.'

Alice-Miranda appeared in the doorway. Everyone stopped speaking immediately.

'What's the matter?' she asked.

'Nothing,' the group chorused.

The girl frowned and clearly didn't believe them.

'I spoke to Miss Wickham. You're right, Mummy, she's lovely. She said that she'd let

Mr Turner know that we're all very excited to be coming to his party,' Alice-Miranda said. She glanced at the clock on the mantel. 'We'd better get moving if we're going to get our shopping done.'

Cecelia nodded and the others did too – though a sly wink from Neville probably didn't go anywhere to helping keep the surprise present situation under wraps.

Chapter 27

The children decided to split up to do their shopping then meet back at the cafe at Kennington's at one o'clock.

The village was a hive of activity with people dashing about, in and out of stores, laden with parcels.

'We'll see you all soon,' Alice-Miranda said and hurried off with Millie, who was on a mission to find something for her grandfather first.

'What about socks?' Alice-Miranda suggested.

Millie shook her head. 'Boring.'

'A book?' the girl tried again.

'Grandpa's eyesight isn't what it used to be, so he mostly listens to audio books now,' Millie said. The pair walked along the high street past Kennington's, which seemed a lot busier than usual. There was a menswear shop a little further along. Millie wondered if a hat might be a good idea.

Across the road they could see Lucas, Neville and Sep lurking outside the antique shop. Lucas was pointing at something in the window before the boys disappeared inside.

Further along, Britt, Chessie and Caprice had just gone into the newsagency, which also had a bookshop at the back, and Jacinta and Sloane were outside the gift shop.

Over the course of the next hour, the group crossed paths a number of times. Going by the shopping bags they were all carrying, it seemed that the expedition was proving successful.

Alice-Miranda had almost checked everyone off her list – except for Mrs Oliver. That is until she spotted the perfect present in the window of the charity shop. She also spied someone she recognised inside behind the counter.

'Come on, Millie,' the girl said and grabbed her friend's hand.

The bell tinged as they entered. The woman looked up. She was wearing a beautiful yellow silk blouse with a pussybow at her neck and tailored grey trousers. Alice-Miranda couldn't see her shoes, but she imagined they were stylish too. Her bobbed silver hair was trimmed to perfection, and she wore large pearls in her ears.

'Hello, Miss Appleby,' Alice-Miranda said with a beaming smile. 'Or should I say Mrs Pertwhistle?'

'Godfathers, child, I might have married the old coot, but I didn't take his name. I've been Violet Appleby all my life – I wasn't about to change it. Besides, Pertwhistle is such a silly name – even though it does suit him rather well. You're home from school already, I see. My parents used to say that the more you paid, the less you stayed – quite right, I think. Clemmie finishes this afternoon and not a minute too soon. Honestly, the child is exhausted,' the woman said, raking a strand of hair back behind her left ear.

'Yes, we finished on Wednesday morning after our concert and Christmas dinner on Tuesday night,' Alice-Miranda said. 'Do you remember my friend Millie? I think you met at one of Mummy's garden parties.'

'Vaguely,' the woman replied. She gave Millie a look up and down while at the same time wrinkling her lip.

Millie almost laughed. The woman's rudeness was legendary, so it was good to see that although Miss Appleby had softened a little after her recent marriage, she was still her usual crusty self. A complete turnaround would have been concerning.

'How's Lady Clarissa and Clara?' Alice-Miranda asked. Her mother said that she'd run into the woman not long ago and the little girl was absolutely gorgeous.

'They're both well – though Clarissa still does far too much. They're concentrating on weddings at the hotel these days.'

'Is Mr Smote still helping out?' Alice-Miranda asked. 'He's such fun.'

Violet Appleby rolled her eyes. 'Such a buffoon, did you say? Although, to be honest, I'm not sure how he puts up with some of the bridezillas he has to contend with. There was one girl recently who wanted a white rabbit on every table.'

'I suppose they're probably not that easy to come by – white china rabbits,' Millie said.

'Not china, my dear. This batty girl wanted a real rabbit on every table – dressed in a cerise-coloured bow to match her bridesmaids. Can you imagine it? Anyway, Smote told her that the white rabbits were all taken and she could only have grey ones, so she changed her mind.'

Alice-Miranda and Millie both giggled.

'And Clara is a darling child – not nearly as disagreeable as her older sister – at least, not yet,' Violet said.

'Clementine is a lovely girl,' Alice-Miranda rebuffed. 'I've always found her the sweetest and that little pig of hers, Lavender, is darling.'

Violet nodded. 'Mostly, I'd agree with you, but lately Clementine has become obsessed with craft. I can't tell you how many hours I've spent pointing out pieces of glitter on the floor and if there's one thing I like even less than weddings, it's a hot glue gun.'

The girls exchanged wry looks.

'Are you working here?' Millie asked.

'I volunteer a couple of days a week. It gets me out of babysitting duties. Digby loves drool and dirty nappies, but I can think of nothing worse – except weddings, glitter and hot glue guns. Although it's hardly glamorous here either, is it? Sorting through people's cast-offs,' Violet replied.

'I think it's wonderful,' Alice-Miranda replied. 'A very important job, especially as all the money goes to charity. I might have found the perfect present for Mrs Oliver in the window.'

Alice-Miranda hurried to take the teapot from the table. It was very much like the one that had sprung a leak at home.

'That's a rather nice piece – I suspect it's probably Japanese or Chinese. I have a feeling it might be a genuine antique, so if that's the case you're getting yourself something of a bargain. I was considering buying it myself,' Violet said, raising her left eyebrow. 'But you can have it. We've got enough teapots at home.'

Alice-Miranda smiled. 'Mrs Oliver will love it. Do you know where it came from?'

A frown appeared on Violet Appleby's forehead. She paused and tapped her cheek. 'Now that you mention it, I think it was among the box of things Delia Wickham dropped off at the start of the week. I'm here on a Tuesday and Thursday. It belonged to her sister, but clearly held no sentimentality for Delia. I think the two were on tricky terms. Happens so often in families, doesn't it? I mean, Clarissa and I didn't speak for such a long time and look at us now. It's never too late to mend fences. Although Delia's sister passed away and I'm not entirely sure they were reconciled. Pity, really.'

'That's sad,' Alice-Miranda said, while Violet wrapped the teapot in layers of tissue paper. 'I wonder if the teapot was special to Miss Wickham's sister.'

'Who knows?' Violet said. 'And we probably won't ever find out now.'

Alice-Miranda thought that was likely true though Mrs Oliver was going to love it. She was looking forward to getting home and wrapping all of the gifts she'd bought.

Millie had been browsing while Alice-Miranda paid for the teapot and found a perfect gift for her father. A pair of binoculars. He'd recently mislaid his and told Millie on the phone the other week that he needed to get some more. It was how he kept check of the sheep in the top fields from the house.

Millie took them to the counter and paid as well.

'Have a lovely Christmas, Miss Appleby,' Alice-Miranda said, as the pair turned to leave. 'Will we see you at the Christmas light ceremony this evening?'

'Godfathers, is that happening again?' the woman replied, then rolled her eyes. 'I suppose the children will want to come along.'

It was hard to imagine the woman was unaware of the event, given the village was crawling with workers putting the finishing touches to the display. There was a man up a light pole right outside the shop and across the road in the village square, a scissor lift had two people inside hanging the last of the baubles on the giant tree.

'We'll see you tonight,' Alice-Miranda said.

'Oh, I suppose so,' the woman replied with a sigh.

The girls exited the shop and walked out into the chilly air. At least today the sun was shining and the forecast was for a clear night – that would help draw a crowd.

Millie giggled. 'It's good to see some things never change. I remember when you first introduced me to Miss Appleby. I thought she made the old version of Miss Grimm look positively angelic.'

'I don't think she's nearly as awful as she makes out,' Alice-Miranda said. 'Mummy said that she saw Mr Pertwhistle and Miss Appleby in the village a little while ago with baby Clara and they were both goo-ing and gah-ing over the child as much as each other. I suspect she likes people to believe she's mean and then when she happens to do something kind it's far more shocking.'

The pair walked across to Kennington's and inside to the little coffee shop that formed part of the shopfront, where the rest of the group were already sipping hot chocolates and devouring ham and cheese toasties.

'Sorry, we're late,' Millie said. 'But at least we got everything we wanted.'

It sounded like the outing was a success all round.

'Oh, blow,' Alice-Miranda muttered to herself.

'What's the matter?' Sloane asked.

'I forgot to bring the donations box. It's still sitting in my room. I'll have to remember to tell Mummy and see if anyone's coming back later today or bring it myself,' the child said. 'I'll be back in a minute.'

The girl ducked through the rear door that led to the supermarket section of the complex, where she was surprised to see a new donations box sitting on the counter. She didn't feel quite so bad now – knowing that people could still dispense of their spare change if they felt inclined. Alice-Miranda turned to leave and noticed two boys, dressed in dark overcoats and heavy boots, standing just inside the entrance to the shop. They were pointing at the counter. She had a feeling she'd seen them before somewhere.

'I don't reckon she ever took it in the first place,' one of the boys said. He had long strands of greasy hair and a pimply complexion.

'Anyways, doesn't matter much, she's given us a great idea – and we'll see how good she is at coming through on that one,' the second lad said. 'Should be a doddle with everyone here at the light-up.'

Alice-Miranda realised then that the lads had been standing out the front of Hoxton Manor when they'd been driving home the other day. She frowned and wondered exactly what it was they were planning. The pair gave her a strange feeling and she was often right about those.

The child hurried back to her friends where Millie had ordered them some toasties and hot chocolates too.

Chapter 28

'My goodness,' Dolly Oliver exclaimed as the children tumbled through the kitchen door laden with bags. 'Is there anything left in the shops?'

'I think my dad is going to be very happy with the gift I got him,' Neville said. 'Who knew that I'd find a squirrel nutcracker? He's wanted one forever.'

Dolly grinned and after several more excited revelations about their purchases, she ushered the children into the side sitting room where Cecelia had left rolls and rolls of wrapping, sticky tape and ribbons. Given that some of the gifts were for each other, the children quickly hurried away to different parts of the house to wrap their presents.

Alice-Miranda headed to her room, while Millie asked Mrs Oliver if she could help her wrap the tweed flat cap she'd purchased for her grandfather. Dolly was thrilled with it and said that it would match the tweed tie she'd bought him perfectly. What a lovely combination and they hadn't even conferred.

Upstairs, Alice-Miranda pulled out the teapot. She unwrapped it from the tissue paper to check that Miss Appleby had removed the price from the bottom. It really didn't look as if it had been used terribly much at all – which caused her to wonder if perhaps it didn't pour particularly well. Alice-Miranda decided she'd test it in the bathroom. There was no point giving it to Mrs Oliver if it didn't work – although perhaps she could plant herbs in it instead.

Alice-Miranda turned on the tap and held the pot underneath, and lo and behold when she tried to pour the water out – nothing. Not even a drop.

She tipped the pot upside down and the water cascaded into the sink from the large opening.

'I wonder what's blocking that spout,' she said to herself, as she dried the pot and took it back into her bedroom to examine the inside with her torch. Oddly, there was something. It looked like a glass bottle – of all things – and a tiny one at that. Alice-Miranda tried to dislodge it with her finger, but she couldn't get a grip. There just wasn't enough space but a pair of tweezers might do the trick.

She ran back to the bathroom and located what she was looking for. After much poking and prodding, she realised that perhaps the best way to come at it was from the other end of the spout. She pushed the tweezers inside and within a minute she could feel the bottle coming loose. Eventually it fell into the pot and she pulled it out.

'Good gracious – whatever are you doing in here?' the girl said aloud as she realised that inside the bottle was a piece of paper.

There was a knock on the door.

'Alice-Miranda, do you have any more sticky tape?' Jacinta called.

'Of course – come in,' the girl replied.

Jacinta opened the door and ducked her head around. A long row of gifts was lined up along the wall – there were things the girl had been collecting all year for their neighbours and people who worked in the village, as well as some of the gifts she'd bought today.

Alice-Miranda was holding the little glass bottle she'd just removed from the teapot's spout.

'What's that?' Jacinta asked.

'The most delicious mystery,' Alice-Miranda said and explained about the teapot she'd bought for Mrs Oliver and what she'd just found inside.

'Have you opened it yet?' Jacinta asked.

Alice-Miranda shook her head. 'Shall we?'

The girl pulled the tiny stopper from the top of the bottle and was about to grab the paper with the tweezers when Jacinta yelled, 'Stop!'

Alice-Miranda looked up. 'What's the matter?'

'I think everyone should be here. What if it's something important – like the location of a buried treasure or a death bed confession?'

'I'm sure that it's probably nothing like that,' Alice-Miranda said, but it was quite exciting, nonetheless.

'Oh, come on,' Jacinta said. 'Let's have some fun – we can be like those spy kids you love so much.'

'Fine – we'll round everyone up,' Alice-Miranda said. She pushed the page back inside the bottle and put it in her pocket, then the pair hurried away to find their friends.

'Meet you back here in ten minutes,' Jacinta said. 'And no peeking before we're all together.'

Alice-Miranda grinned and nodded. 'You know I wouldn't.'

'Yes – I'm not sure why I even said that. If it was me on the other hand – I wouldn't trust myself for a second,' Jacinta said.

The girls split up and raced away. Alice-Miranda flew downstairs while Jacinta checked the bedrooms upstairs. Soon all ten children were back inside Alice-Miranda's bedroom waiting for the big reveal. Jacinta hadn't told them what was going on – just that there was something thrilling they needed to see.

Alice-Miranda had told the others much the same.

When everyone was seated on the floor and on the bed and the rocking horse, Alice-Miranda regaled them with the tale of the bottle inside the teapot spout.

'Did you check that it works now?' Neville asked.

'Who cares?' Caprice said. 'Alice-Miranda has a secret message to reveal.'

The others agreed.

'Okay – so this is what I found,' Alice-Miranda said, pulling the bottle from her pocket and holding it up. She popped the top and, using the tweezers in her other pocket, removed the paper. It was rolled around and around. As she unfurled it, she could see that the writing was tiny script – beautifully written but very small.

The girl squinted. 'This isn't going to be as easy as I thought.'

'Hurry up! What does it say?' Sloane gasped.

'Okay,' Alice-Miranda said, then began to read.

My darling, if ever you find this, then you will know two things. One, that I am no longer here on earth and two, that I have done a despicable thing. For that I am truly sorry. You deserved so much better. My actions were unforgivable – but you must remember that I only did it for you.

The girl paused.

'Wow – this is deep,' Millie said.

'So, it is a deathbed confession – of sorts,' Jacinta added, surprised that she had forecast the contents. 'Amazing.'

'Come on – keep going,' Caprice ordered.

The children were all on the edge of their seats.

'It might just be a joke, you know,' Lucas said. 'Someone being funny.'

'I don't think so,' Sep said. 'Why would they go to all that trouble to hide it? This isn't sounding as if it's going to end in a laugh.'

Alice-Miranda continued.

Our daughter was ill. I knew she wouldn't live past a few years. And we'd tried for a baby for so long. I couldn't bear it. Not knowing that this was our last chance. Their child was healthy and they were planning to have more. It didn't seem fair. I did what I had to do.

The children were all leaning forward, hanging on Alice-Miranda's every word.

'What did they do?' Sloane demanded.

'Yes, please keep reading,' Britt said.

But the truth is . . .

'What?' the group chorused.

Alice-Miranda looked up. 'It's smudged. I can't read it.'

'You have to,' Caprice jumped up and ran to the girl's side. 'It can't stop there – we need to know.'

'Yes – who wrote it and why was it hidden inside a teapot spout?' Neville said. 'This is the greatest mystery ever.'

Alice-Miranda scanned the rest of the page. It must have been wet at some stage because the ink bled into the page and was now faded beyond recognition. There was one thing near the end she could just make out.

I love you, my darling, and I beg your forgiveness. Ast

The group was on the edge of their seats.

'That's it – I can't read anything more and the last sentence starts with three letters, a-s-t,' Alice-Miranda said.

'But that doesn't mean anything,' Millie said. 'What's a-s-t? Astonishingly, astoundingly?'

'It could be a name,' Britt said. 'Perhaps it's Astrid.'

'Good thinking,' Sep said.

'Do you know anything about the teapot?' Jacinta asked.

Alice-Miranda nodded. 'I do, actually. Miss Appleby said that it was among a box of things that Miss Wickham – she's Mr Turner's housekeeper – dropped off that had belonged to her sister. Her sister passed away recently and the pair weren't on good terms – at least, that's what Miss Appleby said.'

'We should take it to her and see whether she has any ideas,' Millie said.

Alice-Miranda frowned. 'I was planning to give the teapot to Mrs Oliver for Christmas. I could call Miss Wickham and see if we can meet – although I suspect she's very busy with the party preparations, given that it's tomorrow night.'

The others agreed that's exactly what she should do, but in the meantime most of the children had to get back to their wrapping. They weren't as speedy as Alice-Miranda.

'We've got the Christmas light ceremony tonight too,' the girl reminded everyone. 'Mummy says that we'll leave at half five so we can get something to eat beforehand.'

The children disappeared but Millie stayed behind.

'I wish we could read that smudged part of the note,' the girl said.

'I'm almost afraid of what we might find out,' Alice-Miranda said. 'It sounds as if whoever wrote it was extremely upset about whatever it was they did.'

'True – but it could be important too. They talk about a baby being sick – that's pretty drastic – and someone else's child was healthy,' Millie said, as she hopped up onto Alice-Miranda's bed. She picked up Brummel Bear and hugged him tightly. 'If it was something that affected your entire life then I think you'd want to know. It's a bit like those long-lost family shows on television. Grandpa and I were watching one of the episodes a while back and we were both blubbering.'

Alice-Miranda unfurled the page again. She walked across to her desk and pulled a magnifying glass from the drawer.

'You're right. Let's not give up yet,' she said.

Chapter 29

Ellie arrived home, surprised to find her mother and brother in the kitchen drinking hot chocolate and listening to Christmas music on the radio. She thought Juliette would have been at work and her brother was supposed to be in after-school care.

The cloying smell turned Ellie's stomach – she'd been feeling sick all day.

'Hungry?' Juliette called, as Ellie stormed into the hallway and threw her backpack into her room.

'No!' the girl yelled back.

'I swapped a shift so I could pick Myles up from school because today's the last day before Christmas holidays. Unfortunately, that means I have to work tomorrow.'

Ellie's heart hammered. She knew that was code for, 'And you're on babysitting duties.'

She could hear Myles singing along loudly to 'Rudolf the Red-Nosed Reindeer'. He sang every word and yet he only spoke when he chose to.

'Remember, we're heading out to see the Christmas light ceremony tonight,' Juliette said, as she appeared in Ellie's doorway. 'Myles is so excited. I told him I'd buy you some sparklers to celebrate together.'

'I'm going to Hazel's,' Ellie said, bluntly. 'And I'm not babysitting tomorrow if that's what you were getting at.'

Juliette frowned. 'But we talked about this, Ellie. You said that you'd come with us and Myles is really looking forward to it – and you know I have to work.'

'I promised Hazel I'd go with her,' the girl said. 'And we've got stuff on tomorrow too.'

Juliette took a deep breath. The last thing she wanted was to fight with her daughter, but it seemed par for the course these days.

'I need you to look after Myles tomorrow,' Juliette said.

Ellie could feel the heat rising up her neck.

'Why can't you get a sitter? I shouldn't have to do it, Mum. I'm fourteen and for the first time in my life I have friends. Why is that so hard to understand?' Ellie gritted her teeth.

'I'd really like to meet these friends of yours,' Juliette said.

'They're busy,' Ellie said. She sat on the end of her bed, facing away from her mother.

'Ellie – honey, what's wrong?' Juliette asked, walking over and putting her hand on her daughter's shoulder. The girl recoiled and spun around.

'Don't,' she spat and stood up. 'Just leave me alone.'

Juliette Byers could feel the tears prickling the back of her eyes, but she wouldn't cry.

'Ellie, come on, darling. This isn't like you at all,' the woman tried again.

'Go away, Mum. I'm not worth worrying about,' Ellie said. 'And I'm not looking after Myles tomorrow – I won't.'

'What's the matter, Ellie?' Myles said, appearing

in the doorway. 'Don't you want to be my friend anymore?'

Ellie's heart sank. Myles padded into the room and over to where she was standing with her arms crossed and her back to the door (and to her mother).

'Ellie – we're going to see the lights,' he said. 'And there're going to be decorations too.'

The fact that he was telling her all this – it meant something to Myles.

She bit her lip and pressed her eyes together tightly, willing the tears that were building to stay away.

She turned to look at the boy. He had that goofy grin on his face – the one that always made her smile too.

'I'll see you there a little later,' she said and pulled him into her embrace. 'I promise. And make sure that you take your decorations with you.'

It was a tactical comment. If he had his own things, he might not want to pocket others that didn't belong to him.

Myles nodded and pressed his forehead hard against hers.

'Thank you,' Juliette mouthed at her daughter.

She steered Myles back into the hallway with the promise of more hot chocolate and some Christmas craft.

Ellie walked over and looked at the mirror on the ancient dressing table. The silver inside the glass had bled around the edges and it was cracked in one corner. She stared at her reflection, wondering who the girl staring back at her even was.

'Hurry up, everyone,' Caprice called, as Millie arrived in the kitchen.

'Keep your hair on,' Millie retorted. 'Jacinta's just gone back to get her scarf and the boys are already outside.' They were kicking a football around on the driveway. 'Alice-Miranda's looking for her parents and I'm not sure where the other girls are.'

'We'll be late,' Caprice said.

'No, we won't,' Millie replied. 'We're getting food first. There's this amazing crepe truck and a burger van and pizza. Speaking of food, have you talked to your mother at all?'

Caprice shook her head. 'No, I'm sure that she doesn't have time to be worrying about me.'

'And you still don't know where she is?' Millie asked.

'No,' Caprice said. 'And vice versa.'

Millie frowned. 'But you said that you called and let her know that you were coming here. You told her about the accident too, didn't you?'

Caprice's eyebrows jumped up. She swallowed hard. 'Of course. I didn't mean it like that.'

Millie frowned again and this time the lines were even deeper. 'Caprice – you know I can read you like a book. There's something you're not telling me.'

Caprice grabbed the girl's arm. 'Please don't say anything. Cecelia will kill me – and then if I'm not already dead my mother will too.' There was a frightened look in her eyes.

'What are you worried about?' Millie asked. 'Surely your mother would want to know where you are?'

Caprice sighed. 'I was so mad that she dumped me at the last minute to work. Then I was worried that she wouldn't let me come, so I didn't tell her. She's called a few times and I've ignored her.'

Millie grinned. 'I suppose I'd be pretty annoyed if my parents changed their plans like that too – but you really should let her know where you are. And I'm surprised that Mrs Clarkson let you get away with it.'

'I think she was desperate to get rid of me, and I might have lied and told her that I'd spoken to Mummy. But please don't tell anyone else,' Caprice said and bit her lip.

Millie nodded. 'I won't. But your mother might be a bit cross when she finds out.'

'I'm not even sure that she will be. Mummy's so preoccupied with work at the moment,' Caprice said.

'Is everything all right?' Millie asked.

Caprice shrugged. 'I know I tell everyone how famous and successful she is, but I have a feeling that things aren't going too well. In fact, I know they aren't.'

'How bad is it?' Millie asked.

'Let's just say it's lucky I'm on a scholarship at school or I'm fairly certain my parents would have to pull me out,' the girl replied. 'I think *Sweet Things* is about to be axed. There's this new chef, Sophie Garceau – she has a show called *Pressure Cooker* and everyone loves it, and her. To make matters even worse, the restaurants aren't doing well either. They don't think I know, but I overheard Mum and Dad talking. That's why I was so excited about going to Italy – I thought we could all escape and forget about things for a while and just have a good Christmas.'

Millie's eyebrows jumped up.

'I'm sorry to hear it, but my lips are sealed,' Millie said, as Alice-Miranda bounced into the kitchen.

'Thank you,' Caprice mouthed.

'Where is everyone?'

'Coming!' Jacinta called out as she charged into the room, followed by Britt, Sloane and Chessie.

'We'd better get a move on,' Alice-Miranda said. 'Mummy said to go ahead and she'll catch us up in a bit. Daddy's still not home from work, but he said that he'll meet us there.'

Dolly Oliver walked through from the side sitting room where she and Mrs Shillingsworth had just been doing some gift wrapping of their own.

'Come along then,' Dolly said. The group walked outside where a chill wind had sprung up.

'Make sure you've all got enough warm clothes on,' Shilly said.

The children set off along the driveway, collecting Mr and Mrs Greening on the way. Everyone was off to the light ceremony, including their stablehand, Max, who had already gone on ahead.

When they reached the barns at the edge of the farm, they were joined by Jasper and Poppy Bauer and their parents, Heinrich and Lilly. The woman greeted Lucas with a hug and a kiss. (No one was shocked, given he was her nephew.) And Poppy swiftly hitched a ride on the boy's back. Jacinta loped along beside the pair, letting herself imagine life when they were older. Maybe she and Lucas would have a little girl like Poppy themselves one day.

'Did you get a chance to call Miss Wickham?' Millie asked Alice-Miranda.

'I did but she was out,' Alice-Miranda replied. 'I'll try again in the morning, though I'm sure I'll see her tomorrow night at the party, or perhaps she'll be at the light ceremony too.'

Millie nodded. She looked ahead and realised that Neville was walking beside Chessie. The pair seemed deep in conversation. She wondered where Sep was and if he knew that yet again, he and Neville were competing for the one girl's affections.

Alice-Miranda began talking to Britt, who was on the other side of the trio. Millie turned around and was surprised that Sep was right behind her. She stumbled and almost fell backwards, but Sep grabbed her before she landed in a puddle.

'Oops,' she said.

'That was close,' Sep said, grinning. 'Couldn't have you covered in mud, Millie – especially not in that lovely coat.'

Millie felt her insides turn to mush.

'What? This old thing,' she said, rolling her eyes. She hardly dared to imagine that Sep had actually noticed her – but her coat was rather nice. Her parents had bought it for her last winter and she'd loved it more than anything she'd ever owned before.

'You know you don't always have to put yourself down, Millie,' Sep said.

'Okay,' the girl squeaked. In her head she was telling herself off for being so stupid. Sep was talking to her – he was saying nice things and she needed to say something sensible. Millie drew herself up taller and smiled.

'So, did you get all the gifts you were after?' she asked.

Sep nodded. 'I think so. Though there was one that I'm still not sure about – I really want it to be perfect.'

The pair fell back behind the others and talked all the way to the village. Millie felt as if a swarm of butterflies had invaded her tummy and she couldn't have loved it more.

Chapter 30

Kane Hendrix held onto the steering wheel and looked across at his younger brother beside him. 'Are you sure that they're all going out?'

'She said they were,' Jake replied, turning to look at Ellie. She was sitting on the floor in the back of the van, leaning against the side wall. Hazel was next to her and Liam opposite.

Ellie had been wondering how they were going to steal the baubles, but it had now become clear. Kane had arrived home a while ago in a black van that belonged to the parcel delivery company he worked for.

'But what if there *is* someone home?' Ellie asked. Her mind was a whirl of worries.

'Well, then you're a liar,' Kane said. 'But I've got it covered. I'm delivering a parcel – then I realise I've messed up the address and it's for someone else on the estate. I've been here heaps of times before, so it's not as though seeing me would be a surprise.'

Ellie couldn't believe the situation she'd got herself into.

'What if they have an alarm system?' Ellie asked quietly. 'And cameras?'

Kane scoffed. 'From what I've seen on my rounds, rich people – I mean properly rich people – don't seem to be that worried about security. Back door's never locked here, as far as I know – not even when they're away. I've popped a parcel inside a couple of times – there was a note from one of the staff to do it. And I've never seen any evidence of cameras or the like.'

Ellie picked at the skin around her fingernails and bit the quicks. The family was super trusting, that's for sure – especially with dirtbags like Kane and his friends around.

'Are you excited?' Hazel asked, raising her eyebrows at the girl.

Ellie nodded but didn't say a word.

'Don't look so scared then. Enjoy it,' Hazel said. 'It's not as if we're doing anything wrong. Think of it as a community service.'

Ellie had started thinking that it wasn't like that at all. Stealing was stealing – wasn't it?

The van drove on and Ellie could hear Jake and Kane chatting away in the front seat. They were talking about when they were going to start decorating all the houses with the stuff they'd stolen so far and that it was all stored in a shed – but they didn't say if it was at their house or Liam's, or somewhere else. Jake said something about having a map of the addresses that were in for a Christmas surprise. Ellie almost died when she heard him mention the row of terraces she lived in.

'No, not there,' she blurted.

'Why?' Liam said. 'Those places need cheering up more than anywhere in the village.' A smirk appeared on the boy's lips. 'Do you live in one of those dumps?'

Ellie shook her head. 'No – of course not.'

Hazel turned to look at her. 'Actually, I just

realised I don't know where you live either – and you've never invited me over.'

The girl had been dreading the question for ages but fortunately they were interrupted by Kane, who said that they'd arrived at their destination.

'Looks like the coast is clear,' the lad said. He parked the van down beside a brick barn, out of sight. Liam opened the sliding door and he jumped out, followed by Hazel. Ellie was still sitting on the floor with her arms wrapped around her knees.

'Hurry up, slow coach,' Hazel said. 'We haven't got all night.'

Ellie stood up and exited the vehicle. She followed the others and almost died when she caught sight of the size of the house. Hazel's house was big enough, but this was like a palace.

'I'll never find the charity box in there,' the girl gasped.

'Of course not,' Jake said. 'Just take something else and we'll know you can be trusted.'

Ellie gulped. Somehow that seemed even worse.

Kane told everyone to stay close to the barn while he scouted the perimeter. He took a parcel to the back door and rang the bell, then waited. But after a while he decided there was no one home.

'Come on,' he motioned to the rest of the group to follow him. They rounded the edge of the house and spotted the Christmas display.

'Paydirt,' Liam declared. 'These baubles are mad. They're going to look fantastic in someone's front garden – way better than here.'

'Yeah – I reckon,' Jake said. 'But I hope they're not heavy.'

Ellie had followed the rest of them.

'What do you think you're doing?' Kane whispered. 'Aren't you supposed to be proving your worth?'

Ellie swallowed hard and scurried back to the porch where Kane had been ringing the bell. She tried the handle and was surprised that, like the boy said, the door opened and she found herself in a huge old-fashioned kitchen with a scrubbed-pine table and the biggest cooker she'd ever clapped eyes on. The place smelled like a hug. Ellie had never been inside a house like this before – so grand – and warm. What a dream, not feeling chilled to the bone every winter. That would be heaven.

But she wasn't there to enjoy the Highton-Smith-Kennington-Jones family's hospitality. She had to find something to take and fast.

Unfortunately, it wasn't that simple – everywhere she looked there were 'things', but what could she take that no one would miss?

She decided on a teaspoon – that seemed inconsequential enough.

Ellie pulled out a couple of drawers before she found what she was after.

Then she slipped the silver spoon into her jacket pocket and headed for the back door. She could see Hazel holding a giant bauble with her brother and racing back towards the barn to load it into the van. Liam was carrying a reindeer made from wire.

Ellie was about to leave when her stomach cramped violently. Could the timing have been any worse? She needed the toilet and fast. She looked around, wondering where there might be a bathroom. Surely, there had to be one somewhere close by. Ellie raced into a small sitting room off the kitchen but there was nothing. So she headed back through the kitchen door into a hallway that led to some of the most magnificent rooms she'd ever seen. Still nothing. If there was a powder room somewhere, it was certainly well hidden. She passed by an enormous Christmas tree and raced up the staircase, turning the handle of the first door she came to. It was a bedroom – and a beautiful one at that. There was another door and thankfully a bathroom. Ellie unzipped her jeans and sat down, feeling a flood of relief wash over her.

'Oh my gosh,' she mumbled and quickly put herself back together and washed her hands. She stepped out into the bedroom with its gorgeous four-poster bed, a doll's house that looked as if it belonged in a museum and a giant rocking horse with a mane that she could have sworn was real.

This must be Alice-Miranda's room.

Of course, it was. Spoilt brat. The kid had everything. Imagine growing up and never wondering where your next meal was coming from or if you'd have a warm bed to sleep in. It must have been the best feeling in the world.

Ellie noticed the bookcase with so many of her favourite titles. There were copies of *The Secret Garden* and *A Little Princess* side by side. Ellie pulled them both out. She flicked to the imprint page and realised that the volume she was holding was a first edition. And then she spotted the presents all lined up along the wall between the huge double height windows. Ellie knelt down to take a closer look. There must have been fifty gifts at least and she was shocked to see the label *Juliette Byers and Family* on one of the tags. Why was the kid giving her family presents? That was ridiculous. The child was ridiculous.

Or was she? Juliette said that she thought Alice-Miranda was lovely and kind — and her parents too.

Ellie stood up and glanced out the window, then realised that there were lights heading along the driveway. She had to get downstairs and out to the van before whoever was coming arrived.

She turned to leave and spotted the thing she'd been sent to get in the first place. The donations box. It was sitting right there on the bookshelf. Ellie scooped it up and raced back out the door and down the stairs. She hurtled along the hallway to the kitchen, but the sound of tyres crunching on the gravel pulled her up.

The van was out of sight of the driveway and there was no sign of her friends.

Ellie ran back into the main part of the house. She'd seen the huge double front doors in the entry foyer past the staircase.

She charged down the long hallway and found what she was looking for, then turned the handle. She pulled the heavy door open, then closed it as quietly as she could before stuffing the donations box under her coat and running along the veranda towards the side of the mansion. Surely the others hadn't gone without her.

Ellie turned the corner and realised that the driver of the sports car was still sitting inside of it. And he had just looked straight at her.

The door opened and he hopped out.

'Hello. May I help you?' the man asked. His clothes looked expensive – a beautiful woollen jumper in a sage green with taupe-coloured pants and the coolest trainers Ellie had ever seen. She had a feeling that this was her mother's boss.

Over near the sheds she couldn't see if the van was still there, but she assumed so. She had to distract this guy so the others could make their getaway.

'H-h-hi,' Ellie stammered. 'I was looking for Alice-Miranda.'

'Oh, I'm sorry you've missed her. Everyone's gone to the village for the light ceremony. I'm on my way there myself in a few minutes – been held up at work,' the man replied. 'I'm her father, Hugh Kennington-Jones, and you're . . .'

The girl gulped. 'Ellie,' she said quietly.

'How do you know Alice-Miranda?' Hugh asked.

There was no point lying.

'We met at the supermarket. My mother works there,' Ellie said.

'Oh – you're Juliette's Ellie,' the man said. 'Delighted to finally meet you. Your mother is terribly proud of you and your brother. She's very clever too – management material.'

Ellie gulped. Why was he being so nice to her? He wouldn't once he realised why she was there.

'Are you heading to the village?' Hugh asked. 'Would you like a lift? I just have to collect something from inside.'

Ellie nodded. 'Thanks – that'd be great.' She had one eye on the gap between the sheds.

'Would you like to come in?' Hugh asked. 'It's chilly out.'

'I'm fine. I'll wait here if that's okay,' she said.

Hugh gave a nod and hurried away inside. Ellie was clutching the donations box under her coat. As soon as he was gone, she raced across the driveway to see if the van was still there. It was.

She ran to the driver's door. Kane was inside with the others.

'What are you playing at?' he hissed.

Ellie took the donations box out and thrust it through the window.

'I'm going with Mr Kennington-Jones to the light ceremony,' she said. 'He thinks I came to see Alice-Miranda and he's offered me a lift. I have to get there to meet Mum and Myles anyway. Stay here until we leave.'

Hazel was jammed in the back of the van with all of the stolen goods and didn't like any of what she'd just heard.

Her head popped through the gap in the seats. 'What? So now you're best friends with that toff. You're supposed to be with us.'

'I am – but if I do a runner now, he'll tell my mother, and I don't want her knowing we were here,' Ellie said.

Hazel pouted. 'So you're going to get a ride in that gorgeous sports car and I have to hang out with these losers. That's not fair.'

'I'll meet you in the village, Hazel,' Ellie said, ignoring her friend's disapproval. She turned and scampered back across the driveway and up the steps to the veranda.

Hugh Kennington-Jones headed out the back door at almost the exact same time.

'Well then, we'll be off,' he said. 'Hop in.'

Ellie had never been in a car anything like the one that was parked in the driveway. She wasn't sure what make it was, but it looked like it cost more than her mother would have made in fifty years.

Hugh opened the door for her and she climbed in. It smelt amazing too – like new leather. She was worried about getting dirt on the carpet.

When Hugh turned the ignition, Ellie jumped. The growl was like something you would have heard on a wildlife documentary.

'Sorry – I should have warned you that it's a bit loud,' the man said. 'One of my follies – sports cars.'

'It's lovely,' Ellie said quietly.

Hugh was about to take off when his phone rang. 'Excuse me, Ellie, but I have to take this. Hello, Detective Inspector Freeman.'

Ellie swallowed hard. It was the police. Hugh must have watched some surveillance footage of her inside the house and the others taking the

Christmas decorations and called them. Ellie was half expecting a convoy of patrol cars to come screaming down the driveway at any minute, ready to take her and the others into custody. But that's not what happened at all.

'Evening, Hugh. Just wanted to update you on the investigations,' the woman said. 'Is now a good time?'

'Hang on a tick – I'll take you off speaker,' Hugh said.

There was a pause as Hugh listened to the detective on the other end of the line.

'Interesting,' Hugh said. 'Have you got any idea how they're intercepting the stock?'

There was another long break. Hugh ummed and ahhed and said that it sounded like they were on the verge of a breakthrough.

'So you think that the people taking the goods are quite a way down the food chain,' Hugh said.

Ellie wondered what he was talking about. It must have had something to do with the shops. The other day when they met Alice-Miranda, she'd asked her mother if anything had been wrong – if things were missing from Kennington's. It must be a big problem.

'We've not long ago taken up a new transport contract with Freightliners. They've been brilliant, so far — at least that's what the reports have said. Now I have to wonder,' Hugh said. 'Sounds as if it's the most likely scenario as to how things are going missing.'

Ellie knew that name. It was on the invoices she'd seen at Hazel's house in her father's study.

'Keep me posted and tell your man to be careful. I want these people prosecuted,' Hugh said, then hung up.

'Sorry about that, Ellie. Just some trouble at work,' the man said.

'It sounds bad,' she said.

'Yes, much worse than I originally thought. It's not only us who have been affected. Someone is very cleverly skimming goods from a whole lot of supermarket chains. Not enough that we've noticed until recently — it was Alice-Miranda who mentioned something about the Kennington's close to her school having no Christmas supplies. Then we did a little more digging and it seems that, while Christmas appears to be the thieves' favourite time of the year, small amounts have been going missing for months and the same for our competitors. We think the inventory that is being reported in the trucks is not what's actually going out – I'm confident the police are close to discovering who's behind it all.'

Ellie nodded and glanced back towards the end of the shed where the van was still parked – loaded up with the family's Christmas decorations. Ellie hated what she'd just done. It felt wrong on every level. She'd tell Hazel that she was busy the next time they wanted her help. She wasn't a thief – and even if some people had a lot more than others, this was no way to level the playing field. Besides, she had a terrible feeling that Hazel's father might have been involved in something much worse than what his children were up to.

Chapter 31

Alice-Miranda munched on a couple of fries that she'd earlier declared to be the best she'd ever had. She and her friends had done the rounds of the food stalls as soon as they'd arrived in the village.

'Thith ith delithus,' Sloane muttered, as she shovelled another huge bite of burger into her mouth. Chessie pointed to the blob of sauce that was now decorating the side of the girl's face, while trying not to lose the contents of her own dinner.

'Oops,' Sloane said and wiped at it with her napkin, only serving to smear the offending condiment even further across her cheek.

Lucas had just presented Jacinta with a cloud of pink candy floss on a stick that was twice the size of the girl's head – they'd already devoured tacos and were now onto dessert – while Sep and Neville were wolfing down plates of chocolate crepes. Millie and Britt had opted for cod and chips. Britt said that fish was one of the foods she was missing from home. Caprice was eating a margherita pizza – to remind herself that she'd soon be in Italy with her family.

Festivities were in full swing, with food trucks and a Christmas market in the square.

'Is Daddy coming soon?' Alice-Miranda asked her mother, who was sipping a hot chocolate. Dolly Oliver and Mrs Shillingsworth were both enjoying mugs of mulled wine – the scent of the cinnamon and cloves unmistakable.

'He called and said that he's on his way. He's bringing Ellie, the girl you met the other day at the supermarket. Juliette's daughter,' the woman replied.

Alice-Miranda frowned. 'Why?'

'Apparently, Ellie was on the veranda when your father arrived home. He said that she was looking for you,' Cecelia said.

'Oh, really?' Alice-Miranda's eyebrows jumped up. She wondered if the visit had anything to do with the donations box. It would be good to be able to talk to her again and get to the bottom of things.

Most of the group had wandered away to check out the market stalls when Alice-Miranda spied Elliot Turner in the distance. He was talking to a young boy – probably only six or seven years old.

'Who's that with Mr Turner, Mummy?' Alice-Miranda asked. It looked as if the child was showing him something – there was a shiny glint coming from the boy's hand.

'Oh, I think that's young Myles – he's Juliette's son. I've met them a couple of times in the village when she's been walking him to and from school. He's a dear little boy – completely obsessed with Christmas baubles, or "bubbles" as he calls them, according to his mother.'

Alice-Miranda watched as Mr Turner smiled at the lad and then Myles turned and ran off, leaving the man on his own. Alice-Miranda wondered if she might have a word with Mr Turner – he could tell her if Miss Wickham was about.

'Do you fancy getting some more of those lovely linen tea towels?' Dolly Oliver said to Cecelia Highton-Smith. 'I've just seen Matilda Salisbury is there with her stall again. Shilly, is there anything you're after too?'

The three women were busy conferring.

'I'll be back in a minute, Mummy,' Alice-Miranda said and dashed away to see Mr Turner, who was now chatting to Violet Appleby. The woman had a huge smile on her face and was standing beside her husband, Digby Pertwhistle, who was in charge of a young girl in a pushchair. The woman's granddaughter, Clementine Rose, was playing tag nearby with Poppy Bauer. The two girls were at school together and were the best of friends. Clementine often had sleepovers with Poppy at the farmhouse at Highton Hall.

Alice-Miranda appeared in front of the group. 'Hello, Miss Appleby,' she said. 'I'm glad to see you came along after all.'

'Godfathers, it's ghastly, isn't it?' the woman replied, rolling her eyes, but Digby Pertwhistle smiled and gave his wife a nudge.

'Good heavens, Violet – you've been looking forward to tonight more than anyone,' he teased, garnering himself another eye roll from the woman.

'Hello, Mr Pertwhistle,' Alice-Miranda said.

'Look at you, my dear,' he said. 'You must have grown an inch since you were last home.'

'I don't think I've grown as much as Clara,' the child replied. The toddler smiled for a second, then went back to sucking on her iced lolly.

'Hello, Mr Turner,' Alice-Miranda said and looked at the man. 'Thank you for the invitation to your party. My friends and I are all terribly excited.'

'It's my pleasure,' he said. 'You reminded me that Christmas really is all about children. Sebastian has planned some lovely surprises.'

'Is Miss Wickham here?' the child asked. 'I was hoping to speak to her.'

Elliot Turner shook his head. 'No, I don't believe so. She's had a lot on her plate lately.'

Violet Appleby *tsk*ed loudly. 'Not the least being the death of her sister – and trying to find her missing niece.'

Alice-Miranda frowned. 'Her niece is missing?'

'The girl ran away fifteen years ago and hasn't been heard from since,' Violet said. 'Poor Delia was telling me about it when she dropped that box of things into the charity shop last Tuesday. Her sister died never knowing what happened to the girl.'

'Do you know her name?' Alice-Miranda asked.

'No, I'm afraid I don't,' Violet Appleby replied.

Elliot Turner cleared his throat.

Alice-Miranda sensed that the conversation was uncomfortable for the man. Miss Appleby probably shouldn't have been sharing Miss Wickham's secrets with her – Alice-Miranda didn't really know the woman at all. She decided not to say anything about the mysterious bottle inside the teapot. But tomorrow night at the party she'd see Miss Wickham and show her what they'd found.

'Hello, darling!' Hugh Kennington-Jones called to his daughter, interrupting the conversation.

The girl spun around. 'Oh, hello, Daddy.' Her father was walking towards her with Ellie beside him. She was dressed in the same coat Alice-Miranda had seen her in the other day and she looked just as cold as she had then too.

Hugh gave Alice-Miranda a quick hug and shook Elliot's hand before Violet Appleby began talking to Hugh at a rate of knots about cranberry sauce and why it wasn't available at Kennington's – not in Highton Mill or anywhere else she'd been. Ellie hung back almost as if she was hiding.

'Daddy said that you were at home looking for me,' Alice-Miranda said to the girl.

'Um, yes,' Ellie replied. 'I . . .' she began, but Alice-Miranda was distracted.

She'd noticed that Elliot Turner was staring at the girls, the colour having completely drained from his face.

'Are you all right, Mr Turner?' Alice-Miranda asked.

'Yes, of course,' he said, but it was clear now that it was Ellie he was interested in. He couldn't take his eyes off the girl.

'This is Ellie. She's just moved here a little while ago with her mother Juliette and her brother Myles. Juliette works at Kennington's here in the village,' the child explained.

Ellie's face was ashen too. Alice-Miranda wondered if they were suddenly both unwell. Hopefully there wasn't a bug going around.

'Juliette, you say. How odd. I'm sorry to stare – it's just that Ellie reminds me so much of someone,' the man replied. 'It's uncanny.'

Alice-Miranda was intrigued. 'Who is it?'

'My wife,' Elliot muttered then excused himself and quickly hurried away.

Alice-Miranda turned to speak to Ellie but surprisingly she'd disappeared too.

'Well, that was strange,' Alice-Miranda said to herself.

Her father looked at her – the Appleby-Pertwhistles had moved off as well.

'What's strange, darling?' the man asked.

'Ellie just vanished and before that Mr Turner looked as if he'd seen a ghost,' the girl said, then explained what the man had said about Ellie reminding him of his wife.

'The poor chap,' Hugh said. 'I'm not sure that we've ever told you this before, but Elliot Turner's wife died about fifteen years ago – before you were born. It was a terrible tragedy. She fell from the top of the stairs at Hoxton Manor, but there were rumours that perhaps there had been another party involved.'

'She was murdered?' Alice-Miranda gasped.

'Possibly – though no one was ever charged. Elliot wasn't there so he was never a suspect. It was a terrible thing. On the very same day, one of our local doctors was killed in a car accident not far from Hoxton Manor. He had a connection to the Turners too, as his wife was Miss Wickham's sister.'

'That's awful,' the child said. 'Poor Mr Turner and Miss Wickham, and now her sister's died and her niece is missing. Some families have an awful lot of tragedy, don't they?'

'It didn't end there for the Turners,' Hugh said. 'Elliot's only daughter was poorly from the beginning and she passed away not terribly long after his wife died.'

'Oh, Daddy, that's horrible,' Alice-Miranda said. 'Yet he seems such a happy man.'

'Yes, Elliot has been quite incredible through it all. I admire him very much,' Hugh said. 'The mere fact that he puts on that fabulous party every year is testament to him living each day to the fullest, despite the things he's endured. If anything happened to your mother, I'd probably lock you up and throw away the key.'

'No, you wouldn't, Daddy. And nothing's happening to Mummy,' the girl replied.

Hugh put his arm around the girl and gave her a squeeze. 'As if I could even think about trying to rein you in. The daughter who organised to go to boarding school at the ripe old age of seven and one quarter. There's no stopping you, and your mother and I both know it. We couldn't be prouder.'

'I love you, Daddy,' Alice-Miranda said.

'And I love you too, my darling girl,' the man replied.

Alice-Miranda nodded. But she couldn't stop thinking about Ellie. Where had the girl gone and why? She really wanted to talk to her and Miss Wickham – there were just so many things on her mind.

'Alice-Miranda!' Millie shouted from where she and the rest of her friends were standing by the Christmas tree. 'They're about to turn the lights on.'

The girl ran over to join the group while the countdown began.

'Five . . . four . . . three . . . two . . . one!' The crowd cheered as the Christmas tree in the centre of the village square lit up in a blaze of colour. Fairy lights sparkled in the surrounding trees and on the lamp posts. The place looked magical and then the most magical thing of all happened. Fat snowflakes began to fall, much to everyone's delight.

Millie was standing beside Alice-Miranda. 'Beautiful,' Millie gasped.

Behind her, Sep said the same thing – though he wasn't looking at the Christmas display.

Millie turned around and he smiled. Her heart felt as if it was about to beat right out of her chest.

With the village lights on and their stomachs full, Cecelia gathered the children together and they all set off for home. Hugh was going to meet them there and Dolly had decided she would go with him in the car, as her arthritis was playing up.

Britt and Chessie walked ahead with Sloane – the three girls arm in arm. Neville and Sep were deep in conversation, while Jacinta held Lucas's hand and rested her head on his shoulder.

'Is everything okay?' Millie asked Alice-Miranda, who was silently staring off into the distance.

The girl nodded.

'No, it's not,' Millie said. 'You can't put anything past me.'

'I was just thinking,' Alice-Miranda replied.

'Care to share?' Millie asked.

Caprice appeared on her other side. 'Yes – spill.'

Within a few seconds, the girl was surrounded.

'Has this got anything to do with the mystery note inside the mystery bottle inside the mystery teapot?' Caprice asked. 'I haven't been able to stop thinking about that myself.'

'That's one thing,' the girl said. 'I've also been wondering about Ellie.'

'Who's Ellie?' Millie asked.

'The girl we met at the supermarket yesterday – the one whose mother works there,' Caprice reminded her.

'Oh – okay. Why?' Millie said.

'Because Daddy said that when he came home, she was standing on the veranda and she said that she'd come to see me. Then he gave her a lift to the light ceremony, but when I went to talk to her, she disappeared,' Alice-Miranda explained.

The snow was coming down much heavier now and starting to settle on the ground. Millie wiped some flakes from her eyelashes.

'So what was she doing at your house, then?' Caprice said.

Alice-Miranda shrugged.

The children reached the back entrance to the Highton Hall estate, where they said goodbye to the Bauers who had caught up to them.

They trundled on past Rose Cottage, where Granny Bert used to live before she went into care at Pelham Park – her father's old family home, which had been converted some years ago to an aged care facility. Granny Bert's granddaughter, Daisy, lived at Rose Cottage but she was away at the moment, visiting her parents in Spain.

The Greenings had headed home a few minutes before the others and the children could see Mrs Greening in the kitchen as they passed by their gatehouse home.

Hugh's car was already parked by the side entrance.

'Hey, let's look at the baubles – they'll be covered in real snow now,' Britt said.

The children charged off around to the front of the house to see the display. But they were soon stopped in their tracks.

'What?' Millie exclaimed. Where only hours earlier the giant baubles and their reindeer friends adorned the garden, now there was nothing.

'Oh my goodness, they've been stolen!' Britt gasped.

The children were all talking over the top of each other, speculating that it must have been the work of the gang that had been taking all of the other Christmas decorations.

'Check for footprints,' Jacinta urged.

'I think the only ones are ours,' Sloane replied.

Further investigation revealed that the snow had covered any potential evidence – either in the garden or on the driveway.

Alice-Miranda led the charge inside, where Mrs Oliver had just put the kettle on and Mrs Shillingsworth was busy making hot chocolate for the children. Hugh was there too.

'Daddy, the Christmas bandits have struck again. We've been robbed,' Alice-Miranda said, as the rest of the group spilled through the door behind her. 'The baubles in the garden and the reindeer – they're all gone.'

Hugh jumped up and led the charge back outside to the front garden.

'Good heavens – who steals Christmas decorations?' Hugh said, shaking his head.

Alice-Miranda looked at her father. 'Do you think Ellie could have had anything to do with it? I never got to talk to her in the village. She disappeared.'

Hugh frowned. 'She's a teenager – I hardly think that likely. I'm sure that it must have happened after Ellie and I left. The baubles aren't heavy and neither are the reindeer. It wouldn't take long for them to be whisked away – though whoever took them would need a van or a small truck.'

'Do you have cameras, Uncle Hugh?' Lucas asked.

'We do, but I'm afraid they're currently being upgraded – we hardly ever think about them. Being out here, there's always someone around,' the man replied.

'Except tonight. I wonder if anyone else was robbed and if they're planning to nick the lights from the village too?' Neville said.

'I'll call my police contact and let them know – we need to make sure that there's no chance of Highton Mill losing their display as well,' Hugh said.

'It's not right,' Shilly said, shaking her head. 'What are they planning to do with all those lovely decorations anyway? They must surely be Grinches.'

'I think we should set a trap,' Caprice said. 'A really good one so that they get caught and go to jail. And I agree with Alice-Miranda that Ellie probably had something to do with it.'

'How?' Millie asked.

'Well, I don't know the details. I haven't worked them out yet, but if we could come up with a plan to catch them, wouldn't that be amazing?' the girl said.

Everyone nodded.

'Come on – let's get back inside and have some hot chocolate before bed,' Cecelia said. 'Remember we've got Mr Turner's Christmas party tomorrow night and we've still got to get all your outfits sorted for the party.'

'Oh, yes,' Britt clasped her hands together. 'I can't wait. You know I live for fashion.'

'Me too,' Sep said.

All eyes turned his way.

'Oh, right,' Sloane said. 'You're being ironic.'

Sep looked wounded. 'No. I thought I was pretty stylish these days.'

'Stylish? You?' his sister teased.

'You always look great as far as I'm concerned, Sep,' Millie said, earning herself some raised eyebrows.

'Thanks, Mill – at least I can rely on you to make me feel better,' Sep said.

Millie's face turned the colour of her hair and she bit her lip.

'Oooh – do I detect some chemistry?' Caprice whispered.

'As if,' Millie retorted and shook her head.

But no one was buying it. Maybe there was a new Christmas romance on the horizon – but in the meantime, there was a gang of thieves to catch – two in fact. The Kennington's crims and the bauble bandits.

Chapter 32

Alice-Miranda was lying in bed, staring at the canopy above her.

'Millie, are you awake?' the girl whispered.

'No,' Millie grumbled and buried her face in her pillow.

Alice-Miranda rolled over and tapped her friend's shoulder. 'Are you sure?'

'I wasn't but I am now,' Millie replied, wriggling to sit up then stretching her arms above her head. She yawned loudly. 'What's the matter?'

'I can't stop thinking about Ellie,' Alice-Miranda replied. 'I need to talk to her.'

'Why?' Millie asked.

Alice-Miranda explained about the charity box and how she had her suspicions concerning the way it ended up in her bag. And the boys she saw standing near the counter at Kennington's yesterday – the same ones who were outside Hoxton Manor on the afternoon they arrived home from school. 'But I don't want to accuse Ellie of anything until we've had a chance to talk. Perhaps we can go and see her before the others are up.'

Millie closed her eyes and nodded vaguely. 'Do you know where she lives?'

Alice-Miranda realised that she didn't but maybe Mrs Oliver would. Her father would definitely be able to find out, given he had access to all of the Kennington's staff records. She didn't want to invade the family's privacy, but Mr Turner had looked like he'd seen a ghost when he spotted the girl last night and there was just something that didn't sit right. She'd spent the other half of the night thinking about the message in the teapot and when she'd be able to talk to Miss Wickham about that.

'Highton Mill isn't that big and her mother did mention that they lived in the village,' Alice-Miranda said as she pushed the covers back and dropped down to the floor. 'I'll get dressed.'

Millie nodded. 'Where did you leave the charity box?'

'It's on the bookcase,' Alice-Miranda said. She walked over and was perplexed to find that it wasn't there. 'You didn't move it, did you?'

Millie shook her head. 'Not me.'

'I wonder if Mummy or Shilly saw it and one of them has taken it – though surely they'd have said something,' Alice-Miranda said. She scanned the length of the shelves and realised that two of her books had been removed and were sitting on the bench. *A Little Princess* and *The Secret Garden*. 'Millie, did you take these out?'

'Again, not me,' the girl replied.

It couldn't have been a coincidence. Alice-Miranda was sure that Ellie had been in her room. There were so many more valuable things she could have taken, so why only the charity box? It didn't really make any sense at all.

'Okay – let's get a wriggle on,' Alice-Miranda said as she dashed into the bathroom.

Alice-Miranda and Millie arrived in the kitchen minutes before seven and were surprised to see Hugh Kennington-Jones sitting at the table with Detective Inspector Fenella Freeman. Mrs Oliver had just delivered the pair some tea and toast.

The girls had first met the detective a few years ago when they were at a school camp that turned out to involve much more than just the usual high ropes and orienteering challenges. At the time, Fenella had mistakenly arrested Hugh and his brother Ed for art theft. With the children's help, the mystery was solved and all charges against the pair were dropped. Surprisingly, the detective had gone on to become good friends with the Highton-Smith-Kennington-Jones family. The woman's elderly father lived at Pelham Park.

'Hello, girls,' Fenella said with a smile. 'It's lovely to see you both.'

'Good morning, Inspector,' Alice-Miranda replied. 'Has there been a breakthrough in the Kennington's case?'

The woman frowned and chewed her lip. 'There've been some developments.'

Millie poured herself a bowl of muesli and sat down while Alice-Miranda scooped some porridge from the saucepan on the stove, then walked to the table where she added a drizzle of honey.

'That sounds promising,' Alice-Miranda said.

'Not exactly, darling,' Hugh said.

'Why not?' Millie asked, as she raised the spoon to her lips.

Fenella set her teacup down. 'I wouldn't normally discuss things but, given it's you girls who helped crack the case that got me promoted in the first place, I can tell you a little bit. Unfortunately, our man on the inside is missing – we need him to corroborate the evidence he's collected about the manager of Freightliners and those higher up the food chain.'

'That's terrible,' Alice-Miranda said. 'And you have no idea what's happened to him?'

'One of our team intercepted a radio message but it was incomplete, and we haven't heard from him since,' Fenella said.

'Do you know how they're stealing the goods?' Millie asked.

Fenella nodded. 'We have a pretty good idea that there are two fleets of trucks – one where the vehicles are legitimately owned by Freightliners and then there's another smaller number of lorries supplied by the criminal gang in charge of the operation. They're dressed up to look like Freightliners and driven by Freightliners drivers – but the records of what they're hauling are fake and the destinations too. The manager of the trucking company orchestrates all the deliveries, making sure that goods are diverted from the legitimate trucks to the gang trucks and the goods are taken to docks all over the country for redistribution on the black market overseas.'

'That sounds complicated,' Alice-Miranda said.

'We believe it's been going on for a while now – the man in charge has gotten sloppy and if he doesn't watch himself, we have fears for what the people at the top will do to him too. And before you ask – no, I can't tell you any names.'

Millie frowned. Pity, she thought to herself. This was just getting good.

'What about the bauble bandits?' Millie asked.

'Probably locals having a laugh at everyone's expense, but they shouldn't be too hard to track down,' Fenella said.

'We've got some ideas,' Millie said, earning herself a glare from Alice-Miranda.

Hugh looked across at the red-haired girl. 'Care to share?'

'We're off to do some investigating and we'll let you know if we find anything,' Alice-Miranda replied.

Fenella nursed her teacup. 'Please don't go getting yourselves into any trouble. It's the last thing I need.'

'We won't,' Millie said.

Fenella raised her eyebrows. 'You do remember I know how you two operate.'

'We promise,' Alice-Miranda said. She finished her last bite and stood up to take the bowl to the dishwasher. 'We're just off to visit Ellie – I didn't get to talk to her last night. You don't happen to know where she lives, do you, Daddy?'

'It's a bit early, darling,' Hugh said. 'And no, I don't.'

Dolly Oliver interjected. 'Is that Juliette's daughter, Ellie?'

The girls nodded.

'I can tell you her address. I saw that poor woman walking home in the rain the other day with her young son,' Dolly replied. 'You can take her a cake too. I don't think she has an easy time of it. I was going to ask if we could have Mr Greening deliver her a load of firewood, Hugh – I didn't see any smoke coming out of her chimney and those terraces are terribly cold.'

'Of course,' the man replied. 'I'll organise it this morning.'

Dolly bustled away to the pantry and returned with a slab of cake wrapped in cellophane and tied with a bow. 'And you can take one too,' she said, looking at Fenella who grinned.

'It's no wonder I gain weight every time I come through the door here.'

The girls put on their coats and hats and gloves and scarves.

'We won't be long,' Alice-Miranda said. 'I've left a note for Jacinta to keep everyone entertained until we get back.'

'Good luck with finding your man,' Millie said to the detective.

The woman nodded gravely. 'Thank you, Millie – and remember what I said about your sleuthing. If you discover anything, call me – immediately.'

The girls nodded and trotted out the door.

Chapter 33

Millie drew her scarf up around her neck and thrust her gloved hands into her pockets. Alice-Miranda was carrying Dolly's cake in a Kennington's bag.

'It's really cold this morning,' Millie said as she and Alice-Miranda crunched their way across the snowy ground. The flakes had stopped falling during the night, but the temperature was so low that none of the snow had melted.

'What exactly are you going to say to Ellie?' Millie asked as they walked down the avenue of poplar trees towards the main gates of the estate. 'You said yourself, you don't want to accuse the girl – makes it a bit awkward.'

Alice-Miranda bit her lip. The more she thought about it, the more she realised that she wasn't actually sure either.

'I'd like her to tell me the truth about why she was at our house,' Alice-Miranda said.

'You already know that – she stole the donations box,' Millie replied. 'It's pretty obvious – seeing that it was there yesterday and gone this morning.'

'I want her to tell me,' Alice-Miranda said, then realised the likelihood of Ellie confessing was probably not very high. The girls walked on for a way before they reached their destination. 'Is that it?' Millie asked.

'Mrs Oliver said it was the end one,' Alice-Miranda replied.

The row of Victorian terrace houses looked pretty in the snow – even with their patchy paintwork and crumbling exterior details.

Millie glanced at her watch. It was just after eight thirty. A dull glow lit one of the front windows but there was no smoke coming from the chimney.

Alice-Miranda opened the squeaky front gate and walked onto the porch. An ancient scooter stood at the end beside some moving boxes.

'I hope we're not too early,' the child said as she raised her hand and grabbed the rusty door-knocker, giving it three sharp bangs.

She could hear someone shuffling about inside and then the door swung open.

'Oh, hello,' the woman said, obviously surprised. 'Alice-Miranda, what can I do for you?'

'Hello, Mrs Byers, – sorry to call by so early,' the girl replied. 'This is my friend, Millie. We were wondering if Ellie's home. There's something we need to talk to her about. And this is for you – from Mrs Oliver. She said she met you at the store and she's been doing so much baking, our house looks like a cake shop – she needs to pass some on.'

Alice-Miranda handed her the bag.

'Oh, that's terribly kind,' the woman replied. 'Ellie's in the shower. She won't be long. Myles is still asleep. I think the light ceremony was a little overwhelming. He was so excited. Shiny things are his favourite. I was just about to head off to work in a few minutes, but please, come in.'

Late last night, when Juliette had reminded Ellie that she needed her to look after Myles today, she'd expected a war. Surprisingly, though, the girl said she was happy to stay home.

'Would you like something to drink? I've not long boiled the kettle and there's tea in the pot. It's cold out there,' the woman said.

Millie couldn't help thinking it was about the same temperature inside too. The load of firewood Mrs Oliver suggested would be welcome, for sure. But she wasn't about to mention it and neither did Alice-Miranda.

'That would be lovely, thank you,' Alice-Miranda said. 'But please don't let us hold you up.'

'It's fine. I promise you won't make me late,' the woman replied.

Juliette busied herself pouring two cups of tea. She offered the girls sugar and milk though both declined, noticing she didn't seem to have much of either.

'Weren't the lights beautiful last night?' Juliette said as she ushered the girls to the kitchen table and the three of them sat down.

'Gorgeous,' Alice-Miranda said. 'It's always such a festive evening. And the food was delicious too.'

'Yes, it was wonderful,' the woman replied. 'I'm growing fond of this community.'

Alice-Miranda bit her lip. 'Daddy gave Ellie a lift from our place into the village, but I didn't get to catch up with her properly last night.'

'And someone stole the Highton-Smith-Kennington-Jones family's Christmas display while we were out,' Millie added.

Juliette Byers frowned. 'What was Ellie doing at your house?' Knowing her daughter's attitude towards Alice-Miranda and her family, she was more than a little surprised to hear it.

'I'm not sure. That's why I wanted to talk to her. See if I can help with anything. I spotted her at the light ceremony, but then I was talking with Mr Turner and, when I turned around, Ellie was gone. And Mr Turner's face was the colour of a sheet. Do you know him at all? He's a lovely man – lives at Hoxton Manor just a mile or so from our place.'

'Hoxton Manor?' Juliette said. 'My aunt Delia worked there – before I was born. But my mother said she died when I was a child. I don't remember her at all.'

'Oh, I'm sorry,' the child said. 'Mr Turner was very taken with Ellie. He said that she reminded him of his wife.'

'She died too,' Millie said. Alice-Miranda had filled her in on all the details of Mr Turner's tragic history before the pair had fallen asleep last night.

'Goodness – that's sad and odd about Ellie. They say we all have doppelgangers out there somewhere – it's funny, but I think Ellie's mine. I'm afraid I've never met the man,' Juliette said.

'He was talking to your son last night too,' Alice-Miranda said. 'I spotted them when I first arrived. It looked like Mr Turner gave Myles something shiny then Myles ran off.'

'Oh – he came charging back to me with a gorgeous little silver bauble in his hand. I thought he might have taken it from somewhere he shouldn't, but then he said that a man called Mr Turner found it in his pocket and gave it to him. I didn't realise he was Mr Turner from Hoxton Manor,' Juliette said. 'It's not a particularly unusual name.'

Millie looked around the kitchen. There was the small round table where the three of them were sitting, a row of cupboards with an ancient cooker and a dresser with crockery for four. A framed photograph was the only personal item. In it was Ellie, her mother, Myles and a man.

'Is that your husband?' Millie asked, motioning at the picture.

'Yes, Bronson. He's away a lot.'

Alice-Miranda stood up to take a closer look.

'He looks kind,' she said. 'What does he do – that takes him away?'

Juliette chewed her lip. 'He is – kind, I mean. He works in transport.'

At least, that was the last job he'd told her about before he disappeared this time. She just wished he'd come home. Prove to Ellie that he wasn't the deadbeat dad and stepdad she thought he was. He still loved them – she knew that from the money he deposited into her account each week. She used it for Myles and to keep a roof over their heads.

'Do you know who he works for?' Alice-Miranda asked.

Juliette shook her head. 'He's changed companies a bit – I'm afraid I can't keep up.' She actually had no idea – Bronson could have been training to be an astronaut for all she knew.

There was the sound of a door closing and footsteps in the hall.

'Ellie, darling, you have some visitors,' Juliette called out.

The girl stopped in her tracks. If it was Hazel, she'd die – or worse – that greasy little slimeball, Liam. When he was talking about where she lived last night, she felt sick.

'It's Alice-Miranda and Millie,' Juliette said.

That was potentially worse.

Ellie wondered if she could sneak off out the back without anyone noticing, but that probably wasn't a good idea. It took her another couple of minutes to muster the courage to walk into the kitchen.

'Good morning,' Alice-Miranda said brightly. 'Sorry to call so early but I was hoping we could talk. We didn't get a chance last night.'

Ellie cleared her throat but didn't say a word.

'Ellie,' her mother prompted.

'Sorry, yes, hello,' the girl said.

'Oh, and I found this in your jeans pocket when I put them in the wash this morning,' Juliette said, holding up a silver teaspoon. Ellie snatched it from her hand and quickly put it in a drawer.

'I was just wondering where it had come from, darling. It's not one of ours. I thought you might have accidentally taken it from Hazel's,' her mother said.

Ellie shrugged.

Juliette glanced at her watch and said that she'd better be going. 'Myles is still asleep. You'd probably do well to leave him until he wakes up on his own,' the woman said.

Juliette stood up to leave.

'It's been lovely to chat, girls. Ellie, there's some bread for toast and your brother's breakfast is in the cupboard. Please make sure that if you take him out anywhere, he's got at least four layers on. You know how he loves to underdress,' the woman said.

She blew her daughter a kiss from the doorway then disappeared. Ellie walked to the toaster and put a single slice of bread into the slot. 'Have you had breakfast?'

'Yes, thank you,' Alice-Miranda replied. 'We came to see why you were at Highton Hall last night.'

Ellie bit her lip. She couldn't tell them the truth. What if her mother got the sack because of her?

There was an awkward silence. Millie tapped her foot and jiggled her leg.

'Fine – I'll say something then – did you take the decorations from the Highton Hall garden?' Millie asked, an accusatory tone in her voice.

Alice-Miranda looked across at her and frowned. 'Millie!'

'No,' Ellie rebuffed. 'Why would I?'

'But you were there,' Millie said. 'And there's something missing from Alice-Miranda's room.' Millie stood up and walked to the drawer where Ellie had put the teaspoon. It wasn't hard to locate given there were only a couple. She pulled it out and held it up.

'This is from the Highton-Smith-Kennington-Joneses' kitchen. See that,' she pointed at a mark on the underside. 'Their cutlery is monogrammed,' Millie said.

Alice-Miranda frowned. Ellie swallowed hard and nursed her head in her hands.

She'd hardly slept a wink last night wondering how she was going to tell Hazel that she no longer wanted to be involved with the gang and their activities – no matter how much they thought they were doing people a favour. Besides, so far no one had benefited from the thefts. And there weren't that many more days until Christmas.

'I didn't want to do any of it,' Ellie said. Tears welled in her eyes. 'You have to believe me.'

Alice-Miranda reached out across the table and gave the girl's hand a squeeze while Millie pulled some clean tissues from her pocket and offered them to her. The two girls exchanged concerned glances.

'It's okay. We'd just like to know what happened and why?' Alice-Miranda said gently.

Ellie squeezed her eyes shut tightly and two fat tears spilled onto the top of her cheeks.

'You don't know what it's like – always moving around, never having any friends. She made me feel special. I knew what they were asking me to do was wrong – but I couldn't stop myself,' Ellie said with a sniff.

Alice-Miranda looked at Millie who shrugged.

'So can you tell us what happened?' Millie asked.

'I don't want to get into trouble,' Ellie said.

'But you know who's stealing the Christmas decorations?' Alice-Miranda said.

Ellie nodded. 'I promise I didn't take them, but I did borrow the spoon from your kitchen. No, I stole it. I wasn't intending to give it back.'

'And the donations box from the counter at Kennington's?' Millie said.

Ellie nodded. 'It was a test – to see whether they could trust me. It was so stupid, but they said the money would get to the people who needed it most. I started to have doubts about that almost straight away, but I was already in too deep. Liam said that if I didn't do as they asked then they'd set me up to take the fall. I can't get into trouble. Mum would kill me and besides, I want to go to university one day and be a lawyer – I don't think having a criminal record would help with that.'

Alice-Miranda bit her lip. 'Do you want to stay friends with these kids?'

Ellie shook her head. 'Not if the only reason Hazel likes me is because I do bad things with them.'

'Do you know where they're hiding all the stuff they've taken? I mean there must be quite a bit. Those baubles aren't exactly small,' Millie said.

'I think in a shed at Hazel's house, but it might be at Liam's, and I don't know where he lives,' the girl said, shaking her head. 'Actually, they just said a shed so it could be anywhere.'

'Without any evidence, it's your word against theirs,' Alice-Miranda said.

Ellie nodded. 'They're planning another raid.'

'When?' Millie asked, her eyes widening.

'Tonight, at Hoxton Manor,' Ellie said.

'But Mr Turner's having his Christmas party tonight. There'll be people everywhere,' Alice-Miranda said.

'They're planning to take those giant wreaths from the front gate and some things from the garden. I think they have this idea that everyone will be busy inside and no one will notice, but it sounds risky to me,' Ellie said.

'What are they going to do with it all?' Millie asked.

Ellie explained about the plan to decorate the houses that didn't have any obvious Christmas cheer.

'Some people might not want that,' Millie said.

'Like me,' Ellie said with a nod. 'It's embarrassing enough living in this dump without someone lighting it all up.'

Millie took a sip of her tea. 'We should set them up tonight – the gang,' she said.

'But I'll go down too,' Ellie said, horrified by the thought. 'Or they'll know I dobbed them in. Either way I'm dead.'

Millie and Alice-Miranda thought for a moment.

'I've got an idea,' Alice-Miranda said. 'If you're willing to run with it.'

Ellie took a deep breath. Two days ago, she couldn't stand Alice-Miranda – even though she didn't know her at all – and now she was about to make plans with her. Could she trust the kid? Probably more than she could trust Hazel and her brothers and that slimy weasel, Liam. Ellie hated what she'd allowed herself to become. If there was some way she could make things right, then she really had no other choice.

Chapter 34

Bronson Byers knew full well that there were larger forces at play. He just didn't think they'd twigged to anything. Clearly, he was wrong.

The throbbing above his left eye felt like someone was using his skull as a timpani drum. It was a wonder the tyre lever hadn't punched a hole straight through – obviously there were some benefits of having a thick head. Or at least that's what his father had always told him. Now, strapped to a chair, his arms and legs tethered with rope, he wondered how long it would be until they'd be back. It had been a long drive to get here. The voices had been eastern European – no one that he recognised – and now the thing that worried him the most was the silence. It was deathly. He thought he was being held in some sort of bunker, but where, he had no clue.

None of this was what he'd had in mind when he took this job. And all the others. Juliette had no idea. He hated that he'd been lying to her all these years, but it came with the territory. The fact that he had to keep up the pretence in every aspect of their lives was beyond tricky – she deserved more. So did Myles and Ellie. This was supposed to be his last job. He'd told his boss that was it. No more undercover work. His plan was to retire, buy a house and live a quiet life. Maybe he'd become a postman or a greenkeeper. Office work wasn't ever going to cut it – not after the life he'd led.

Everything had almost fallen apart when he and Juliette got together. He'd not long gone into undercover operations, and it was only because she was a woman who asked few questions that he had been able to continue. She had no idea how much money he'd saved over the years – he was going to tell them he won the lottery and that's how they could afford to start again. He sent her as much as he could without attracting attention, but it was never enough. Especially not with all the bills she had to pay for Myles and his care. That was something he felt guilty about every single day.

No one had expected this job to last as long as it had – and now they were so close to the head of the snake. If they'd wanted to wrap it up six months ago and take down the middlemen, they could have. But not now. His bosses were going for the big guns, which is why if they killed Bronson at this point no one would ever know. He'd be involved in a horrible accident. That's what his family would be told. Juliette and the children would be none the wiser.

He had to get out of here before they realised that Bobby Lambert and Bronson Byers were actually the same person, or he was a dead man.

Chapter 35

Alice-Miranda and Millie hurried home, leaving their footprints in the snow.

'Do you think she'll do it?' Millie asked.

'She hasn't really got a choice,' Alice-Miranda replied. 'Not if she wants to come clean and avoid too much trouble. I'm sorry Ellie's been caught up in all of this.'

'Do you think we should tell the others what's going on?' Millie said.

'I have a feeling the less people who know, the

better,' the girl said. 'Imagine yourself in Ellie's situation. She doesn't need everyone's judgement. Her life's been hard enough – constantly moving, never being able to make a proper friend. I can see why she was taken in by Hazel. It's only natural, really. We all want to feel as if we belong.'

The two friends linked arms. 'Like the way you and I belong together,' Millie said with a smile. 'You do know we're going to be best friends until one of us kicks the bucket, even if you decide to move to the other side of the world for some reason.'

'I'm not going to do that, Millie – not unless you come with me,' Alice-Miranda said.

They squeezed arms and gently knocked their heads together.

The girls walked down the tree-lined driveway towards the house where curls of wispy smoke rose into the sky from at least half a dozen of the chimneys.

Mr Greening drove past in the pick-up truck with Betsy sitting beside him and a load of firewood in the back. He gave the pair a wave.

Alice-Miranda and Millie raced up the stairs to the side porch and into the kitchen only to find it empty.

'Mummy!' Alice-Miranda called as they ventured into the hallway where the sounds of laughter and clapping filled the air.

'What's going on?' Millie asked as they headed towards the noise that seemed to be coming from the front hall.

'Hello!' Alice-Miranda called in a singsong voice.

'Where have you been?' Sloane asked, as she spun around and struck a pose with one hand on her hip.

Millie giggled.

'Are you the new cook?'

'Oui,' the girl replied in a French accent, 'I will be whipping up some crepes for your lunch.'

'Crap for lunch – well, that doesn't sound appetising,' Millie teased.

'You know what I meant! I can't help it if my accent is appalling – anyway, you didn't answer my question. Where have you been? We've had breakfast and chosen our outfits for tonight. Sorry, Millie – you're getting last pick.'

'That's okay,' the girl replied.

'We went for a walk and took some of Mrs Oliver's baking to the neighbours,' Alice-Miranda said. It wasn't technically a lie – but she and Millie had decided that it was better for Ellie if they didn't mention anything about having seen her or what she and the others had been up to.

'Hello, darling,' Cecelia said, gliding across the room. 'I thought we'd get started with the outfits for tonight – which we did and everyone is going to look gorgeous – and then I remembered the old dress-up boxes in the attic. Your father and Mr Greening have kindly brought them down and we've been having the most wonderful time seeing who can put together the most outrageous ensembles.'

Just as Cecelia finished explaining, Sep emerged from the doorway off the entrance hall dressed in full military uniform, including a ceremonial sword.

Millie wolf-whistled then clamped her hands over her mouth. 'Sorry.'

'It's okay, Millie,' the boy said. 'I'd agree – I look absolutely dashing.'

Everyone laughed except Sloane, who pretended to throw up.

Chessie, Sloane and Neville made up the audience, along with Cecelia, while the rest of the girls were getting changed in the room to the left of the hallway. Lucas was changing in the room to the right.

Chessie looked gorgeous in a long lilac gown that looked like something from the 1800s, Sloane was wearing a chef's uniform and Neville was dressed in tartan plus-fours with a matching vest and cap and looked ready to hit the golf course.

'Is there enough for us to dress up as well?' Millie asked.

'There's enough for half the village,' Chessie said with a smile. She twirled the umbrella she was holding and tugged on her long white gloves.

'Come on then,' Millie said, and she and Alice-Miranda hurried off to join the others.

Chapter 36

'Myles, this isn't funny,' Ellie yelled as she ran down the hallway searching each room. It was such a tiny house, there weren't many places he could hide. Her mother was due home soon and the last thing Ellie needed was to have lost her little brother.

Ellie had fallen asleep for less than twenty minutes. Given she'd hardly slept a wink last night and spent most of the day entertaining Myles, she'd laid down for a second – at least, that's what it felt like. When she woke up, he was gone. They'd played hide-and-seek twice during the afternoon, so she assumed he was just getting a head start on another game. But no amount of calling had lured him from his spot – not this time.

All day she'd tried to forget about what was happening tonight. She was supposed to meet Hazel at her house in an hour. Last night, after she'd got a lift to the light ceremony with Mr Kennington-Jones, the girl had sought her out and made the arrangements. Ellie wanted to tell her that she was done – she couldn't help them again – but the words wouldn't come. Then, after she'd confessed to Alice-Miranda and Millie this morning, she had to go through with it now. It was a good plan, but who knew if it would work.

'Myles – where are you? I'm coming,' Ellie sang. She'd already opened every cupboard. She'd even looked in the fridge and the washing machine, but thankfully he was too big to get stuck in there these days. It had happened once before.

He'd shown her his collection of Christmas decorations three times – painstakingly pulling out each piece and lining them up on the kitchen table before he told her where he got them. The shiny new bauble from last night held the greatest fascination, though. It always made Ellie smile the way Myles called them his 'Christmas bubbles'. He said that the man who gave it to him promised he could have another. Obviously, Mr Turner didn't know who he was dealing with. Myles wouldn't forget that in a hurry.

Ellie could feel her heart hammering. She pulled off her hoodie and threw it on the bed – beads of perspiration trickling down her neck.

Myles had disappeared once before and it had been the worst three hours of her life. A lady at the ice-cream parlour had said he could come whenever he liked for a treat and he'd taken her at her word. Trouble was, he didn't tell anyone, and he was four years old at the time. How he hadn't been killed crossing the road was a complete mystery. He had the road sense of a baby otter and still did to this day.

'Come on, Myles, where are you?' Ellie could feel the tears welling. He might have been a pain sometimes, but she would literally die if anything happened to him.

Outside, the snow had begun to fall. Surely, he wouldn't have gone to see their mother at work. He didn't do things like that.

Ellie heard the key turn in the back door.

'Hello, my darlings, I'm home,' Juliette called. Ellie met her mother in the hallway.

'What's wrong?' her mother asked, her brow furrowed.

'I can't find Myles,' Ellie replied then began to sob.

Hazel looked at her watch again.

'So where's Ellie?' Liam asked. The group was sitting upstairs in Jake's bedroom, having just devoured two family-sized pepperoni pizzas.

'She'll be here,' Hazel replied. 'Anyway, we don't have to leave for ages.'

'No – but we need to make some plans. We know the party kicks off at six,' Kane said.

'Won't there be security?' Liam asked.

'Duh. That's why we're security too, remember, you moron,' the young man said, shaking his head. 'We discussed this already.'

Liam sneered. He didn't like being told off, least of all by Kane who always thought he was in charge of everything.

One of Kane's friends worked for the firm that was on duty tonight and he'd managed to procure enough jackets for them all to be in uniform. With plain black pants and a black T-shirt and jacket, no one would spot the difference.

There was a knock on the door. 'Can I come in?'

'What do you want, Mum?' Hazel called out.

'That's a lovely greeting, isn't it?' Keeley said as she poked her head around. 'Has anyone heard from your father? He should be home by now.'

Liam wolf-whistled and Keeley stepped into the room properly. She was wearing a gold gown – long to the floor with a slit up the thigh and a plunging neckline. Her long hair tumbled in curls halfway down her back and her makeup was perfect if not a little heavy.

'Oi!' Jake gave the boy a thump on the arm. 'Inappropriate.'

'Really, Jakey, darling – you think Mummy looks inappropriate? That's the best compliment I've had in years,' the woman replied.

'I didn't say that, Mum. I meant Liam shouldn't be whistling at you – he's a pimply teenage boy – it's gross,' Jake said.

The woman smiled at her son, then gave Liam a sneaky wink.

'Where are you going?' Jake asked.

'Party of the year. Mr Turner's invited everyone who's anyone from the village – and he knows your father's a big deal in the transport business. But your father had better get here soon, or I'll be heading there on my own – he won't like that one bit and I won't care,' the woman said.

'You're going to Hoxton Manor?' Liam asked, a quiver in his voice.

'You never mentioned you were going to *that* party,' Hazel said.

'Well, the invitation only came the other afternoon, and I'd already accepted my Pilates Christmas party, but then I thought about it and there was no way I was going to pass this one up,' Keeley explained. 'The girls will be so jealous when I tell them about it. Though I think a couple of them might be invited too – the Pilates party numbers seemed way down when I phoned to say I couldn't make it.'

Hazel looked at Jake who looked at Liam who stared at Kane.

'You'll be the most gorgeous woman there,'

Liam said. 'I mean that very respectfully of course, Mrs Hendrix.'

The other three pulled faces at the lad.

Downstairs, there was the sound of the back door opening.

'Griff, is that you, darling?' Keeley called. 'You'd better hurry up and get changed. I've got your suit laid out in the bedroom. We're due at the party at six.'

And with that, she turned and hurried out of the room.

'I hope you've got a plan B, boys,' Hazel said.

'Mum would be mortified,' Jake said.

Kane shook his head. 'Dad wouldn't care if he caught us – he hates that rich sod anyway. It just makes the whole thing a bit more fun really.'

'Fine,' Hazel replied. She glanced at her watch. 'Ellie had better hurry up then – because I'm not going to be the only girl there.'

Chapter 37

With Cecelia having kept the children busy all day, it seemed that everyone had forgotten about last night's robbery. Although Alice-Miranda certainly hadn't and neither had Millie. They just weren't reminding anyone about it.

After their fashion spectacular, Cecelia suggested the group head into the garden and build some snow people, which ended up in a vigorous snowball fight, followed by lunch and a hilarious Christmas movie about some criminals who try to ruin a family's Christmas – perhaps a little too much like art imitating life at the moment. There was also an impromptu dance lesson from Shilly and Mrs Oliver in the ballroom that had everyone up enjoying themselves – there would be dancing tonight and Caprice suggested they get in some practice.

Jacinta and Lucas surprised the group with their cha-cha moves, while Sep asked Millie if she'd be his partner in a waltz. Alice-Miranda giggled when she realised that the girl's face was about the same colour as her hair, but it was lovely to see the two enjoying themselves. When the clocks around the house echoed their four-thirty chimes, Shilly shooed the children off to get ready for the party – though the boys argued that they'd be changed in no time flat. The woman suggested they do some reading while they waited for the girls – and to get used to the fact that they'd spend a lot of time in the future doing exactly the same thing. Neville dissented, saying that he also took ages to get ready, these days – taming his hair into exactly the right style was something of a m-a-n-e event. That joke caused him to laugh out loud. Sloane just shook her head.

Mr Greening was organised to take the children, Cecelia and Hugh in the minivan at quarter to six.

'Don't you all look gorgeous,' Cecelia gasped as the children walked down the stairs into the entrance foyer. She'd asked Mr Greening to bring the van to the front of the house for a change. They almost always used the kitchen entrance and tonight she wanted to make things a little more special.

The group was a kaleidoscope of colour from Chessie's ballerina-length pale-pink gown with silver sparkles to Sloane's silver A-line halter-neck with a faux fur stole. Jacinta was in a gorgeous cobalt-blue off-the-shoulder number while Britt had opted for white on white with sequins and a knitted shrug. Caprice drew a gasp in her fairytale princess dress with a full skirt in pale blue. Millie was in her favourite forest-green, in a gown that perfectly complemented her hair and eyes. Britt looked sweet in a feathered skirt and sequinned top in red.

Alice-Miranda wore a calf-length tulle skirt in silver with a matching cashmere cardigan with pearl buttons. Her hair was pulled back off her face and she wore a jewelled headband.

Cecelia was a picture herself in a navy floor-length gown with a deep V neckline and an attached cape. The dress was covered in sequinned stripes.

'Mummy – you look so tall,' Alice-Miranda said.

The woman grinned. 'Helped by heels and this dress.'

'Yes, vertical stripes give the illusion of height,' Britt said.

'Look at you, you little fashionista,' Caprice said.

The boys looked smart in their tuxedos too. Lucas wore a cobalt-blue bow tie to match Jacinta's dress, while Neville had added a natty tartan waistcoat to his ensemble and Sep was resplendent in mint-coloured accessories, including a lovely cashmere scarf.

'Hugh!' Cecelia called out.

'Coming, darling,' he said, though from the pinched look on his face, Alice-Miranda decided that there probably hadn't been any good news since their visit this morning from Detective Inspector Freeman.

'Don't you all look festive,' Hugh said. He was as handsome as always in his formal attire.

'Well, have a wonderful evening,' Dolly Oliver said, as she and Shilly snapped photographs of the group.

'Shilly and I are going to put our feet up and watch a movie – before the rest of the family arrives tomorrow night.'

'Don't you wish you were coming?' Jacinta asked.

Shilly shook her head. 'My dancing days are long gone, dear. My idea of a perfect Saturday night usually involves supper in front of the television, a movie and early to bed. I know – boring – but one day you'll be old like us and you'll understand what I'm talking about.'

'I'm looking forward to seeing Mummy and Anthony,' Chessie said. 'I'm glad that they're coming. Mummy says she's been so busy with guests, they've hardly had time to think about Christmas. And I can't believe I've been here since Wednesday and haven't seen them yet.'

Millie nudged Caprice. 'Speaking of parents,' she whispered. 'Have you spoken to your mother?'

The girl bit her lip. 'Um, no, but I'll call her from the party – then I won't be able to talk to her for too long and she won't be able to tell me off as much either,' she replied.

Millie grinned. That seemed like a good strategy.

'Now, has everyone got everything?' Shilly asked. 'Handbags, handkerchiefs, ham sandwiches?'

'What?' the children chorused, followed by a staccato firing of, 'Why would we need to take ham sandwiches?'

'Just checking to see if you were all paying attention,' the woman replied to guffaws of laughter.

'Shilly – you're in a cheeky mood,' Hugh said. 'But you did pack me one, didn't you – in case the food's ghastly?'

Alice-Miranda's jaw dropped. 'Daddy! Now who's being cheeky? The food will be amazing, I'm sure.'

'Actually, I ran into Miss Wickham at the shops this morning and she mentioned that their chef is recuperating from a nasty appendicitis. I'm not sure who'll be cooking, but I can't imagine that Mr Turner will scrimp,' Shilly said.

'It'd be funny if it's your mother, Caprice,' Jacinta said. 'Though surely you'd know that by now.'

Caprice looked at Millie and swallowed hard.

'Mr Turner said that he was visiting one of his staff members when I saw him at the hospital the other night. It sounds like poor Miss Wickham has had a lot on her plate too,' Alice-Miranda said. The girl was carrying a clutch purse and inside it was the bottle and the letter she was hoping to show Miss Wickham tonight. She had a feeling it was important, but it was also Christmas and she wondered if now was the right time – especially if Miss Wickham was also dealing with a sick staff member on top of all her other worries. She didn't want to upset anyone, so she'd decide what do to when she got there.

'Well, off you go, you lot. Enjoy the evening,' Dolly Oliver trilled.

And with that, the group headed out the door to their waiting ride.

Chapter 38

'What's the matter with you?' Keeley asked her husband, who was pulling up his trousers and looked in a right old sulk.

'I've got a few things on my mind,' Griffin replied. 'I don't know why we're going to this do – you know I can't stand all those rich toffs.'

Keeley handed him his shirt, which he shrugged on, then buttoned up. She grabbed the tie from the end of the bed and passed it to him.

'We're going because we were invited and

it would be bad manners to say no – besides, I've wanted to get a look at Hoxton Manor for years. Everyone says it's even more gorgeous than Highton Hall and that's one of the most beautiful houses I've ever seen. At least the Highton-Smith-Kennington-Joneses have the good grace to host an annual garden party so us mere mortals can get a squiz,' Keeley said.

Griffin finished doing up his tie. To say he had a few things on his mind was an understatement. His star driver, Bobby, had been intercepted chatting to people he shouldn't have been. Griffin didn't know where they'd taken him, but he had a nasty feeling that Bobby was about to disappear for good. From the messages on his phone, the boss wasn't very happy with Griffin either – given he was the one who gave the bloke the job. Griffin was in way over his head and he knew it.

He wriggled the Windsor knot into position around his neck and raked a hand through his hair.

'You look very handsome, darling,' Keeley said. She looked at him with her hand on one hip. A moment later he realised that she was staring.

'What?' he asked.

'You're supposed to tell me what a knockout I am,' Keeley harrumphed. 'At least Liam thinks I'm hot.'

'You are, Keeley – but you don't want the likes of that greaseball teenager telling you so,' Griffin said and rolled his eyes. 'You'll be the most gorgeous woman there – unless Venetia Baldini turns up, because she's off the charts,' he said with a smirk.

'Thanks a lot,' Keeley said and gave him a playful smack on the arm before grabbing her feathered coverlet from the back of the chair. 'That's not likely now, is it? She's probably off in her villa in Italy getting ready for Christmas – like that show we watched about her family Christmas last year.'

'Oh, yeah – you're probably right. So you'll be the most beautiful woman there, for sure,' Griffin said, earning himself a peck on the cheek.

Juliette Byers had checked under all the beds and in every cupboard.

'I told you, Mum, he's not here,' Ellie said.

The woman was pacing the hall. 'Think, think, where would he go? Why would he go?'

Ellie checked her brother's room for the umpteenth time.

'It's gone,' she called out, suddenly realising that her brother's box of treasures was missing.

Juliette raced to the door.

'He told me last night that the man who gave him the bauble said he has something else for him,' Ellie said.

Juliette nodded. 'He did. But that was Mr Turner from Hoxton Manor. It's a long way from here and how would Myles even know how to get there?'

Ellie raced into her room and pulled the hoodie over her head, then grabbed her coat from the end of the bed.

'Myles has heard you telling us about Hoxton Manor. We never go past the place without you mentioning you had an aunt who worked there and you've said that it's owned by Elliot Turner. Last night Myles said his name and where he lived. He's gone there – to get his next trinket. I'm sure of it,' Ellie shouted as she raced back into the hall.

'I'm calling the police first,' Juliette said. 'They can meet us there. Oh, Ellie – I hope you're right. I'll never forgive myself if anything happens to him.'

Ellie nodded. She felt exactly the same way. And then she remembered that Hoxton Manor was where she was meant to be going tonight anyway. Surely Hazel and the others would understand. Her brother's safety was far more important than a couple of Christmas wreaths and some decorations in the name of misguided charity.

Chapter 39

A fleet of vehicles entered the driveway at Hoxton Manor, forming a procession around the circular drive at the front of the sparkling mansion.

'What a beautiful house,' Alice-Miranda gasped.

'And look at that!' Britt added, pointing.

The giant Christmas tree in the middle of the driveway provided the most perfect centrepiece.

The children's eyes were on stalks as they took it all in.

'Are you sure we're not on a movie set?' Neville asked.

'Oh no – this is not like the movies at all,' Caprice began to explain. 'For a start, there'd be cameras everywhere and catering trucks . . .'

'I was kidding,' Neville said with a grin.

'Sorry – you know I love Hollywood, right?' Caprice smiled back.

'Have a good night, all,' Mr Greening said as he closed the van door. 'Hugh – just call and let me know what time I should be here to pick you up.'

'Thank you, Harold,' Hugh Kennington-Jones replied.

Chessie spotted her mother and stepfather arriving too. She raced over to greet them while Millie realised that the Applebys were there, as well as some other people from the village she'd met before.

'Come on, everyone,' Alice-Miranda said, leading her friends inside where the interior decoration was even more gorgeous than what they'd seen outside.

There were waiters offering drinks and canapes, and Christmas music playing through unseen speakers.

The group drifted away in pairs and threes, exploring the house and its finery.

Alice-Miranda's eyes were drawn upwards on the staircase to a portrait of a strikingly beautiful woman. She had long dark hair and emerald-green eyes. She gasped when she realised who it must have been. Mr Turner was absolutely right when he said that Ellie reminded him of his wife. The resemblance was uncanny.

Alice-Miranda had to talk to Miss Wickham – if she could find her, that is. She asked one of the wait staff, who told her to look for a lady with short grey hair wearing a black suit. So far, she couldn't see anyone bearing that description at all.

Then she spotted a face in the crowd she knew.

'Hello, Mr Smote,' Alice-Miranda said.

'Oh, darling girl – how wonderful to see you and what a gorgeous Christmas outfit that is. So, what do you think?' the man asked.

In his long green pants with a matching jacket, red vest and silver bow tie, he reminded Alice-Miranda of a shiny Christmas ornament.

'You look very festive,' the girl said with a smile.

Sebastian frowned. 'Not me, darling – the house – what do you think? The ice sculpture – is it too much?'

The centrepiece in the front room was an ice sculpture paying homage to the song 'The Twelve Days of Christmas'. There were geese and swans and even a partridge in a pear tree.

'No, not at all – it's wonderful. I love it! Tell me, Mr Smote – you haven't seen Miss Wickham, have you? I need a word with her.'

Sebastian fiddled with his hands, then looked left and right. 'The last time I saw Delia she was in the ballroom.'

This time it was Alice-Miranda's turn to frown. 'Did you say Delia? Is that Miss Wickham's first name?'

'Yes, dear girl, it is. And a lovely one at that.' The man's eyes opened wide and he swallowed hard.

'No, children, stop – please don't lick the swans!' he cried and with that he disappeared.

Alice-Miranda's mind was whirling.

Juliette Byers said that her aunt's name was Delia, but she'd died when she was a child. She couldn't ever remember meeting her.

'Is everything all right?' Britt Fox asked. She'd been watching Alice-Miranda with the nattily dressed man before he ran away.

'I don't think it is,' the girl said. 'We need to find someone – it's important.'

★

Juliette turned the key in the ignition of her ancient hatchback, only to hear a horrible grinding noise.

'Seriously, now the car packs it in!' Ellie thumped her hand on the dashboard.

'I'm sorry, Ellie!' her mother shouted. 'I don't drive it very often – the battery's gone flat. We'll just have to wait for the police.'

But that wasn't an option as far as Ellie was concerned. When her mother called and reported her brother missing, they said that all available officers were currently busy – there was a major incident unfolding and it would take time to send someone from out of area. This wasn't good enough. Myles was out there – it was freezing and who knew how many layers of clothes he had on. Last Ellie had seen him he'd been running around the house in a long sleeve T-shirt.

'I know someone who can take us,' Ellie said. 'Come on, Mum.'

The pair jumped out of the car and ran down the street.

'Where are we going?' Juliette asked, as they charged along through the snow that was now coming down in fat flakes.

'Hazel's place,' the girl replied. 'Just let me do the talking, okay?'

Juliette nodded.

Chapter 40

Millie found herself wandering the house with Caprice and Sep in tow. This wasn't just a party – it was more like a carnival with a Christmas-themed carousel in the orangery, a mechanised Santa's workshop in the sitting room with life-sized elves making all manner of toys, and real reindeer outside, hitched to a sleigh.

'Wow!' Caprice whispered. 'I'm glad I'm not in Tuscany.'

Millie spun around. 'Speaking of which, please call your mother. You promised.'

The girl rolled her eyes, then leaned closer to Millie. 'What if she's here?'

'Seriously – I can't imagine Mr Turner's the only wealthy person in the world hosting a Christmas party,' Millie replied.

'Okay – but I need to go somewhere private so if she yells at me and I have to yell back, people won't hear. I wouldn't want anyone to think I'm some sort of brat or anything,' Caprice replied.

Millie smiled and asked Sep if he wouldn't mind getting them both some more lemonade. She told him they were going to freshen up, which Millie realised made her sound like a granny.

Caprice and Millie ducked into what appeared to be a guest bedroom to make the call.

Venetia Baldini pushed her sleeves up and began cracking the first dozen eggs, separating the whites. She'd been on her feet all day and couldn't see herself sitting down anytime soon. At least the bulk of the dinner was done and she just had to get this last dessert underway.

Caprice still hadn't returned her calls, which niggled, but the girl was a champion grudge-holder and Venetia had more on her plate than she'd imagined when she'd agreed to this job. At least the payday would provide a lifeline to the restaurants. She and her husband had decided they'd still put the villa on the market. Although the family loved spending time there, there were other more pressing priorities and having a holiday home in Italy was a luxury beyond what they could currently afford. But at least Christmas would be brighter now.

Venetia wiped her brow with the back of her hand and decided to make herself a cup of tea. The meringues could wait another few minutes.

While Venetia watched the kettle boil, contemplating the vagaries of life – the fact that less than a year ago she was on top of the world doing better than she'd ever thought possible, and now she was fighting to keep the business she'd worked so hard to build afloat, she became aware of a tapping sound. It started softly but was building to quite a crescendo and it seemed to be coming from somewhere beyond the kitchen – perhaps in one of the butler's pantries.

She wandered off to investigate. Despite having been in the house now for several days, Venetia realised that she'd barely seen any of it, apart from the guest room where she was sleeping and the kitchen. Everything she needed to cook for the party was there – which was fantastic given the weather hadn't been at all conducive to outside activities, and the forecast was only getting worse.

Venetia walked out of the kitchen and down the hall, poking her head inside the various pantries and storerooms along the way. The tapping sound wasn't as loud anymore. Perhaps it was the pipes in the main part of the kitchen. And now it had stopped anyway.

She headed back to the kitchen and had just finished making her tea when she was grabbed from behind. A hand covered her mouth. A tiny gasp escaped from her lips.

'Don't move or make a sound,' a man whispered. 'I'm not going to hurt you. My name is Bronson Byers and I'm an undercover police officer. I've been held here against my will. The man you are working for is not who you think he is. We need to get out of here – now. You must believe me or we're both dead.'

Footsteps echoed outside the room. There was someone coming.

Venetia prised his hand from her mouth, unsure whether he was telling the truth, but what choice did she have? She spun around and looked into his eyes. She could feel his desperation.

'I'll help you, but you need to hide,' she whispered and pointed to the butler's pantry at the end of the room.

Bronson nodded and made a run for it.

'Hello, Miss Baldini,' a man in black said. 'Is everything all right?'

She turned and pulled a large carving knife from the block on the bench.

'Yes – perfect. Busy, busy,' she said, trying to calm the wavering notes in her voice as her heart raced wildly.

'Please don't let me hold you up,' he said. 'And if you need anything, be sure to let me know.' She heard his footsteps fading down the long hallway.

Venetia's phone rang, causing her to drop the knife which clattered onto the bench. Her heart was still pounding. She looked at the screen. It was

Caprice – finally. At the other end of the room, she could see Bronson Byers' head poking around the door – staring at her.

'It's my daughter,' she whispered. 'I have to take it.'

He nodded.

'Hurry – I need that phone,' he said.

'Hello, Mummy,' Caprice said.

Millie gave the girl a glowering look and mouthed, 'Apologise for not calling her.'

'I'm sorry I haven't returned your calls. I've been busy.'

There was a lengthy silence and Caprice pressed the button to put the speaker on. She rationalised that if her mother got angry, then she could say she was with Millie on speaker and she'd calm down. Venetia would never lose her temper if she knew someone else was listening.

'Where are you?' Caprice asked. 'What was this amazing job you had to take?' The girl bit her lip, hoping that the answer wasn't what she thought it could be.

'I'm cooking for a party at a beautiful home just on the edge of Highton Mill. Not far from Highton Hall,' the woman said.

Caprice looked at Millie, her eyes wide.

'You have to tell her. She's going to find out that you're here,' Millie whispered.

'That's amazing, Mummy – what a coincidence,' Caprice said brightly. 'I'm at the party right now with Millie and the girls and some of the boys too. They invited me to come to Alice-Miranda's for the week when you dumped me.'

'I didn't dump you, darling. This job was too good to refuse. It's going to help Mummy and Daddy get out of a bit of a bind,' the woman said. 'And what do you mean you're here? You can't be.'

Caprice rolled her eyes. 'Of course, I can. And you're on speaker phone, Mummy – Millie's here with me.'

'Hello Ms Baldini, happy Christmas,' Millie said.

'Mummy, are you in the kitchen?' Caprice asked. 'We'll come down.'

'What are you talking about, Caprice?' Venetia said. 'Where are you?'

'We're at Mr Turner's Christmas party at

Hoxton Manor. Isn't that who you're cooking for?' the girl said.

There was a short pause before Venetia spoke.

'No, I'm at Loff's Folly – I think it's actually next door to Hoxton Manor. I remember passing the estate on the way here. It's on the Highton Mill side. I'm working for a man called Sergey Koloff –'

Suddenly there was the sound of heavy footsteps.

'Venetia, please, I need that phone,' a voice said.

'I have to go, darling,' Venetia said.

'Mummy, what's going on?' Caprice asked. 'Who's that man?'

'Bronson Bye–' she said, but her words were drowned out by the sound of people running and another woman shouting.

'Who are you?' a voice demanded.

'I'm Bobby Lambert,' the man replied. It was followed by a scuffling sound and shouting.

Then another man yelled. 'How did you get out of there?'

The girls could hear gasps and thuds and it sounded like a fight.

'Mummy! What's going on?' Caprice demanded.

'Caprice! You need to call the –' Venetia yelled before the line went dead.

Caprice looked at Millie in alarm. 'What just happened?'

'Come on,' Millie grabbed the girl's arm. 'Your mother said that she's next door and it's obvious she needs help. Give me your phone!'

Sep spotted the girls as they were racing towards the back door. 'I've got your lemonade,' he called, but there was no stopping them.

All the while, the pair had no idea that someone had been listening to their conversation from the ensuite bathroom right next to them.

Griffin Hendrix could hardly believe his ears. What was Venetia Baldini doing at Loff's Folly? He absolutely adored that woman and now it sounded as if she was in serious danger. At least he knew where his star driver, Bobby, had disappeared to – although what they had planned for him, Griffin didn't even want to think about. And who was Bronson Bye? It sounded like the same voice that said he was Bobby. Griffin's head was spinning. Sergey Koloff was not a man to cross. He had to do something, but what? And if Sergey didn't kill him, Keeley probably would.

Chapter 41

Alice-Miranda and Britt had been in and out of almost every room and still hadn't managed to find Miss Wickham. They headed downstairs to the kitchens, where it was a hive of activity. A team of chefs were haring about. But there was one who was obviously in charge. A commanding woman in a tall chef's hat and white uniform. Her long blonde hair trailed halfway down her back and, despite the frenetic pace, she looked as if she'd just stepped out of the pages of a magazine.

'Is that Sophie Garceau?' Britt asked.

Alice-Miranda nodded. 'Yes, I think so.'

'They say she's the new Venetia Baldini,' Britt said.

The woman was barking orders at her team, snapping and snarling like an angry terrier.

'She might be beautiful like Venetia and a good cook, but I think that's where the comparison ends,' Alice-Miranda said. 'Venetia would never yell at her staff like that.'

One poor young girl had dropped something on the floor and the woman was towering over her, screaming like a banshee.

'It sounds like *Pressure Cooker* is the perfect name for her show,' Britt said, as the girls dashed along the hallway.

'Excuse me,' Alice-Miranda asked a waiter, who was carrying a huge platter of meat. 'Have you seen Miss Wickham?'

The fellow nodded. 'She's in the cellar. At the end of the passageway.'

Alice-Miranda grabbed Britt's hand and the two girls hurried away.

They reached a door through which a set of circular stone steps led down into the deepest recesses of the house.

'Miss Wickham, hello? Are you down here?' Alice-Miranda called.

A woman with stylish short grey hair, wearing a black pants suit, looked up from where she was checking a list.

'Yes, hello,' she replied.

'Hello,' Alice-Miranda said, then proceeded to introduce herself in the usual way. 'This is my friend, Britt Fox.'

'Shouldn't you girls be upstairs enjoying the party?' the woman asked.

'I think this is more important,' Alice-Miranda said. She opened her clutch purse and pulled out the tiny bottle with the note inside, then proceeded to explain about the teapot she'd bought for Mrs Oliver for Christmas from the charity shop and what happened when she checked to see that it poured properly.

'I found this jammed into the spout. I think it might mean something, but part of the note is smudged.'

Alice-Miranda pulled it out with the tweezers she'd also remembered to pack.

Delia Wickham leaned in to get a closer look.

'I'm afraid my sister and I weren't close the past

fifteen years. She wasn't well and before that, when her husband died, she upped and moved to the other end of the country. I have a niece, but she's been missing for a long time,' Delia explained. 'I've tried everything to find her, but I think she must live abroad.' The woman shrugged sadly.

Britt's eyebrows jumped up.

'I'm not completely sure, but I think your niece lives here in Highton Mill,' said Alice-Miranda. 'And if I'm right, she works for my parents at Kennington's but has no idea that you're still alive. And if what's written in this letter means anything, then I think it could be more complicated than I first thought,' the child explained.

'What?' Delia gasped.

'Really?' Britt said. 'When did you discover that?'

Alice-Miranda unfurled the note and handed it to the woman, along with a magnifying glass she'd brought with her.

'It's been like a jigsaw,' Alice-Miranda said. 'There are still pieces missing.'

Delia Wickham studied the paper. 'That's my sister's handwriting. I'd recognise it anywhere. She had the most perfect script – it was always so tiny – as if she was hiding something.' She began to read the letter and gasped again.

'Oh, my word!' Delia's hand flew to her mouth. 'Surely she didn't . . . swap the babies.'

'We can't make out all of it,' Alice-Miranda said. 'But those last letters – do you have any idea what they mean?'

'Aster – it's my niece's name. Is that the name of the woman you know in the village?' Delia asked.

Alice-Miranda shook her head. 'Her name is Juliette.'

Delia Wickham looked as if she was going to faint.

Britt pulled over a chair and she sat down.

'What's the matter?' Alice-Miranda asked.

'That was the name of Mr and Mrs Turner's beautiful girl. The one who died not long after Mrs Turner fell down the stairs,' Delia said, cradling her head in her hands. 'But why would Aster have changed her name to Juliette? Do you think she knows?'

Alice-Miranda shook her head. 'I don't think she has any idea.'

Delia Wickham looked up at the girls. 'What on earth did my sister do?'

Chapter 42

Griffin Hendrix stood on the patio at the back of Hoxton Manor considering his options. He couldn't just leave Venetia Baldini at the mercy of Sergei Koloff and his thugs. And – he wasn't sure exactly what they had on Bobby Lambert, but as far as Griff was concerned, whatever it was, it didn't warrant the man disappearing. Griffin's temples began to throb. He was surprised to see a delivery van, the same as the one his son drove for work, fly around the corner to the parking area behind the mansion. But what he saw next was even more perplexing.

What were his children and that little ferret, Liam, doing dressed as security guards? They were supposed to be at home watching Christmas movies. He was shocked to see Hazel's friend Ellie emerge from the back of the van with a woman in tow.

'Oi, you lot!' Griffin called out, hurrying over to the group. 'What are you doing here?'

'Looking for my son,' the woman said. 'Have you seen Myles? He's about this tall,' she held her hand at about the one metre mark, 'and he's wearing a long-sleeved T-shirt and he's probably carrying a tin.' She was talking a million miles a minute.

'What's she on about?' Griffin asked. 'Is that your mother, Ellie?'

The girl nodded. 'My brother's missing and we think he might have come here.'

'Why?' Griffin asked.

'It's a long story, Dad,' Hazel said.

Ellie looked at Hazel. 'Are you coming, or have you still got more important things to do? I mean, finding a lost nine-year-old would seem to trump your other plans, wouldn't it?'

Hazel narrowed her eyes. 'I thought you were my friend,' she snapped.

'Friends don't ask people to steal things to prove their worth,' Ellie retorted. While a showdown had been brewing in the van, Ellie had held her tongue until now. She didn't need them turfing her and her mother out before they got to their destination.

Juliette looked at Ellie. 'What are you talking about, darling?'

'I'll tell you everything later, Mum – and I'm sorry. I really am.' She grabbed Juliette's hand and the pair raced away to the mansion.

Griffin glared at the teens.

'What did Ellie mean? And why are you dressed like that?' he asked. Then he remembered something he'd heard on the radio on his way home from work about the robberies of all the Christmas decorations. Finally, the police had a lead on a black van.

'Oh, for the love of everything good in this world, tell me you're not the Bauble Bandits?' Griffin said.

Hazel smiled. 'How did you know, Dad? Are you proud of us? We're like Robin Hood and his Merry Men – we're going to nick those wreaths from the front gates tonight. Then we're going to decorate all the poor houses round the village that never get any love.'

Griffin felt sick. 'Why would I be proud? You're nothing but common criminals.'

Hazel recoiled.

'But you're always banging on about rich people and how life isn't fair and that we need to level the playing field,' Jake said.

'I didn't mean you should steal things,' Griffin said, the weight of his words almost causing his legs to buckle beneath him given his own sordid track record. 'You're not taking anything from this place and you're going to return everything you've nicked and then you can use your own money to buy decorations for all the houses you decided needed cheering up.'

'But Dad,' Kane griped. 'That's, like, heaps of money and it will take us hours to give everything back – and then what if someone sees us?'

'You'll be lucky I don't give you away to the police,' the man said. 'But then again, your mother won't be impressed if the whole family is locked up at the same time.'

Hazel frowned at her father.

'What are you talking about, Dad?' she asked.

'Nothing – but you need to come with me. There are some people in trouble and we're going to help them – no questions asked.'

He glared at the four youngsters. 'You've obviously got your thieving ways from someone, and I need to make things right.' He pulled his phone out and made the call he should have when he'd overheard those girls talking. For the first time in his life, he needed to be smart about what he did next. He only hoped that he hadn't left things too late.

Chapter 43

Sep looked around and spotted Neville with Lucas, Jacinta, Sloane and Chessie at the other end of the hall.

'Hey,' he called.

The five friends looked up and hurried towards him.

'There's something weird going on. Millie and Caprice have just bolted outside. I think we need to go after them,' Sep said.

'Did they say anything?' Sloane asked.

Sep shook his head. He was still trying to work out where to put the drinks – fortunately, a waiter walked past, and he deposited the glasses back onto the man's tray.

'Do you know where they were going?' Chessie asked.

'No – but they were in a hurry,' Sep said.

'Come on, then,' Lucas said, and the group dashed out through the rear doors into the darkness. Problem was, they really had no idea where to look.

They asked a couple of the valet drivers who'd been parking cars if they'd seen the girls, and some security guards too, but without any luck.

Snowflakes whirled on an icy wind. 'Maybe they've gone back inside,' Jacinta suggested. Her teeth were chattering and she was shivering uncontrollably.

'Yeah,' Lucas agreed. 'It's freezing out here. Come on.'

It didn't take much to convince the others. Lucas wrapped his arms around Jacinta and Neville, Chessie and Sloane hurried after them. Sep bit his lip. He had more clothes on than the girls and wasn't feeling the cold quite as much.

'Sep!' Sloane called from where she was standing further up the driveway.

'Be there in a minute,' he shouted after her.

Sep spun around and saw lights over by the fence that separated Hoxton Manor from the neighbours. He wondered if it was Millie and Caprice and, if it was, what they were doing there. He called out but his voice was carried away by a sudden gust of wind. He'd go and take a look just in case. He hurried across the driveway and down a path towards the boundary, but was disappointed to see it was only some more security guards. Though he might as well ask them too.

'Excuse me, I'm wondering if you've seen my friends. Millie is kind of short with fiery red hair and freckles, and Caprice is tall with long copper hair and blue eyes.'

'No, we haven't,' a young girl snapped, spinning around. He was surprised that she only looked about the same age as him. The boys she was with were young teens too – although one was older. 'Go back to the party.'

He noticed that she was holding a pair of binoculars looking towards the mansion next door.

'Is there a problem?' Sep asked.

'There's Dad,' the older boy said, snatching the binoculars from the girl. 'He's going inside.'

'What's happening?' Sep asked.

'None of your business,' one of the younger boys spat. 'Now, get lost.'

'Are you really security guards?' Sep asked. It didn't seem likely.

'We told you, nick off,' the other boy, who reminded Sep of a ferret, barked.

But Sep wasn't going anywhere. Especially not after what he saw next.

'Millie!' Sep shouted, before being punched in the stomach. He doubled over and lay in the grass gasping for breath. 'What did you do that for?'

He'd just caught sight of Millie and Caprice being manhandled by a pair of men and it looked like they were heading inside the mansion too.

'Shut your trap!' the older boy hissed.

'But those are my friends,' Sep said, clambering to his feet. 'We've got to help them.'

'What do you think we're doing?' the girl said. 'Our father's in there too and so's Venetia Baldini.'

'Venetia!' Sep gasped. 'She's Caprice's mother. Have you called the police?'

'No – Dad says these guys aren't your everyday criminals,' one of the boys said.

But Sep didn't care. His friends were in danger and he needed to help. Without another word he took off, hurdling the fence and sprinting towards the house.

'Are you kidding me?' the girl said. 'Come on! We have to go after him before he gets everyone killed.'

Millie was opposite Caprice, both tied to the chairs they were sat on. At least the thugs hadn't covered their eyes. The men who had grabbed them were gone. The girls were alone in a room that looked like a cellar – though there wasn't any wine in this section of it. Millie couldn't help thinking what a cliché that was – the bad guys always took their victims to the cellar. There had been more than one occasion when she and Alice-Miranda had found themselves in a bit of bother in similar surrounds. Although what this lot were up to and why they'd grabbed Venetia – especially after she said that she was working for the man who owned the house, and he was supposedly paying her a fortune – was anyone's guess. It must have had something to do with the fellow on the telephone – what was his name? Millie racked her brain thinking of it. Then she remembered. Bronson. Millie realised she'd heard that name only this morning. Juliette's husband was called Bronson. It wasn't very common. And Venetia had said Bronson Bye before she'd been cut off – it had to be Bronson Byers. But what on earth was he doing here? Caprice was wriggling about when suddenly she rocked her chair forward. Her feet touched the floor and much to Millie's amazement she managed to hop over and position herself back-to-back with Millie, close enough that the girls' hands could touch, which hopefully meant that with a lot of pulling and fiddling they'd be able to undo each other's ropes.

Without a word – only because they were gagged – the pair set to work. Sometimes being stubborn paid off and, though neither of them could say it, they were both hoping that what was often their worst attribute was about to become one of their most valuable.

Chapter 44

Sep had almost reached the back of the mansion before the others caught up.

'Stop!' the older boy hissed.

Sep slid under a hedge and lay on his stomach, relieved to have got this far without being intercepted.

They all lay down beside him like soldiers in a row, trying to catch their breaths and wondering what was going to happen next.

'You shouldn't have come here,' the girl said.

'Fine – probably wasn't my best plan,' Sep mumbled, wondering how he was ever going to find Millie and Caprice and Venetia inside the huge modern house. But he hadn't really been thinking straight.

'We have to wait and hear from Dad,' the older boy said. 'Until then, no one moves, okay?'

Sep wasn't keen on that idea, especially now that the snow was coming down in fat flakes. It wouldn't take long before they were buried with a dose of hypothermia.

Meanwhile inside, Millie had managed to get her fingers through the knot and with one last tug she freed Caprice, who quickly pulled the gag from her mouth and took a deep breath.

She undid the ropes from her legs and quickly finished untying Millie.

'They're not very smart,' Millie whispered. 'Cable ties would have been far harder to get out of.'

Caprice nodded, then did something completely unexpected, wrapping her arms around Millie tightly.

'Thank you,' she mumbled. 'Now we have to find Mum and get out of here.'

The girls didn't have to look far before they found *someone*. They peered around into the main part of the cellar and at the end of the room, among thousands and thousands of bottles of wine, a man was tied to his chair just as they had been.

At the sound of their footsteps, he looked up. It was clear he'd taken a beating, with two black eyes and a nasty cut to the side of his face. Millie pressed her finger to her lips and the girls crept towards him, their footfalls silent on the stone floor.

Working together, they quickly released him from his bonds.

'I'm Millie and this is Caprice – she's Venetia's daughter,' the girl whispered.

He nodded.

'Are you Bronson?' the girl asked. 'Bronson Byers? Myles and Ellie's dad?'

'Yes, you know my children?' he said.

Millie nodded.

'Are they okay?' Bronson asked.

'Yes, they're fine,' Millie said. Although she had to wonder if Ellie was still going through with the plan the girls had hatched to bring down Hazel and the boys. It wasn't exactly the right time to bring that up now.

'Good,' Bronson said with a tight smile. 'You mustn't say my real name if we happen upon any of the thugs who are guarding this place. I'm an undercover police officer – I don't know how they found out, but I've been on this case for over a year now. My cover is Bobby,' he said.

'That explains a lot,' Millie said. 'The police are on their way. I called Detective Inspector Freeman before we got here. But they're coming quietly. No sirens.'

Bronson's eyebrows jumped up. 'How do you know her?'

'It's a long story,' Millie replied. 'Has this got anything to do with the grocery thefts from Kennington's and all the others?'

Bronson nodded.

'No wonder Detective Freeman sounded excited when I told her what was going on. She's been trying to crack this case for ages,' Millie said.

'Do you know where my mother is?' Caprice asked.

He nodded. 'Sergey is hosting a party – it's only small, but his nearest and dearest are upstairs in the dining room. Your mother is cooking. I managed to convince them she knew nothing about any of this before they dragged me back down here.'

The girls nodded. This was good news – but now they had to get out of there and make sure that DI Freeman and her team got their man.

The unexpected arrival of Griffin Hendrix at his boss's exclusive Christmas party was clearly not welcome. But, when Griffin said he'd received some information he needed to deliver in person and in private, Sergey Koloff took leave of his guests, leading the man to his study – which is exactly what Griffin had hoped he would do.

During the construction of the mansion, Griffin had made many deliveries here – and not grocery items. Everything in the house was hot – as in stolen – from the tiles and taps to the ovens, sinks, furniture and floor coverings. Another sideline that the trucking company had been involved in. His boss would have been surprised at how familiar Griffin was with the house and its quirks – something he was about to use to his advantage.

Sergey Koloff closed the door. He ran a hand over the top of his bald head, then cracked his knuckles. Yet neither action made him seem any taller than his five-foot-three stature. Two henchmen stood either side of the man. Tactical but good. Now Griffin just had to get the other two he'd seen downstairs inside. As far as he knew, Sergey's security team was only four.

'So, what is it that could not wait?' Sergey demanded.

'I've got news about Bobby,' Griffin said. He wasn't sure where he was going with this, but he had to make something up and knowing that Bobby was somewhere in the house might actually help him to find the man once he had taken care of Sergey and his thugs.

'We have dealt with him already,' Sergey said. 'And next time you employ someone, make sure that your background checks are more thorough. Perhaps it is time we dealt with you as well.'

'What are you talking about? I've been nothing but loyal to you, Sergey. I organise those deliveries and make sure that everything gets where it needs to go,' Griffin said with a gulp.

'That may be true, but I know that you take

a little bit for yourself. You think I don't have someone else keeping an eye on you?' Sergey said, his stare drilling into Griffin. 'Enough of this cat and mouse. Get rid of him.'

The men standing beside Sergey moved towards Griffin, whose hands balled into fists. He looked around for something to defend himself, snatching a silver letter opener from the desk and holding it in the air.

'Don't come any closer,' Griffin threatened, but a loud bang and shouts from downstairs caught everyone off guard.

'Don't tell me those idiots have allowed him to escape again!' Sergey bellowed. 'Find out what is going on!'

The first of Sergey's henchmen hurried to the door and out into the hallway. There was the sound of a scuffle.

'Don't just stand there, you idiot!' Sergey yelled. The second man raced out and before long the pair had both been silenced.

'What the heck is going on?' Sergey yelled as Griffin charged towards the door, hitting the small button on the panel that activated the safe room's capabilities. As a steel panel slid across the exit, he turned sideways and wriggled through, grateful he'd recently started back at the gym.

'What are you doing?' Sergey yelled, but it was too late. The man was locked inside – at least until the police found a way in.

★

'Mum,' Caprice yelled as she sped into the kitchen to find her mother, who had just pulled a tray of baked potatoes from the oven.

'Caprice!' the woman shouted as the tray clattered onto the bench and she tore off the oven mitts she was wearing. 'What are you doing here?'

The girl quickly told her what had happened and how the police were on their way.

'Where's Bronson?' Venetia asked, worried that the threats she'd heard the men making earlier may already have been delivered. She'd expected to end up locked away herself, but Bronson had convinced Sergey that she knew nothing. Given his guests had already begun to arrive, she was expected to carry out her contract and Sergey would think about what came next. She'd been feeling sick to the stomach for the past hour.

'He's gone to find Sergey – the police are on their way, but we have to get out of here,' Millie said.

'Where is everyone?' Caprice asked.

'The guests are upstairs in the sitting room with Mr Koloff. I'm not sure where all the guards have gone – I'm sure there was one lurking around just a few minutes ago.'

But they didn't have to wait long to find him. When they headed out into the hallway, he was slumped down unconscious against the wall. Millie and Caprice recognised the rope that bound his hands and legs. Bronson was good. Moments later, the man reappeared with Griffin Hendrix and guided Millie, Venetia and Caprice towards the entrance doors.

Outside, Sep and the others watched, mouths open, as what looked like an entire tactical response unit surrounded the building, having arrived on foot from who knows where. Suddenly, the mansion door opened and Bronson Byers emerged with his hands up, yelling out who he was and that Griffin Hendrix was with him. Much to Sep's relief, they were soon followed by Venetia, Caprice and Millie.

Sep took off towards them, hugging Millie tightly as soon as he reached her. Millie smiled at him and he kissed her cheek, which turned bright red.

'I was so worried,' he said, then embraced Caprice and Venetia as well.

Griffin's children hurried to see him too, though he was in the middle of being handcuffed by one of the officers.

'Dad, what's happening?' Hazel asked, hugging him before he was helped into the back of the police car that had just sped into the driveway.

'Do what I told you, okay?' he said. 'And go back and help find that missing boy first.'

Hazel, Jake, Kane and Liam nodded.

'Who's missing?' Millie asked.

'Ellie's little brother, Myles,' Hazel said. 'Her mum said they think he walked all the way out here to Hoxton Manor in the snow.'

At the mention of his son's name, Bronson Byers' ears pricked up.

He looked at Detective Inspector Freeman who nodded.

'Go. I'll deal with this lot,' Fenella said. But it looked like her team had things well in hand with a veritable parade of thugs being marched outside in handcuffs.

'Sergey's upstairs in his study,' Bronson said. 'It's a safe room, so you'll need some experts to get in. You might want to go a little bit easy on Griffin. I think he might finally have found his conscience.'

Millie turned to Caprice. 'I'm going back to help look for Myles too. You stay here and help your mum.'

Caprice nodded, then hugged Millie again. 'Thank you, my friend.'

Millie grinned and took off with Sep – Bronson Byers and the Bauble Bandits behind them.

Chapter 45

Alice-Miranda, Britt and Miss Wickham walked upstairs together. They'd agreed not to say anything to Mr Turner until tomorrow – let him enjoy his Christmas party tonight.

But sometimes life had a habit of foiling the best-laid plans.

'I need to check on the band,' Delia said and hurried away to the ballroom, where she hoped the group was set up. They had called earlier to say they were running late because of congestion on the motorway.

'And I need to go to the loo,' Britt said. She dashed down the hall.

Alice-Miranda wandered into a large sitting room. At the end of it, a pair of sliding doors leading to what looked like Mr Turner's study was slightly ajar. When she walked towards them, she was stunned to see Myles, Ellie's little brother, standing in the room. He was staring at something on the desk. It was a photograph of a woman.

'Hello,' she said, letting herself into the room. 'Does your mummy know you're here?'

She could see that his clothes were wet and his shoes looked to be soaked too. He must have been freezing but surprisingly he wasn't shivering.

The boy turned and looked at her, his eyes wary. He was holding a tin in his hands about the size of a shoebox and put it down on the desk.

There was a noise outside the room and the doors opened wider.

'I was told I had a visitor who couldn't wait,' Elliot Turner said as he walked inside and realised who was there. 'Good heavens, how did you get here?' the man asked.

Myles stared at him and held out his hand, unfurling his fingers to reveal the silver bauble

Elliot had given him the night before. 'You said you'd give me another bubble, so I came,' Myles said. 'It was a long way, but I can remember places – I see them in my mind.'

Delia Wickham arrived in the room too – the band was still stuck, and she'd gone to find her boss to see if he had any ideas about an alternative.

'Oh – who's this?' the woman asked.

'Myles,' Alice-Miranda said. 'Juliette's son.'

A small gasp escaped Elliot's lips.

'My daughter's name was Juliette,' he said.

'I know,' the girl replied.

'She's my mummy,' Myles said. 'There.'

He pointed at the photograph on the desk.

Elliot Turner frowned and looked at Delia and Alice-Miranda. 'No, that's my wife, Inez.'

Delia nodded and Alice-Miranda reached into her bag and pulled out the tiny bottle.

'You need to read this, sir, but it's probably best if you sit down first,' Delia said.

The man did as he was bid, before Alice-Miranda handed over the note which she had removed from the bottle.

'What is it?' Elliot asked.

Myles had begun to shiver. 'Does your mother

know that you're here?' Alice-Miranda asked the boy. She grabbed a throw rug from a chair in the corner and wrapped it around him.

But before he could answer there was a commotion outside. A woman was shouting.

'Is my son here?' she called. 'Myles!'

Alice-Miranda hurried out into the sitting room as Juliette and Ellie charged towards her.

'He's here!' she called.

Juliette ran into the study. She grabbed Myles and scooped him into her arms then hugged the boy tightly. Seconds later he was wriggling from her embrace.

Ellie followed her and hugged Myles again.

'Thank goodness, you're okay,' Ellie said, tears streaming down her face.

Juliette looked across at Elliot Turner.

There were tears streaming down his face too.

'Look, Mummy, there's a picture of you,' Myles said, pointing at the framed photograph on the desk.

Juliette gasped. 'What?'

Ellie stared at the photograph, then at her mother.

Alice-Miranda walked over and pulled the doors closed then spun back around.

'There's some things you need to know,' the child said. 'I'm not sure how you're going to feel about it all – but I think it's something of a Christmas miracle. You should probably all sit down.'

And with that, Alice-Miranda began to explain everything.

'My sister did a terrible thing,' Delia Wickham said, shaking her head. 'I can't believe that she stole your baby, Mr Turner – swapped her own sickly babe for Juliette. Do you think my brother-in-law knew too and he came that day to tell Mrs Turner? Maybe it was the shock of it all that caused her to fall down the stairs. And then he was killed in the car accident – the whole thing is horrific.'

'I'm not sure that we'll ever know,' Alice-Miranda said.

Delia took a deep breath. 'I'll pack my things tonight and be gone first thing in the morning.'

Elliot Turner looked at his housekeeper. 'No – of course, you won't. You didn't do anything wrong, Delia. You are not your sister and, goodness, you've lost so much too. Maggie took your family away from you as well.'

A tear slid down Delia's face. 'Sir, I don't deserve your kindness.'

Juliette looked at the man she now knew to be her father. 'Well,' she said, an air of pragmatism in her voice. 'I never thought we'd be getting a whole new family for Christmas – and the chance to be reunited with my aunt. I was just hoping for a hot lunch.'

'But I'm not your –' Delia began but Juliette cut her off.

'You'll always be my aunt, Delia,' the woman said, tears shining in her eyes. She stood up and walked over to hug the woman.

'Myles,' Ellie said. 'Do you understand? This man is our grandpa and that lady over there is our great-aunt.'

Myles walked over to Elliot. 'You said I could have another Christmas bubble.'

Elliot Turner looked at his grandson, his chest expanding with a love he never thought he would know. He opened his desk drawer and pulled out a tiny crystal Christmas tree and handed it to the boy, who gasped with delight.

Alice-Miranda smiled. 'I'm sorry – this must be such a shock to you all,' she said.

Elliot's eyes glistened with tears but there was a sparkle in them too. 'Alice-Miranda, I don't know how we can ever thank you for finding out the truth. And yes, it will take time for us all to get to know each other but I'm sure we will. The fact that Aster became Juliette when that was her real name in the first place and my eldest grandchild has a name so close to my own – some things aren't mere coincidences.'

Ellie looked over at the man, wondering if he was right.

Juliette nodded. 'I saw something one day when I was snooping in my mother's things. There was a card with the name Juliette on it. I don't know why, but when I ran away and changed my name from Aster, it felt like that's who I should have always been. I can't explain it – I know it sounds ridiculous but it's the truth.

Suddenly the study doors slid open and a man stood in the entryway – Millie and Sep beside him.

Everyone turned to look at them.

Myles frowned before he shouted, 'Daddy!' and ran into his arms.

Juliette's hand flew to her mouth. 'Bronson!' she cried and ran to him too.

The man clung to his wife and son but only seconds later he looked over at Ellie and beckoned for her to come to them.

She began to cry, then rushed to hug the only father she'd ever known.

Minutes later, Juliette introduced her husband to her newfound father. To say Bronson was shocked was something of an understatement. And though he had a hundred questions, right now he just wanted to be with his wife and son and daughter.

Elliot Turner looked at Alice-Miranda. 'Well, this is cause for celebration, don't you think, young lady?'

Alice-Miranda looked up at him and smiled. 'What do you have in mind?'

'Why don't we leave this wonderful family of mine to get reacquainted and I think you and I should go and have a ride on that merry-go-round, shall we?'

Alice-Miranda nodded. Elliot Turner held out his hand and she slipped hers inside.

Chapter 46

The fire crackled in the giant hearth as the family and friends gathered in the front sitting room at Highton Hall. Despite an abundance of antique furnishings and Persian rugs, somehow the room was still both grand and cosy at the same time, with enough overstuffed couches, cushions and comfortable armchairs for everyone to find a seat.

Mugs of hot chocolate had just been passed out by Mrs Oliver and Shilly, while Cecelia, Jacinta, Britt and Venetia handed around plates of homemade gingernut biscuits, rum balls, Christmas tree cupcakes, slices of hazelnut log and mince pies.

Dressed casually in jeans and a pale blue cashmere jumper with a snowflake motif (that was as close to an ugly Christmas sweater as the woman would go), Charlotte Highton-Smith sat on the floor with her daughter Imogen on her lap, while the girl's twin, Marcus, sat beside his brother, Lucas, on the couch, babbling about Santa. Their grandmother, Valentina, surveyed the scene from a high-backed armchair, smiling contentedly to herself. Or perhaps she was also amused by the array of terrible Christmas jumpers everyone was now wearing, herself included.

Alice-Miranda took a sip of hot chocolate, unaware of the milk moustache that now decorated her upper lip. 'Who knew that our pre-Christmas celebrations would be so eventful?' she said, frowning at Britt who was miming the need to wipe her face.

Alice-Miranda realised what the girl was getting at and dabbed her mouth with a paper napkin.

Lawrence Ridley grinned at his niece. 'I'm not surprised at all. Your life is full of adventures, Alice-Miranda.'

'Not *all* the time,' she protested.

Millie looked at her friend and raised her eyebrows. 'Are you kidding? There's never a dull moment when you're around. I've lost count of all the mysteries you've solved and that I've had the pleasure of being part of, as well. Maybe you're destined to be a detective. Maybe we both are. We could set up our own business. Although we might have to think of a simpler name than the Highton-Smith-Kennington-Jones-McLoughlin-McTavish-McNoughton-McGill Agency.'

'Good grief – please don't offer me a job as your receptionist,' Britt said to guffaws of laughter.

Alice-Miranda smiled. 'That could be an interesting life.'

'Maybe you could work out why Miss Wickham's sister thought it was okay to steal the Turners' baby and swap her with her own. I mean, who does that?' Caprice said.

'Clearly the woman wasn't well,' Millie said. 'Though that's still no excuse – poor Juliette has had a really tough life. She's a wonderful mother, despite how she was raised.'

'And what about poor baby Aster? The real Aster, who was such a sick little girl? I can't imagine losing my baby,' Cecelia said, casting a loving gaze in Alice-Miranda's direction.

Jacinta hopped up to get a cupcake and plonked back down on the sofa on the other side of Marcus, who immediately put his finger in the middle of the chocolate icing.

'I couldn't agree more. It's all ghastly but thanks to you, Alice-Miranda, the story has a happy ending,' Charlotte remarked. 'A family reunited for Christmas. It feels rather like the plot of a movie, wouldn't you say, Lawrence?'

The man turned to look at his wife. 'Actually, I think it would make a great screenplay. Perhaps I'll have a go at writing it.'

'And I'll play the role of the lead character, because you'll need someone who can sing,' Caprice said, giving a sly wink.

'But Alice-Miranda is the lead character and she doesn't sing . . .' Neville said, then realised that Caprice was kidding.

The others chuckled. Not so long ago, Caprice would have been deadly serious and they'd all be in big trouble for laughing. It was wonderful to see the change in the girl.

'Make sure that you add the Bauble Bandits into the story,' Lucas said.

'Silly misguided kids,' Hugh said with a shake of his head. 'I can see why they thought they were doing something noble, but stealing is never a good idea. And at least it sounds like their father gained a conscience after he realised what his kids were up to.'

'Don't you think they should be in trouble with the police too?' Neville said.

'They're kids – they made a mistake and it sounds like they're going to put everything to rights. That would be far more constructive than dragging them through the courts and I'm fairly sure that Detective Inspector Freeman has given them a jolly good talking to. Hopefully that's enough to keep them all on the straight and narrow from now on,' Hugh said.

Sep looked over at Venetia Baldini who was sitting quietly beside her daughter. 'How are you feeling, Ms Baldini?' the boy asked. 'It must have been a shock finding out what Sergey was up to.'

Venetia smiled at the boy. 'Thank you for asking, Sep. I'm fine. It was probably for the best that I had no idea I was working for a monster. But I must say that I was stunned when poor Bronson Byers appeared in the kitchen. Strangely, though,

I trusted him almost immediately and knew I had to help him somehow. I just didn't imagine it was all so complicated.'

'Did you get paid, Mummy?' Caprice asked. Although her voice was light, Millie could see that it was a serious question, given what she knew about the family's current circumstances.

The woman nodded. 'I'm pleased to say that Sergey transferred my full fee up front. I'm sure I wouldn't have seen a cent otherwise – not now that his assets have all been frozen by the police.'

'Yes, I suspect he won't be around for quite a long time to come,' Hugh said.

After last night's party with all its incredible revelations, the children had slept in this morning and then taken themselves off for a walk after breakfast to see the Greenings, before going down to the farm to play with Poppy and Jasper. Granny Valentina had arrived just after lunch, closely followed by Charlotte and Lawrence and the twins. This afternoon, the children had split up, with Caprice, Britt, Millie and Sep keeping Mrs Oliver and Venetia Baldini company in the kitchen, baking all the treats they were enjoying now, while the others spent the afternoon outside with the twins building a huge snowman. Dinner had been a casual affair of cottage pie and steamed vegetables. Cecelia had forbidden Dolly to do anything fancier, given it was only a couple of days until Christmas.

'I can't believe Sep and Neville and I will be home in Spain by tomorrow night,' Sloane said. 'The week's gone so fast.'

Britt nodded. 'And I'll be in Oslo. Mamma says that it's absolutely freezing.'

'Well, you should all reach your destinations in time,' Mrs Oliver said. 'As long as you get ahead of the cold front that the bureau says is the likes of which hasn't been seen in years. It sounds like there's going to be more snow for Christmas.'

'Sadly, not in Spain,' Sep said.

'I don't mind. It probably won't be warm enough to swim, but I'm looking forward to some sunshine,' Sloane said.

'Daddy says it's chilly in Tuscany too, but it will be fun to have one last Christmas there,' Caprice said, glancing at her mother who gave a nod. She'd told Caprice everything last night after they'd been reunited and had been surprised by how mature the girl's reaction had been.

The children and Venetia were all due to leave in the morning, with those who were flying out being ferried to the airport and others being picked up from the Hall. Chessie was the closest. She and Alice-Miranda had vowed to spend more time together over the break, and Millie too. Although her parents were a bit of a drive away, her grandfather was nearby and she was keen to stay with him.

'Do you think that Mr Turner will ever find out exactly what happened to his poor wife?' Chessie said.

'I doubt that very much, dear,' Valentina Highton-Smith chimed in. 'There are some mysteries that are destined never to be solved.'

Alice-Miranda bit her lip. 'Maybe. But Miss Wickham said something about her brother-in-law George having kept diaries. She wasn't sure what happened to them, but perhaps something will turn up one day. I mean, who would have ever expected to find her sister's confession inside the teapot spout?'

The others all nodded in agreement.

'Yes, wasn't that the strangest thing?' Shilly said.

'And speaking of which – now I don't have a surprise for you for Christmas, Mrs Oliver,' the child said. 'That was meant to be your present to replace the one that's leaking.'

'Oh, dear girl,' Dolly said. 'Please don't worry about me. I've got everything I need right here.' She glanced around at the family and friends.

'Why can't you give it to Mrs Oliver?' Millie asked.

'Because I said that Miss Wickham should have it back. And if she doesn't want it, then I think Mr Turner should keep it – for the sake of the family story,' Alice-Miranda replied.

Charlotte Highton-Smith looked over at her young son, mortified to realise that Marcus's hands were now covered in chocolate. She reached into her cardigan pocket and pulled out a small packet of wet wipes, quickly passing it to Jacinta and hoping that the lad hadn't smeared anything on her sister's couch.

'When are we giving each other our presents?' Caprice asked. 'Just the ones us kids bought for each other.'

At the mention of the word, Marcus clapped his hands together.

'Presents!' he shouted. His sister was asleep on her mother's lap.

'Sorry, I shouldn't have mentioned it,' Caprice said, pulling a face.

'Not for you, darling,' Charlotte said, glad that he hadn't woken Imogen up.

Marcus pouted.

Everyone mimicked the lad sticking their bottom lips out in reply.

Surprisingly, the boy giggled. It was amazing how quickly toddlers could be distracted.

'Why don't we boring oldies leave you youngsters alone,' Hugh suggested. 'I'd like to see if I can finally beat Lawrence at a game of snooker.'

'You're on,' the man said.

'Yes, and I want to chat to Dolly and Shilly about the menu for Christmas,' Valentina said, getting to her feet.

'And these two cheeky monkeys need to get to bed,' Charlotte said.

'I'll help you, darling,' Cecelia said, snatching Marcus up from the lounge while Charlotte stood up cradling Imogen.

'Good night,' the children chorused as the adults made their way from the room.

'Present time,' Alice-Miranda said, as her friends followed her through to the entrance hall where the base of the sparkling Christmas tree was piled high with gifts.

'Bags I be Santa,' Caprice and Millie said at the same time. They looked at each other and grinned.

'Why don't you do it together?' Alice-Miranda suggested.

The girls nodded.

'Together,' they said at exactly the same time again.

The others all laughed.

'Seriously, I don't know what's happened with you two – but long may it stay this way,' Lucas said.

'We finally learned the art of cooperation,' Millie said.

'It comes in handy when someone's planning to kill you,' Caprice said, arching her left eyebrow.

'Well, I for one am glad that you've finally come to an understanding and you're both still alive,' Sep said, earning himself a dig in the ribs from Lucas. When they got back to school, he was planning to ask Millie to be his date for the Fayle Spring Dance.

'I think it's more than an understanding,' Caprice said, looking at Millie.

The girl nodded. 'I'd go so far as to say we might even be . . . friends?'

'It's a Christmas miracle!' Lucas exclaimed and everyone laughed.

Millie and Caprice both donned Santa hats for their duties.

Lucas and Jacinta held hands while Sep, Chessie, Britt, Sloane, Alice-Miranda and Neville sat side by side around the tree. Millie and Caprice read the names on the cards and handed out the gifts.

Alice-Miranda's brown eyes sparkled as she looked at her friends.

'I think this has to be my favourite Christmas ever,' she said.

The others could only agree.

And just in case you're wondering...

Elliot Turner's party was indeed the event of the year, although Keeley Hendrix was not happy to learn later that night that her husband had been arrested and her children were the Bauble Bandits. Griffin cut a deal with the prosecutors and, in exchange for him testifying against Sergey Koloff, he got to do his time in home detention. Hazel, Jake, Liam and Kane did exactly what Griffin asked, returning all of the goods they'd stolen and using their pocket money to buy decorations to spruce up the village and surrounds. Hazel suggested they should tell the newspapers about their good deeds, but their mother thought better of it. Hazel and Ellie are no longer friends.

Keeley Hendrix realised that the only way to keep her family afloat was to get herself a job. When Hugh Kennington-Jones heard about the family's predicament, he offered her a position at Kennington's, which she's finding surprisingly satisfying.

The money Venetia earned helped pay down a chunk of debt on the restaurants and get her company back on track. Interestingly, Sophie Garceau was outed by her staff as a bully not long after Christmas. Her show, *Pressure Cooker*, was cancelled by the network immediately, with *Sweet Things* rocketing to the top of the ratings once again.

Bronson Byers told his family as much as he could without compromising the rest of the investigation into Sergey Koloff. He quit his undercover role in the force and used the money he'd saved to buy a beautiful cottage in the village for them to live in. Not long afterwards, he formed a partnership with his new father-in-law, buying properties to renovate and then rent at a reduced rate to families in hardship. Their first acquisition was the row of terraces where Juliette and the children had lived. Ellie couldn't be prouder.

Juliette has started a management training program with Kennington's and is enjoying being able to use her brain. Hugh says he's never been more impressed with a staff member.

Elliot Turner is enjoying spending time with his family – though they're taking things slowly and making sure that everyone is comfortable with the situation. After all, it was quite a shock to learn the truth.

Alice-Miranda's friends all returned home for Christmas, the weather holding off long enough for everyone to get where they were meant to be. The Highton-Smith-Kennington-Joneses and their household celebrated together on a day when there was more snow than the country had ever seen before.

Alice-Miranda had grinned when she'd opened a special hardback edition of her favourite spy series with a note from the author, which had been organised by Millie the night the children had all exchanged their gifts.

There was another present, however, that made her smile more than any other. A copy of *The Hundred Dresses* from Ellie. It would turn out to be a story she would treasure for the rest of her life – and the beginning of a lovely new friendship.

Cast of characters

Winchesterfield-Downsfordvale Academy for Proper Young Ladies students, staff and friends

Alice-Miranda Highton-Smith-Kennington-Jones	Only child, almost twelve years of age
Millicent Jane McLoughlin-McTavish-McNoughton-McGill	Alice-Miranda's best friend
Jacinta Headlington-Bear	Friend
Sloane Sykes	Friend
Francesca Compton-Halls	Friend
Caprice Radford	Friend, of sorts
Britt Fox	Friend and exchange student from Hartvig Skole, Oslo
Miss Ophelia Grimm	Headmistress
Miss Livinia Reedy	English teacher and deputy headmistress
Miss Benitha Wall	PE teacher and deputy headmistress
Charlie Weatherly (Mr Charles)	Gardener
Mrs Petunia Clarkson	Housemistress of Caledonia Manor

Cornelius Trout	Music teacher
Louella Derby	Personal secretary to the headmistress (on maternity leave)
Mrs Myrtle Parker	Acting personal assistant to the headmistress and town busybody
Mrs Doreen Smith	Cook
Caroline Clinch	Maths teacher
Aldous Grump	Miss Grimm's husband
Aggie Grump	Miss Grimm's daughter
Reginald Parker	Myrtle Parker's husband and Alice-Miranda's drum teacher
Ambrosia Headlington-Bear	Jacinta's mother
Lucas Nixon	Fayle School for Boys student
Septimus Sykes	Fayle School for Boys student
Neville Nordstrom	Barcelona International College student

Highton Hall residents

Cecelia Highton-Smith	Alice-Miranda's mother
Hugh Kennington-Jones	Alice-Miranda's father
Dolly Oliver	Family cook and food scientist
Mrs Shillingsworth	Housekeeper
Mr Harold Greening	Gardener
Mrs Greening	Wife of Harold

Hoxton Manor residents, staff and relations

Elliot Turner	Owner of Hoxton Manor, successful businessman
Delia Wickham	Head housekeeper

Maggie Phillips	Deceased sister of Delia Wickham
Paloma	Chef

Others

Ellie Byers	Fourteen-year-old girl
Myles Byers	Six-year-old brother of Ellie
Juliette Byers	Ellie and Myles's mother
Bronson Byers	Ellie's stepfather, Myles's father
Griffin Hendrix	Manager of Freightliners Transport Company and father of Hazel, Jake and Kane
Keeley Hendrix	Wife of Griffin, mother of Hazel, Jake and Kane
Hazel Hendrix	Fourteen-year-old girl
Jake Hendrix	Hazel's twin brother
Kane Hendrix	Older brother of Hazel and Jake
Liam	Jake's best friend
Miss Violet Appleby	Grandmother of Clementine Rose, wife of Digby Pertwhistle
Mr Digby Pertwhistle	Butler at Penberthy House Hotel and husband of Violet Appleby
Sebastian Smote	Party planner extraordinaire
Venetia Baldini	Caprice's mother and celebrity chef
Bobby Lambert	Driver for Freightliners Transport Company
Sergey Koloff	Owner of Loff's Folly and businessman

About the author

Jacqueline Harvey worked in schools for many years, but has had a passion for storytelling since she was a child.

She is the author of the popular Alice-Miranda, Clementine Rose, Kensy and Max, and Willa and Woof series, which have sold almost two million copies in Australia alone. In 2022, she released a picture book, *That Cat*, illustrated by one of her former students, Kate Isobel Scott. Jacqueline's books have received numerous shortlistings and awards while her picture book, *The Sound of the Sea*, was a CBCA Honour Book.

Jacqueline speaks to thousands of young people at schools and festivals around the world and says the characters in her books are often made up of the best bits of children she's met over the years.

Jacqueline lives between Sydney, Australia, and Queenstown, New Zealand, with her husband Ian and cat, Bally Puss, and is currently working on more Willa and Woof adventures, several picture book projects and an exciting new middle-grade story.

jacquelineharvey.com.au

Jacqueline Supports

Jacqueline Harvey is a passionate educator who enjoys sharing her love of reading and writing with children and adults alike. She is an ambassador for Dymock's Children's Charities and Room to Read, and is the current patron of Somerset Storyfest. Find out more at dcc.gofundraise.com.au and roomtoread.org.

Have you read all of Jacqueline Harvey's books?

For a full list of books
in each series visit
penguin.com.au

Stories jam-packed with mystery, adventure, travel, friends, action, intrigue and more!

Did you know there are twenty more Alice-Miranda adventures to explore?

Turn the page for a peek at *Alice-Miranda in the Outback*.

Chapter 1

Alice-Miranda focused on the long, straight stretch of road. In the distance she could see something flying towards them. She wondered for a moment if it was a light aircraft before realising it was an eagle. Another giant bird swooped in from the left across their path, almost touching the bonnet of the four-wheel drive.

'Wow!' Millie exclaimed, having just seen the creatures from the back seat. 'Was that a pterodactyl?'

Alice-Miranda grinned. 'I was thinking the same thing.'

Hugh Kennington-Jones chuckled. 'They say everything is bigger in the outback.'

Millie grabbed her camera from the seat beside her. She was keen to enter the art and photography competition Miss Grimm had announced just before the holidays. There were great prizes as well as the opportunity to be exhibited at the opening of the new Fayle Art Space. Professor Winterbottom, the Fayle School Headmaster, had initiated the idea with Miss Grimm, amid a flurry of excitement and heightened activity in both schools' art rooms. By the time Millie went to take the photograph, though, the birds were too far away.

Behind them, Hugh could see the second Landcruiser in the distance.

'How about we stop and have something to eat?' Hugh asked the girls. 'There should be a roadhouse coming up. Why don't you let your uncle know that's the plan?'

Alice-Miranda picked up the handset from the cradle of the two-way radio and pressed the button on the side.

There was a crackle of static.

'This is KJ One calling Ridley One, do you copy? Over.'

They'd decided on their call signs before setting off from Alice Springs that morning.

'Loud and clear, KJ One,' Lucas replied. 'What can we do for you? Over.'

'We're taking a break at the Kulgera Roadhouse,' Alice-Miranda said, having consulted the paper map she had spread out across her lap. 'Over.'

'Gotcha,' Lucas replied. 'I'm starving and Dad is too. Jacinta's asleep. Can you hear her snoring? Over.'

There was a pause and the sound of Lucas shuffling around in his seat before the girl's breathy grunts came through the airwaves loud and clear.

'Ask him when they picked up the pig,' Millie giggled.

'That's mean, Lucas and Millie. Over,' Alice-Miranda chided, but Millie and Hugh were both laughing.

'You'd better not tell her that I did that. She'll never speak to me again. Over,' Lucas said.

It was another ten kilometres before a clump of iron-roofed buildings loomed into view.

Discover a world of fun online!

Games

Colouring-in

Recipes

Activities

Party invites

Videos

There's even material for teachers and parents!

Be the first to hear about book launches, events and competitions by signing up to the Jacqueline Harvey newsletter.

jacquelineharvey.com.au